STEALTH

STEALTH

HUGH FRASER

Urbane
PUBLICATIONS

urbanepublications.com

First published in Great Britain in 2018 by Urbane Publications Ltd
Suite 3, Brown Europe House, 33/34 Gleaming Wood Drive, Chatham, Kent ME5 8RZ
Copyright © Hugh Fraser, 2018

A CIP catalogue record for this book is available from the British Library.

ISBN 978-1-911583-66-0

Design and Typeset by Julie Martin
Cover by Julie Martin

Printed and bound by CPI Group (UK) Ltd, Croydon, CR0 4YY

Urbane
PUBLICATIONS

urbanepublications.com

1

London 1967

I'm sitting at a corner table in a pub in Wardour Street waiting for Bert Davis. It's Friday night and the place is heaving. I look at my watch, see it's near closing time and I'm wondering if he's going to turn up. He wants to talk about a bit of work his governor George Preston has got for me. I've been able to stay well out of the game since I scored the money my dad left behind from a blag he pulled off before he got shot, but George, who ran a big firm with my dad, has got so much on me he could have me away for life anytime he wants. Even though I doubt if he'd break the code, I can't risk turning him down. The landlord shouts time and I'm about to finish my drink and leave, when I see a face called Jack Fenton coming through the crowd with his eye on me. He's big man with a long reach and I've seen him do some damage in the ring. He sits down and leans across the table until his ugly red face is close to mine.

'You think you're so fucking clever, you slimy little bitch.'

I put my hand in my jacket pocket and slip my fingers into the knuckle duster.

'I know you offed Charlie and I'll have you screaming

in pain with a blade up your drawers before I do you the same way you did him.'

A bloke at the next table looks our way and when Fenton turns to him, I whip out the duster and give him a straight right to his temple. As he falls backwards and hits the floor, I knock the table out of the way and stamp on his bollocks. When he shouts and rears up, I kick him under the jaw, make a run for the door and leg it up Wardour Street wondering how Fenton got to know about me doing Charlie Hobson months ago. After weaving in and out of the evening crowd, I duck into a doorway and look back towards the pub. I can't see anyone after me, so I hail a cab and get in. I reckon I won't go home in case any of Fenton's firm were in the pub and know where I live, so I tell the driver to take me to Abigail's in Frith Street. As we go past the pub, I see Fenton being carried to a car. He looks like he's out cold.

As we drive round Soho Square I'm looking forward to seeing Lizzie. An ambulance roars past and it reminds me of the night I found her and took her to hospital after she'd been beaten up by a mad punter who was into some weird stuff. When she came out I managed to persuade her to give up whoring and mistressing and after I'd sorted the punter out I bought Abigail's Club for her, so that she'd be on a good earner and have something to keep her busy. It's been going well, with Lizzie knowing so many girls to do the hostessing and a good few hotel doormen to send the punters in for something to spice up the business trip.

George Preston's handling the protection and we've got some good muscle on the door so even though we get a few bad lads coming in for a drink or a meet, there's been no real trouble so far.

The cab pulls up outside the club. I get out, give the driver a ten bob note and tell him to keep the change. Max and a bloke I don't know are on the door.

'Evening, Rina,' says Max, as I approach.

He says something to the other man who flicks his fag into the gutter and opens the door to the foyer for me. I go inside, smile at Jane behind the counter and walk down the stairs as the house band go into the opening bars of 'A Whiter Shade of Pale'. Lizzie and I decided to hire some guys who could rock a bit for the house band instead of the usual boring lounge trio doing the Sinatra and Mel Tormé songbook, like most clubs have. The singer's a good pianist with a fine voice and if I shut my eyes I could be listening to Gary Brooker. The guitarist is a young Mexican lad with black curly hair and a beautiful face who's taught himself every lick that Alvin Lee, Peter Green and Hendrix ever played, and the drummer and bass player are good too. I made them wear suits instead of their hippy gear so they blend in with the punters a bit. They were a bit iffy about it until I told them they were on fifty notes a week and they shot off up Carnaby Street and got suited up.

I stand in the shadows at the back of the club and clock the action. All the tables are occupied, mostly by our girls with punters, their faces lit by the glow from the pink-shaded table lamps and the odd stroke of light from the glitter ball. Waitresses are slipping between the tables with bottles of fake champagne for the girls and straight drinks for the punters. I look at the crowd standing round the bar and recognise a couple of faces from a Clerkenwell firm, who I've not seen in here before, talking to a big fat bloke with a small blond woman hanging off his arm. While I'm wondering what it might be about, Lizzie comes out of the door behind the bar and walks towards one of the tables. She catches the eye of the girl and gives her a nod. The girl says something to the punter and then leads him past the bandstand and through a door at the back of the club. As Lizzie turns to the bar I step forward and she sees me and comes over.

'Hello loveliness,' she says, slipping her arm round me and brushing her lips against my cheek. I want to kiss her full on but two Japanese gents are staring at us, so I give her a quick peck and follow her through the tables as the band go into 'Bring it on Home'. She leads me into the office, we have a quick cuddle, then she pours two whiskies, gives one to me and we sit on the sofa.

'We might have a problem,' she says.

'Yeah?'

'The Murphys are sniffing round for the protection.'

'Those creeps at the bar?'

'One of them is Brian's son.'

Brian Murphy is an armed robber out of Clerkenwell with a lot of form who works with his brothers and their kids. They're a strong family firm with a lot of bent police in their pockets. They've got the protection for quite a few clubs and porno bookshops, which is a good earner and gives them a supply of girls to keep the Old Bill sweet.

'As well as minding the place for a pension they want to put a roulette table and one-armed bandits in here and I've told them it's not that kind of club,' says Lizzie.

'Have you told George?'

Before she can answer, there's a shout from the bar. As Lizzie opens the door, Murphy punches the fat bloke in the face and puts him down hard. The blond woman whips off her shoe and tries to jab the stiletto heel into Murphy's face. He grabs her round the waist, picks her up and lifts her clean over the bar, then he lands on the fat man's chest and hammers his fists into his face. Others start weighing in and swinging punches as Max and his mate from the door pound down the stairs and steam into the ruck. Murphy gets knocked out by a kick to the side of the head and he rolls off the fat man onto the floor beside him. Max and the other doorman set about the rest of the fighters. Most of them back off after taking a couple of quick punches, apart from one who's keeping his end up quite well until Max nuts him and breaks his nose. Blood spurts, then all at once it's over and the main players are being hustled up the stairs and into the street. The little blond woman comes out from behind the bar, finds her shoe, puts it on and goes to the fat man who's coming round and trying to get up on one elbow. She helps him to his feet and holds his hand as he hobbles to the stairs. Max appears, stands back to let them pass and comes down into the club. He grabs Murphy by the collar and drags him to the bottom of the stairs. I go to him and we cart Murphy upstairs, dump him on the pavement and a couple of his mates pick him up and carry him to a taxi.

When I come back down Lizzie is at the far end of the club, talking to the punters who retreated back there with the girls and the waitresses when it kicked off. She's assuring them that it's all over and offering them drinks on the house if they'd like to sit down. A few of them make for the stairs but most of them go back to their tables with the girls and the waitresses take their orders. Lizzie goes to the bandstand, has a word with the boys and they go into 'She's Not There.'

As I'm following her towards the bar, Kelly, one of the hostesses, comes out of the door to the dressing room behind the bandstand, grabs Lizzie's elbow and says something to her. They turn and Lizzie nods to me as they head for the dressing room. The deep pulse of the bass guitar goes through me as I go past the amplifier and through the open door. A girl's body is face down on the floor with her head in a pool of blood.

I lock the door behind me, kneel beside the body and feel for a pulse in her neck but there's none. Blood is seeping from the back of her head. I move her hair off her face and reveal a nasty gash on her forehead. Her nose is broken and her front teeth are smashed. Someone's beaten her to death with a tool. I look around and see a claw hammer lying under one of the dressing tables. She doesn't look more than twenty, her long silky black hair is matted with blood and I feel a blaze of anger and the dire need to smash something as I wonder what kind of fucking monster could do this to a beautiful young girl. Lizzie's standing by the door with her arm round Kelly who's looking as pale as a ghost. I go and join them, knowing we've got to move fast.

'Tell me what you saw, Kelly.'

She wipes her eyes and looks at me. 'She was at the bar talking to Dave Priest. He was giving her a bad time and when the fight started I saw him drag her in here and shut the door. When it died down I came in here to get my bag and I found her.'

I've heard of Dave Priest as a fighter and a feared man but I didn't know he ran girls.

'Do you know why he was having a go at her?'

'She told me he was trying to make her go with some MP who'd been in here and seen her but she'd heard he was into the rough stuff and wouldn't do it.'

'What was her name?'

'Rose.'

She starts to cry again. 'She was so lovely.'

I want to comfort her but time's pressing.

'Thanks Kelly, we'll take care of this,' I say, looking at Lizzie, who takes a fiver out of her pocket and presses it into Kelly's hand. 'You get yourself a cab home now Kel and only come in tomorrow if you feel like it. I'll phone you later and make sure you're all right.'

'Thanks Liz.'

'Off you go now, darling.'

Kelly dries her eyes and moves towards the clothes rail in the corner.

'And Kel…' says Lizzie.

'Yeah?'

'This never happened.'

Kelly nods, takes a fur jacket off the rail and walks round the body to the door, which Lizzie unlocks for her. As it opens I can see it's business as usual in the club. Lizzie locks the door and turns to look at Rose.

'What are we going to do?' she asks.

'We've got to hide her until we can get rid.'

'Where?'

'Is Rico in the kitchen?'

'I think so.'

'Take him out the back for a fag, square him off for what's happening and ask him if anyone left through the kitchen.'

'What are you going to do?'

'Put her in the freezer, while I get the car.'

Lizzie goes through the door at the other end of the dressing room and I wait until I hear her telling Rico she wants a word. When I see them going out the back, I go into the kitchen, lift the lid of the freezer and find I'm in luck as it's almost empty apart from a few packets of frankfurters and some rolls which I take out and put on a nearby shelf, thinking that we must do something about the food in the club. I go back to Rose, grab a couple of towels off the dressing table and wrap them round her head to hold the blood. I'm surprised by how light she is when I pick her up and carry her through. I put her in the freezer and close the lid, then I go to the sink and run some water into a bowl. I take the bowl and a cloth to the dressing room and start cleaning up the blood, thankful that it's a lino floor. It takes three bowls of water and a lot of elbow grease before I've got all the blood off. When I've cleaned out the bowl and washed the cloth, I go to the back door of the kitchen and I can see Lizzie and Rico in the alleyway at the top of the stairs. I give a short whistle, go back inside and Lizzie comes down.

'Is he OK?' I ask.

'I've given him a cockle and he's fine.'

'A tenner well spent. If this gets out, we could be well fucked.'

'Can you sort it?'

'I reckon. Did Rico see anyone?'

'He said a bloke ran out past him and up the steps about half an hour ago.'

'Tell him to finish up any orders, close the kitchen and leave in ten minutes. Then lock both doors and give me a key to the back one. I'll be back to get her in half an hour.'

'Do you want me to close the club?'

'No need. Just say the chef's off sick if anyone wants food.'

Lizzie takes a bunch of keys out of her pocket, takes one off the ring and gives it to me. We have a quick hug and she goes back into the club. I get the hammer from under the dressing table, leave by the back door, climb the steps and say goodnight to Rico. I head along the alleyway to Frith Street, dump the hammer in a bin on the way, hail a cab and tell him to take me to Randolph Avenue.

I pick up the Mini Cooper, drive to my lock-up in Harlesden, pick up some tools, motor back to the club and park a short way away along Frith Street. It's nearly 4am and the street is almost clear apart from a couple of drunks and the odd working girl on her way home. I take my rain-cape out of the boot of the car and go along the alleyway and down the stairs to the back of the club. I open the back door, go to the freezer, lift Rose out and lay her on the floor near the sink. I find a fresh cloth and wipe the freezer out for any blood stains, then I rinse the cloth out and clean her face up as much as I can. She's stopped bleeding and apart from the wound on her forehead she doesn't look too bad. I lay Rose face down on the deck, put her arms into the sleeves of my rain-cape and pull the hood over her head, then I pick her up, hold her by my side, put her arm round my neck and grip her wrist. I take a few steps and with her head lolling forward in the hood, I reckon I might just get away with looking like I'm helping a drunken girl along the street.

I hoist her onto my shoulder and carry her up the steps into the alleyway where I put her in position as before, pull the hood over her face and step out into Frith Street. I get to the car without anyone taking an interest and there's a moment when I nearly drop her as I'm opening the door, but I manage to get her into the passenger seat and she flops forward looking like she's asleep. As I drive past the club, I see Max locking the front door and walking towards his black Mercedes.

I drive up to Euston Road, turn left along Marylebone and then up Edgware Road and onto Harrow Road. When I get as far as Kensal Green Cemetery, I pull over at the corner of Wakeman Road where there's a bus stop that's got its shelter up against the wall of the cemetery. There's no one about so I get Rose out of the car and put her over my shoulder. I put one foot on the ledge that runs along the wall and just about manage to climb onto the roof of the bus shelter and lay her down. I take a spade and a torch out of the boot of the car, get back up beside Rose, lift her over the wall and let her down as gently as I can among the leaves. I pick up the spade, put the torch in my pocket and drop down next to her. I leave her where she is while I walk along the path, keeping the torch down while I flash it left and right. After I've gone a couple of hundred yards I find what I'm looking for. There's a fresh grave a couple of rows from the wall and nicely out of sight of the houses on Harrow Road. It belongs to Harold Beams who was born in 1887, so at least he had a good innings. I go and get Rose, lay her down next to the wall and start digging. The soil is still loose, so I soon get to the coffin. I reckon it's deep enough to put Rose on top, so I lay her down carefully on the mahogany, take a moment to say goodbye to the poor little thing, then I shovel the earth back to cover her. When I've finished and smoothed it over you'd never know the grave had been disturbed.

I walk through the headstones to where my little brother Jack is buried and kneel beside his grave. The flowers I brought a couple of weeks ago are wilted and sad looking. It's more than ten years since he died of the whooping cough that he caught in that dirty slum we lived in. I still feel bad that I didn't take him to the doctor sooner but there's nothing I can do about it now. He'd be nearly sixteen now and I wonder how he'd have turned out if he hadn't passed away. I start crying as I think of what a lovely little boy he was and how he'd laugh when we played silly games and that.

• • •

It's gone six o'clock when I park the car in Randolph Crescent and the sun's just catching the top of the curving white terrace where Lizzie's and my flats are. We moved the short distance from Maida Vale to Little Venice a couple of years ago. I'd had a bit of bother with the Teale family and a heavy mob from Birmingham. Lizzie had got dragged into it and although it got well sorted we decided a move wouldn't be a bad idea. I was looking for places to put my dad's money and when two flats in the same house in Little Venice came up for sale, I bought them for us. Even though they've just made it legal for consenting men to have sex, it's still not too cool for the girls so we reckoned it was better to keep it discreet and have a front door each.

I let myself into Lizzie's flat, see that she's in bed asleep, creep into her bathroom, take my clothes off and hope the shower won't wake her. When I've got the blood and soil off me I go into the bedroom and slip in beside her. She wakes up and we hold each other.

'All done,' I whisper.

'That poor little thing.'

'I know.'

'If I'd had time to get to know her, I might have been able to protect her.'

'You mustn't blame yourself.'

'I'm not allowing girls that young in anymore.'

'Isn't it more dangerous on the street?'

'I suppose so.'

'All we can do is try to keep them safe in the club.'

'We need a man downstairs at all times.'

'That's it.'

We lie quietly for a while and I gently stroke her forehead until I feel her breathing slowing and she drifts off to sleep.

2

We drag ourselves out of bed about midday. Lizzie's still upset about what happened to Rose and I do my best to comfort her. When I've convinced her that I'm going to make sure the man who did it can never do it again, I think she feels reassured and we go and have breakfast at the French café in Clifton Road which has the best coffee and croissants this side of the English Channel. The sun's shining, it's a beautiful day and Lizzie remembers that we've been invited to Granny Takes a Trip, Nigel Weymouth's new shop in World's End, where he's changing the giant face of Jean Harlow that he's got outside the shop, for the front end of a Dodge saloon car. Even though it sounds like fun and Nigel and Sheila have got some amazing clothes in there, after what went on last night I've got some phone calls to make, so I put Lizzie in a cab, tell her to enjoy herself and walk round to my flat.

Bert Davis picks up after a few rings.

'Where the fuck were you last night?' I ask.

'I was coming in the side door when you slapped Fenton and took it on your toes.'

'What happened after?'

'Not a lot. You made him look such a wally they got him out pretty quick. A couple of his firm were asking around about you after but I don't think they got anything.'

'Meet me in the Warrington in half an hour.'

'Only if you won't knock me out.'

'Just don't be late.'

I hear Bert chuckle as I put the phone down. I go into my bedroom and open the wardrobe. I'm still wearing last night's clothes and I need to change. Thinking about Lizzie at Granny Takes a Trip makes me go for my Emilio Pucci flares and a floral blouse which I throw on the bed while I change into fresh underwear. I put on make-up and brush my hair. When I get into the trousers, I notice the waistband's loose and tell myself I need to eat more. I take up the slack with a belt, slip a blade in the back, put on the blouse and a pair of low-heeled shoes.

I walk round to the Warrington, go into the public bar and see Bert at a table in the corner with a pint in front of him. Bert is George Preston's right hand and though he's getting on a bit now he was a feared man in his day. George and my dad had the strongest firm in West London. They had nearly all the protection and nothing went off without a nod from them. Bert was on the firm from the beginning and never took any liberties. He still wears the dark suits and the fedora and he's one of the few people I feel I can trust. I get myself a whisky and go and join him.

'What do you know about a face called Dave Priest?' I ask.

'Cobble fighter out of Limehouse.'

'Any good?'

'See for yourself tonight, if you want.'

'Where's it going off?'

'The Barley Mow.'

'Hoxton?'

'Yeah.'

'How will I know Priest?'

'Ginger barnet.'

'Who's he fighting?'

'Some geezer from Bermondsey.'

The Barley Mow is a pub owned by a Hoxton villain who promotes bareknuckle fights at gypsy fairs and suchlike and sometimes in the back yard of his pub. The fighters don't wear gloves, it's all in and anything goes. People can get badly hurt but a lot of money goes on the result.

'Are you going?'

'No, I'm taking her out tonight.'

'Club?'

'*Sound of Music.*'

'Nice.'

Bert's wife Carol is a lovely woman who likes a good time and won't be kept indoors. Bert would be lost without her and he knows how to keep her sweet.

'You want another?' asks Bert, finishing his pint.

'Go on then.'

He lumbers over to the bar, buys the drinks, comes back and sits.

'Heard you had a bundle in the club last night,' he says.

'Just a bit of a tear-up between a couple of Murphy

boys and some fat geezer. Max had it sorted and chucked them out.'

'How was Terry, the new bloke on the door?'

'He was good, put a couple down quick.'

'I reckoned he'd be OK.'

I finish my whisky and stand. 'I'd better get off.'

'Hang on a minute.'

'What?'

'The governor wants to talk to you about a bit of work.'

'When?'

'He's at the races at Aintree today but he'll be at the Astor, late tonight.'

'I'll try and catch him.'

I leave Bert heading to the bar and walk round to my flat. I go into the house, climb the stairs to the first floor, open the security locks on my front door, let myself in and turn off the alarm. Although the locks are as strong as they get, a pro can make a key to anything but you can't get to the alarm from outside the flat and after a couple of weasels broke into my last place and had my young sister Georgie away, I'm taking no chances. Georgie's at Cambridge University now studying English Literature and I'm so proud when I think of how hard she's worked and how far away she is from the life we were born into. As I go into the kitchen and pick up the knife to cut some bread for a sandwich, I think of the time I sliced a blade across Johnny Preston's throat and killed him when he threw Georgie on her back, wrenched her legs apart and tried to rape her when she was only nine. I press the blade of the knife against my wrist to kill the memory and I just get back to myself before it breaks the skin.

I turn on the radio and Tony Blackburn waffles on a bit about how great it is that Radio 1 has come on the air, then the Beatles give it 'All you Need is Love'. It's a great song and I'm only wishing it was true as I take some ham out of the fridge, put it between two slices of bread, make a cup of Nescafé and sit down at the kitchen table. I've got a great view of the communal garden at the back with its triangle-shaped lawn and the trees and the neat flower beds with everything in bloom and looking lovely. There's a young mum with a couple of toddlers playing ball on the grass and an older couple sitting on a bench. He's reading the paper and she's knitting. It's all so nice and peaceful that I start to feel drowsy. When I've finished my sandwich, I rinse the plate and the cup, put them on the draining board, go through to the bedroom and lie down.

There's a noise from inside the coffin. The lid slides open and an ancient ghoulish head rears up, blood dripping from its eyes and mouth. It stares at me with sightless eyes then turns and looks down into the grave. Its claw hands grasp Rose's body and the ghoul is rising from the coffin lifting Rose above its head then it's up and bounding along between the gravestones with its prize held high. I run after the thing of flayed skin and bones as it leaps from stone to stone swinging the body wildly round. It jumps onto a grave and I grasp its ankle as it springs into the air, then we're soaring up above the earth and flying into blackness, on and on through freezing cold and round and back and up and down until all at once the blinding golden sun appears and the ghoul lets go of Rose and streaks off towards it and I dive after her and clasp her to me and she's alive and clinging and now we're plunging down and down towards the earth which gets bigger and bigger and we're falling faster and faster and we hit the ground and everything goes black.

I feel something stroking my forehead. I open my eyes and Lizzie's face comes into focus in front of me. 'It's all right, my lovely. Just a nasty dream.'

She lies next to me on the bed. I take a moment to dissolve the spectre of that ghoul, then I put my arms round her and we kiss. When my hands move down over her body she pulls away a little.

'I'd love to, naughty girl, but I need to get to the club.'

'Can't you be late?' I say, nuzzling into her neck.

'I can't, darling. I'm seeing a couple of new girls before we open and they'll be hanging around on the street if I'm not there to let them in.'

'They're used to it, aren't they?'

'These two are posh escorts, well off the pavement.'

'Going up in the world, are we?'

'After what went on last night, I'm trying to keep the flesh peddlers out.'

'Good move,' I say, reminding myself that I need to

get to the Barley Mow shortly to settle up with one of that species myself.

Lizzie goes to the dressing table and checks her make-up in the mirror. I go and join her, pick up my hairbrush and draw it slowly through her hair.

'Will I see you later?' she asks.

'I've got meet George at the Astor but I'll try and drop in after.'

I don't want to tell her what I'm hoping to do before I meet George. The less she knows the better, in case it goes sideways. She dusts her face with powder and picks up her handbag. We go into the hall, share a quick kiss and she's off.

I go back into the bedroom, take off my floaty clothes and my bra and put on a tight T-shirt, black jeans, a black polo neck sweater and motorcycle boots. I put a blade in each boot, the Smith & Wesson .38 in my belt and the brass knuckles and lock picks in my pocket. I wipe off my make-up, pin my hair up and put on a black woolly hat, a pair of National Health glasses and my leather biker jacket. I turn up the collar, pull the hat down to meet the top of the glasses and have a look in the mirror. When I put my hands in the jacket pockets and hunch my shoulders forward to keep my tits out of the action, I reckon I can pass for a bloke. I go back to the wardrobe, take out my dark red Dior cocktail dress, a pair of fishnets, a Triumph bra and four inch heels and put them in a carrier bag along with my Hermes handbag, some make-up and a hairbrush, for the Astor later.

I lock up the flat and go downstairs. On the way to the car I see the woman who lives on the ground floor, who I know to say hello to, coming along the pavement. I look her in the eye as we pass and I'm glad when she gives me a quick glance and ignores me. I walk on past my Mini, until she goes through the front door, then I go back to the car, put the carrier bag in the boot, and drive down Edgware Road. I turn left onto Marylebone and on through Islington to the Old Street roundabout, then along Old Street into Hoxton, do a right into Rivington Road, then a left and I can see the Barley Mow on the corner. There's a crowd of drinkers on the pavement outside making quite a bit of noise while I park the Mini out of sight of the pub behind a coal lorry. As I walk towards them a couple of blokes start arguing about something and while a bit of pushing and shoving goes on, I slip round the side of them and into the pub.

It's packed to the rafters and heaving with half-pissed geezers shouting to be heard over the racket. Apart from two or three women that I can just see over by the juke box, which is pumping out the Stones' 'Let's Spend the Night Together', it's all lairy looking men with a load on. I nick an empty glass off a table and I'm squeezing through the crowd to a corner where I can lie low when the time bell rings behind the bar, the noise dies down and a voice tells us that the show is about to start in the yard and to have our tickets ready. A door opens at the back of the pub and I join the crowd as it moves towards it. There's a bloke selling tickets at the end of the bar and I buy one for a fiver and give it straight to a ratty little guy on the door.

In the yard, men are marshalling the crowd to leave a clearing in the middle. In one corner an ugly looking type, who's well over six foot, broad with it, and completely bald, is stripping his shirt off to show us he's spent time behind the door with prison tattoos all over him. They do them really badly inside with a razor and ink pulled out of a biro. He's got 'Kill' on one hand, 'Hate' on the other and 'Cut here' round his throat. He's throwing black looks at ginger-haired Dave Priest, in the other corner, who's bobbing up and down, weaving punches in the air and looking the other way. Priest isn't as big as the other man but he's bristling with muscle and he's got a steely look in his eye as he warms up. All around me the crowd are getting excited, shouting to the fighters to get started, rip each other's heads off, gouge each other's innards out, and similar words of encouragement. A little old bloke beside me is taking bets, scribbling slips for punters and stuffing notes in his jacket pocket. When the crowd are getting so loud that I'm thinking they're about to kick it off themselves, the landlord of the pub gets on a chair and announces the fight between "The Bermondsey Bullet... Bruce McDade" and "The Limehouse Legend... Mister Dave Priest."

The crowd cheer and before the landlord can get down

from his chair Priest rushes at McDade and tears into him with a hail of left and right hooks to his head and body. As he reels back Priest kicks him hard in the bollocks and when he goes down he boots him in the ribs, kneels on his chest and starts pounding his face with his bare fists. McDade's cornermen grab hold of Priest and drag him off and while he's swinging punches at them McDade gets up, wipes the blood off his face and catches Priest with a blistering kick to the kidneys that sends him staggering. McDade grabs his shoulders, spins him round, puts both hands round the back of his head and smashes it down on his knee. Priest hits the ground, McDade kicks him in the ribs and the stomach then he lands on top of him and 'Hate' and 'Kill' grab his ears and he's banging Priest's head on the deck. As the crowd go mad and fists start flying, McDade's cornermen drag him off and try to hold him back while Priest's team check their man's out cold, wrap a towel round his bleeding head and carry him away through the crowd towards the door. The punters scream and shout while McDade dances around with his fists in the air. A Bermondsey boy spits on Priest as he passes and gets nutted and kicked to the floor for his trouble. I push my way back into the pub and watch Priest being carried through the bar and out of the door. When I get outside he's being laid in the back of a Ford Transit parked in Curtain Road. I run to my car, turn it round and just manage to get to the corner in time to follow the Transit as it drives away.

Priest's taken a good hammering and I reckon he must have at least broken a few knuckles in that opening whirlwind so I'm wondering if they're taking him to The Royal London Hospital as I follow the van down Commercial Street, but they go on into Cable Street so it looks like we're headed for Limehouse. The van does a few quick turns as we get near the river and pulls up in a street of terraced houses that have seen better days. I park up and watch the men get out of the van and open the back doors. They help Priest out but when he tries to walk he collapses and two of them carry him to the front door, while another one opens it and they get him inside. Lights go on and I wait. Just as I'm beginning to wonder if they're staying there and I'm wasting my time, the lights go off and all three men come out of the house, get in the van and drive away.

After I've waited a while I take a pencil torch from the well under the seat, get out of the car and approach the house. It's all dark, the street's quiet, and there's an alleyway between the houses a couple of doors down. I walk to the end of it and turn along a path that runs behind the gardens. There are no lights on in Priest's house so I climb over the wooden fence, pick my way over a pile of old rubbish to the back door and take out my lock picks. I turn on the torch and hold it in my mouth while I put the cut-down key into the mortice lock and slide a wire pick in on top of it. When I can feel the levers with the pick, I lift them one by one and turn the key. The door scrapes on the floor when I open it, so I grip the handle, lift it up and manage to get it open quietly. I take my boots off, put the knives in my belt, put my hand over the torch and bleed just enough light to see my way through the tiny kitchen. I stop and listen for any sound of breathing before I go on into the back room. It's empty apart from a small wooden table and two folding chairs. I move into the hall, open the front room door a crack and when I can't hear anything I have a look in and see a ratty old rug on bare floorboards, an old sofa and a TV in the corner. As I'm thinking it looks like he's on his own here, I hear a snore and a groan, then some coughing from above. I wait until it quietens then I pad slowly up the stairs to the landing. Heavy breathing is coming from the front room. The door's open and by the light from a street lamp outside the window I can see Priest lying on his back on the bed, still in his singlet and trousers. His mates have just dumped him, without even taking off his shoes.

Once I've checked the other room and made sure he's alone, I go to the head of the bed and look at the upturned face of the evil bastard, now covered in bruises and dried blood. I think of little Rose in her new grave and take out my gun. I hold it by the barrel, raise it up high, smash the butt down on his nose and hear it splinter. He cries out, gets up on his elbows and I swing the gun at the side of his head and knock him out. He falls back on the pillow and I sit astride him, get my hands round his neck and dig my thumbs into his windpipe. In a moment he comes to, thrashes his legs about and tries to pull my hands away but his fingers are busted and weak. I tighten my grip and stare into his terrified eyes until they glaze over and he snuffs it.

I rest a minute then I pull him off the bed onto the floor, take hold of his ankles and drag him along the landing to the top of the stairs. I get one of his shoes off, scrape the sole against the edge of the top step until I've shaved a bit of wood off, then I put his shoe back on, pull him down to the bottom of the stairs and position him to look like he's fallen. I bash his forehead against the floor and nick it with a blade so that he's lying in a pool of blood, just like Rose.

3

I drive up West feeling the buzz I always get when I've put another rotten scumbag out of the game. I turn Radio 1 up loud and Steve Winwood tells me to 'Keep on Running'. I thump the wheel along with him for a bit and then the Swinging Blue Jeans get into 'The Hippy Hippy Shake'. Mike Raven keeps some good records coming and I'm just about rocked out by the time I park in Great Windmill Street. I put my gun and blades under the seat, take the carrier bag out of the boot and head for the Ladies in Piccadilly Tube Station to change into my Dior dress and fishnets. When I've put on make-up, brushed my hair and checked the whole look in the mirror, I feel like I'm about ready for the Astor.

I leave the car in Berkeley Square and walk round the corner to the club. I hang back while a Daimler pulls up outside and the chauffeur gets out and opens the back door for an old bloke in a dinner jacket and a silk scarf, who looks like he might have had a few. He seems familiar and I think he might be some politician that I've seen on TV. He waits while a beautiful younger woman in a full-length silver ball gown gets out of the car. She takes the old boy's arm, the chauffeur tips his cap, the minders open the doors for them and they go in. I tweak the front of my dress to give a bit more cleavage and approach the club. One of the minders steps in front of me.

'You working?' he says.

I nod and he lets me in. I go through the second set of doors into the club and Anita Harris is onstage and coming to the end of 'Swinging on a Star'. She accepts a good round of applause with a bow, takes a quick look at the band behind her and goes into 'Just Loving You'. The tables are all occupied, mostly by toffs and gangsters. You can spot the toffs by the evening wear on the men and the long dresses on the women, while the gangsters favour expensive lounge suits with big shoulder pads and mostly leave their women indoors. I spot George at a table on the other side of the stage with a young blonde beside him and two other couples. In spite of his age George still looks good. He's a big bloke and he's kept in shape since he stopped boxing. One of the men with him is a blagger from Catford who's not long out of Parkhurst and the other's a bent lawyer. I try to keep my dealings with George discreet and I don't want to go over to the table, so I stand at the bar.

'Good evening,' says a voice behind me.

I turn and it's the politician from the Daimler.

'That's a beautiful dress.'

'Thanks.'

'Are you available for a fuck at all?'

'Not just at the moment I'm afraid.'

'Right ho,' he says and totters off to try his luck

elsewhere. Judging by the number of hostesses in the club tonight, he shouldn't have any trouble. I can see the woman he came in with at a corner table sitting close to a young good-looking type, so I reckon they both know why they're here. A gent along the bar is chuckling at what he's just heard.

'I'm afraid Sir David can be a little tactless,' he says.

I give him a smile, get the barman's attention and ask for a large whisky.

'Can I get that for you?' says the gent.

'I'm all right, thanks.'

When the barman puts my drink in front of me I give him a quid, tell him to keep the change and ask if I can get a message to someone at a table. He speaks to a young waitress who's collecting two bottles of champagne and when she's taken them to the table she comes over to me. I point George out and ask her to tell him discreetly that a friend of his is at the bar. She goes to his table, gets his attention, speaks to him and he looks across and sees me. He says something to his guests, stands up and walks through the tables and past the bandstand. The gent at the bar still has his eyes on me as I finish my drink and follow George, who's gone through a door at the back of the club.

The minder on the door won't let me through at first but George's name does it and I walk along a corridor and see him at the far end talking to Bobby Grant, a right old villain who owns the Astor and promotes bands who he rips off and treats like shit. I don't want him to know I work with George but he's seen me and it's too late.

'Well… look at Miss World coming along to join us,' he says, as I approach.

'This is Rina, Harry Walker's girl,' says George.

'How did old Harry produce a beautiful piece like this?'

'I reckon her mum might have had something to do with it, eh?'

'Right enough. Alice was fucking gorgeous.'

I manage to control myself and look suitably modest and demure while they discuss Mum and me like prize cattle and I'm thinking it's no wonder she went on the bottle and ended up topping herself, surrounded by men like these.

'Any time you want a job here Rina, you just say the word, girl.'

I manage a brief smile as he walks past me towards the club.

'I'll see you later, George.'

'OK to use your office?' asks George.

'Help yourself.'

'Cheers Bobby,' says George, opening the door and showing me inside.

There's a desk with a leather chair behind it, two upright ones in front and an array of bottles on a shelf behind. George picks up a bottle of whisky.

'Usual?' he says.

'Go on.'

He pours two large ones, hands one to me, sits behind the desk and loosens his tie. I take a chair opposite him.

'You broke Fenton's jaw last night.'

'Good.'

'Too right. His brother Charlie was a filthy fucking grass. You did right to off him and Fenton's been told to swallow it and keep clear of you.'

'Cheers.'

'That fucking family.'

'South London aren't they?'

'Peckham mostly.'

I take a pull on some very good whisky. 'What did you want to see me about?'

'I've got one for you.'

'What is it?'

'I seen Jack Drake in Broadmoor last week.'

'I thought he was in Belmarsh.'

'He was until he'd battered so many screws they had him put in the Moor.'

'How's he doing in there?'

'He hates it and he's going raving fucking mad. His wife Millie went to see him and told him it was over. He went for her and it took four of them to pull him off her. Then he found out she's taken the kids and shacked up with some young geezer and he wants him done.'

Years ago, George and Jack Drake robbed a security van

together down in Kent. George rammed the van with a Land Rover and Jack held a shotgun on the guards while they opened up. It was going well until a squad car turned up out of nowhere and two coppers laid into Jack while George got away in the Land Rover. Jack had a lot of form and got a fifteen for it. They offered to halve it if he'd give them George but he stuck to the code and took the fifteen, so George has got no choice but to do what he wants.

'Who's the new bloke?'

'Some builder, he reckons. She's moved out to Romford with him and the kids.'

The work George gives me almost always involves people who are well in the game and know what could happen to them if they take a liberty but this one sounds like a straight who may not know that he's gone across one of the most dangerous men in London. He'd probably back off with a frightener but of course Jack Drake'll need to be known to have done him to keep his reputation.

I really don't want to be chasing round Romford for some builder but I don't have much choice. I have to do what George puts my way because he knows I killed his eldest son when he was raping Georgie and he could put me up for it. Even though he can't do that without letting it be known that his son was a nonce, I can't afford to take the chance.

'It'll cost you two large,' I say.

'Putting your price up?'

'Have you been to Romford?'

He laughs, takes a sheaf of notes out of his jacket pocket and hands it to me. 'There's a monkey, expenses.'

I put the notes in my bag. 'Have you got an address?'

'Ray's working on it. He'll call you.'

George finishes his drink, gets up from the desk, opens the door and follows me along the corridor. The door to the club opens and a young hostess in a short lurex dress dashes past us followed by Bobby Grant slapping her about the head and cursing her blind for something or other. I'd like to get hold of the old sod and make him lay off her but I know it would only start all kinds of aggravation. George can tell I want to get at him and he puts his hand on my arm and shakes his head. I give him a nod and stand back to let him go into the club before me. I give him time to get to his table and when I go in Anita starts swinging it with 'Watermelon Man'. As I skirt the dance floor I'm aware that the gent who was at the bar has his eye on me. Anita's good at what she does but she's not my cup of tea so I leave by the main door and enjoy a nice bit of fresh air as I head for Berkeley Square.

I sit in the car a moment and think about what George wants me to do. I've never met Jack's wife Millie but I know she's a good bit younger than him and I can see how she wouldn't want to wait ten years to welcome back a nasty violent bear of a man who's finally gone off his rocker and ended up in Broadmoor. On the other hand, I can see that George has got no choice but to do what he asks. As I'm driving round Piccadilly, on the way to see Lizzie at the club, I begin to get an idea of how I might be able to handle it.

When I get to the club Max is on his own at the door and I notice one of his hands is bandaged. He sees me coming and puts it in his jacket pocket.

'How's the hand?' I ask.

'Still working,' he says, taking it out of his pocket and showing me the small cosh he's holding.

'Did it get broken last night?'

'Just a couple of knuckles.'

'You don't need to be here you know, I can always get someone in.'

'I'm all right, thanks.'

'OK,' I say, as he opens the door with his good hand. I go into the foyer, smiling at what hard men will put up with before they'll lose respect.

The band are getting into 'The Wind Cries Mary' as I go down the stairs and I'm looking forward to hearing Caesar playing the guitar solo better than Hendrix until I round the bend in the stairs and see that it's not him on guitar. The bloke who's standing in is older and nowhere near as good-looking. He's making a reasonable job of it but he hasn't got Caesar's feel. The club's almost full, the atmosphere's warm and friendly and I'm really glad it's going so well, for Lizzie's sake. I see her at the far end of the bar talking to Jane, the assistant manager. As I make my way towards them, Lizzie sees me and comes over.

'You made it,' she says, giving me a squeeze.

'Looks like a good night.'

'We were turning them away round midnight.'

'Where's Caesar?'

'I don't know.'

We move to the bar where there's a bit more light and Lizzie moves closer to me and strokes my face. 'You look a bit knackered, darling. Everything OK?'

'Not as knackered as Dave Priest.'

'Oh yeah?'

'All done.'

'Blimey, that was quick.'

'You know me.'

'I sure do,' she says, putting her arm round me.

I used to try to keep Lizzie from knowing about my dark doings but with her having the club and the battles for the protection and the pimping and all, she's well in the game herself now. There's not a lot I can do about it, so I tell her everything. Especially since she stepped into a bit of bother I'd got into in Spain a while ago and saved my life.

'Did Kelly come in?' I ask.

'No. I'll phone her in the morning and tell her. Jane and Max can take it from here and close up, if you fancy going somewhere to unwind a bit?'

'Sure.'

'The 100 Club's on an all-nighter.'

'Let's go.'

'I'll just tell Jane, then I've got to nip to the office.'

'I'll see you upstairs.'

While she goes to talk to Jane, the boys finish the Hendrix and I go to the bandstand and ask Tim, the piano player, where Caesar is. He tells me he just got a call from him this afternoon to say he couldn't make it but he doesn't know why. I ask about the new guy and he says he's a session player who knows the set and I pass him a tenner to give to the bloke for helping out. When I see Lizzie coming out of the office, I say goodnight to Tim and follow her up the stairs.

After Lizzie's had a chat with Max on the door, we walk round Soho Square and along Oxford Street to the 100 Club. It's six bob to get in and Eric Burden and the Animals are top of the bill with support from The Bakerloo Blues Line, who are on when we get in there and rocking it up nicely with 'Dust my Blues'. It's mostly girls who are dancing and we get in with them. Lizzie whirls me round and we jive it up for a bit, then we move nice and slow to a sneaky version of 'Stormy Monday'. In the break we down a couple of large ones and then the Animals come on and we watch them burn through a great set, with Eric giving it all he's got.

When they finish and the roadies start shifting the gear, we decide we've had enough and it's time for bed. We head for the exit and as we get near it I can hear someone shouting. The voice sounds familiar and it's coming from behind a door beside the ticket desk that's half open. I look in and see Bobby Grant shaking his finger and bellowing in the face of a tall thin bloke in a suit and tie. Behind him, and looking confused, are the Bakerloo boys. I move aside so Lizzie can have a look then we step out of the door, flag down a cab and get in.

'That was Bobby Grant from the Astor, wasn't it?' says Lizzie.

'He can be a nasty piece of work.'

'I know. He came to the club in the week.'

'Was he after something?'

'I don't think so. Just said hello and had a couple of drinks, then I saw him talking to Caesar and he left.'

'Checking the place out.'

'I reckon.'

We sit back as the cab drives through the dawn. When it stops in our street we go into the house and decide on my place. I open the door and see an envelope on the mat. While Lizzie goes into the bedroom, I open it and see that it's a note from George's man Ray, telling me to meet him in the Warwick at eleven o'clock tomorrow, which means he should have the address of Jack's wife in Romford. I drop it on the table beside the phone and go into the bedroom. When Lizzie's finished taking off her clothes, she helps me out of mine and we get into bed and make love.

4

It's another beautiful sunny day and I can see Ray sitting outside the pub as I walk round the corner into Warwick Place. He stands up when he sees me, goes into the pub and I join him at the bar.

'Whisky isn't it?' he says.

'Right first time.'

He buys a scotch for me, a pint for himself, and I follow him to a corner table.

'Have you got the news on Jack Drake's missus?' I say, as I sit down.

'Only an address.'

'That'll do.'

He passes me a piece of paper.

'It's Millie, isn't it?'

'Yeah.'

'What does she look like?'

'Small, blond, dishy.'

'What do you know about the new bloke?'

'He's called Joe. He's a digger driver.'

'Kids?'

'Millie's got two. The boy's about eighteen, done a bit of Borstal. The girl's younger.'

'Nothing else on the new bloke?'

He shakes his head and I drain my glass. 'I'll be off to Romford then.'

'You want me to come with?'

'No, you're all right.'

The last thing I need on this job is a sniffer like Ray looking over my shoulder. He's one of the many faces in the game that I'd never trust and I'm not sure why George keeps him on the firm but I suppose he must have his reasons. I thank him for the drink and he takes a *Daily Mail* out of his pocket and opens it up as I leave.

I look at the piece of paper Ray gave me and as I pass the cabbies' shelter in Warwick Avenue, I ask a couple of drivers drinking tea outside if they know where Olive Street is in Romford. One of them stares at my tits while the other one tells me it's off Mawney Road which is a turning off the A12 just as you get into Romford. I thank him and when I get to the car, I look in my A to Z and plot a route along Old Street, through Stratford and onto the A12.

The Sunday traffic's light and an hour later I'm in Romford and driving down Mawney Road. The cabby was as good as his word and I turn into Olive Street and drive between two rows of small semi-detached houses, mostly grey pebbledash and a bit tatty looking. I'm guessing this is Joe's place, rather than the home of ace bank robber, Jack Drake. I check the address, pull up where I can see number 54 and sure enough there's a white van parked right in front of the house. I look at my watch and see it's nearly one o'clock. I slide my seat back, put on my sunglasses and take my Bob Dylan cap off the back seat.

Half an hour later when I'm fighting to resist sleep and wishing I'd brought something to read, the front door of number 54 opens and a petite blond woman, who looks in her mid-thirties, with a pretty face and a shopping bag in each hand, walks to the van, opens the back doors and puts the bags inside. She's joined by a dark-haired girl of about fifteen who carries a folded rug and a picnic basket which she gives to the woman to put in the van. As I'm thinking this must be Millie and her daughter, a tall good-looking bloke of about thirty, who looks like he could be Joe, comes out of the house, talking to a teenage boy who's got his hands in his pockets and his head down. When the boy turns away and leans on the wall of the house, the man shakes his head, walks to the van, opens the passenger door for the girl and then gets into the driving seat. Millie goes to the boy and after she's spoken to him for a bit she takes his hand and he follows her to the van and gets in.

They move off and I follow at a discreet distance as they drive along Mawney Road and turn east onto the A12. It's a beautiful day for the beach and I'm guessing that's where we're headed.

About an hour later I follow the van into Clacton until it stops in one of the streets near the seafront. I pull in nearby and watch the four of them get out and carry the bags and picnic basket towards the beach. When they're out of sight I drive around a bit until I see a covered market. I park the car, go in and walk around until I see a stall selling bathing suits and beach stuff. When I've got myself a bikini, a towel and a sun hat with a big floppy brim, I drive back to where the van is and park near it. I swap the Dylan cap for the sun hat, roll the bikini up in the towel and walk to the beach. There's quite a few people enjoying the sun, sea and sand and it takes a minute before I spot Millie and the others near the pier. As I lay out my towel a short distance away, with a few people between me and them, I can see Millie sitting on the rug in her bathing suit, watching Joe and her daughter playing about in the sea together. The girl pelts him with water and she laughs as he picks her up, twirls her round and plunges her down into the waves. It reminds me of being here with my dad, when I was a little kid and he took me in the sea and played with me like that, then he put me on a donkey ride and we had candy floss and I'd never been so happy. Dad got drunk later and me and Mum couldn't wake him up when it was time to go so she had to phone Bert to come and get us.

Joe and the girl are still playing about in the sea and Millie's smiling as she watches them, then Joe strikes out for the horizon and the girl swims after him for a bit and then turns back to the shore. I can see how long-limbed and lovely she is as she walks up the beach, picks up a towel and dries herself. She says something to her brother, who's lying fully clothed on his side nearby and he shakes his head and rolls onto his back.

I'm beginning to feel the heat so I take my blouse off, put the towel round my shoulders and execute the difficult manoeuvre of changing my bra for the bikini top, then I stand up, slip my skirt off, put the towel round my waist, and just manage to take my pants off and get the other half of the bikini on without dropping the towel, much to the disappointment of the bloke in the nearby deckchair who's been watching me over the top of his newspaper. I look across and see that Joe has come out of the sea and is sitting next to Millie who is delving into the picnic basket and handing out sandwiches and cans of Coke to him and her daughter. She offers a can to the boy who rolls towards her, takes it and rolls away again. Millie, Joe and the daughter are enjoying their picnic, chatting away, having a laugh and a joke, and looking as if they're having a great afternoon on the beach while doing their best to ignore young moodychops, who's downed his Coke and looks like he's asleep for the duration. After they've finished the picnic they stretch out and sunbathe. Joe lies next to Millie and holds her hand.

I take a dip in the sea and as I swim out towards the end of the pier I make a decision. After however many years Millie's been with Jack Drake, she seems happy with her new man and so does her daughter and no matter what's going on with her son, she's got a right to make a new life for herself and I'm not going to be the one to screw it up for her. All I need to do now is find a way of making sure no one else does.

When I get back to the beach I can see them packing up their stuff so I stay in the water until they pick everything up and head for the van. I take my time drying off and getting dressed then I walk back to the car and buy myself an ice cream on the way.

• • •

After a night of hardly any sleep, agonising about whether I'm doing the right thing and if I've got a snowball's chance of getting away with it, I decide I've got to take a stand against mad Jack Drake and give an honest woman and her kids a chance of a decent life with a good man. After three cups of coffee in the kitchen I reckon I've got a plan. The first thing I need to do is talk to Millie.

I get dressed, drive to Romford and it's just gone seven in the morning when I park in Olive Street with a good view of the house. Half an hour later Joe comes out of the front door, in his work clothes and big boots, climbs into the van and drives off. I've nearly dozed off listening to the radio when I see Millie's daughter come out in her school uniform a while later. As she gets to the pavement, her mother appears and hurries after her clutching an exercise book which she puts in her satchel. I wait a bit after Millie's gone back inside, then I take two hundred quid in fivers out of my pocket, go to the door and ring the bell. After a moment the door opens.

'It's Millie, isn't it?'

'Who wants to know?'

'My name's Rina. I've got something for you.'

'What?'

'From George Preston,' I say, holding the notes out to her.

She looks at the money, then at me, and takes a step back. 'I don't want it. Go away.'

'I need to talk to you.'

'I don't want nothing to do with him or anyone like him so take his fucking money and go.'

She tries to shut the door but I put my foot against it. 'Please, let me talk to you for a minute.'

She puts her weight against the door and tries to shut it. I move closer to her. 'You're in danger and I can help you.'

I feel the door give a little.

'Just hear what I've got to tell you, then I'll go.'

The door opens a bit more.

'It's straight up, I promise you.'

She looks me in the eye, then she opens the door and has a quick look each way along the street. 'All right. Come in, quick.'

I go into the hall and she closes the door, shows me into the front room, points to a chair and sits opposite me on the sofa.

'Say it,' she says.

'Jack knows about Joe.'

'I don't care. I've finished with that bastard.'

'You'll care when I tell you what he's done.'

'What who's done?'

'Jack.'

'What are you on about?'

'He's told George Preston to take care of Joe.'

The colour drains from her face and her hands start to shake.

'You mean…'

I nod and she moves quickly to the window and stares out. Then she turns to me. 'Why are you telling me this?'

'I'm the one he's given the job to.'

She looks at me and her eyes harden. She bolts to the fireplace, grabs the poker in both hands and swings it at my head. I duck just in time, rip it out of her hand, throw her onto the sofa and hold her down. 'I told you I'm here to help you, so calm the fuck down and listen to me.'

Her breathing slows and she nods her head. I give it a moment, then I relax my grip and sit her up.

'I'm sorry,' she says.

'It's all right, but you need to listen to me.'

'Go on.'

'I agreed to do what George told me to do because I've got no choice, but now I've seen you with Joe and your kids and I'm not going to touch him. It's not right and that's the end of it.'

'So why are you telling me?'

'Because if I don't do it, George'll get someone else, because he owes Jack and he can't say no to him. He'll make sure the next one who gets the work won't be bothered and Joe will be at the bottom of Millwall Dock in a pair of concrete trousers.'

'Then what can we do?'

'This is how it needs to go. You and your kids disappear abroad right now. Joe goes where he can't be found and I tell George I've done him. Once the dust settles, Joe goes to where you are and you carry on your life.'

Millie lowers her eyes and seems to study the carpet while she takes in what I've said. After some thought she looks up, 'Where should we go?'

'Somewhere on the continent where you don't need visas.'

'Like Spain?'

'Anywhere but Spain.'

'Why?'

'Too many faces who've taken it on their toes over there.'

'I went to Greece once.'

'Sounds good.'

'Why can't Joe come with us when we go?'

'In case he's seen with you. The airport or somewhere.'

'Right.'

'Are you on?'

She straightens the cushion next to her, looks around the room and then into my eyes. 'I've got a question.'

'Go on.'

'Why are you doing this?'

'I saw you on the beach with him. You looked happy and he looks like a decent bloke.'

Tears well up in her eyes. 'He is.'

'How did you meet him?'

'At his mother's funeral.'

'Yeah?'

'She always used to clean for us in Bethnal Green before Jack went inside. She was a lovely woman and I knew she had a son but I'd never met him, then he was at the funeral and we started talking afterwards and… you know.'

'Your daughter seems to like him.'

'Wendy loves him.'

'Your boy?'

'He misses his dad and he doesn't like Joe being with us but I'm hoping he'll come round.'

She looks a bit wistful for a moment then she takes a deep breath, puts her shoulders back and sits up. 'I've got to thank you for what you're doing. You're right about us getting out of the way, and I need to talk to Joe.'

'When can you do that?'

'He's on a job in Barking. I've got the site office number somewhere, so I can try to get hold of him.'

'Sooner the better.'

She gets up off the sofa. 'Come through.'

She leads me along the hall into the kitchen, picks up her handbag from the table, crosses to the telephone on the wall, takes a piece of paper from her bag and dials a number. After a moment she asks if she can speak to Joe

Mason. She covers the phone and turns to me. 'They're on a tea break.'

I go to the window and look out into the small back garden, with it's neat lawn and flower beds, and wonder what it would be like to live an ordered life, then I hear Millie telling her man he's got to come home.

5

I find a travel agent in Romford High Street and park the car on a meter a couple of hundred yards away. Fortunately both the kids have passports, which I leaf through as I walk. Wendy is fourteen years old. The boy's name is Ronald and he's four years older than his sister. I see that they've been to France a couple of times and Spain too. Millie told me that Jack was prone to taking them out of school and whisking them off abroad for a holiday when the fancy took him, usually after a big prize, and then spending all day and night in the casino, doing his wad and leaving her to look after the kids. Joe was on his way home when I left Millie. We decided it was better for her to tell him the score by herself and that I should get out of the way and phone her when she's had a chance to talk to him and then, if it's all go, get the tickets to Greece. I've got some time to kill and I'm feeling hungry so I go into a café and order myself some scrambled eggs on toast and a coffee.

I pick up a *Daily Mirror* off the counter and take it to the table. There's a picture of a writer called Joe Orton on the front page who's been beaten to death with a hammer by his lover Kenneth Halliwell. The paper says that according to the police, Halliwell hit him nine times, left his head "cratered like a burnt candle", and then took an overdose of sleeping pills and killed himself. Apparently it all happened in Orton's tiny flat in Islington. I think of Dave Priest doing the same thing to poor Rose and I'm thankful I've stopped him. I turn the page and there's an article about the inquiry into the Aberfan disaster, where the slag heap collapsed on the mining village, killing a hundred and sixty-four people. The inquiry, which has taken a year to arrive, blames the Coal Board for not constructing the heap properly and there's a really sad picture of mothers holding their babies outside what looks like a village hall. It's terrible that something like that could be allowed to happen and I hope the people responsible will suffer for it. I'm turning the pages, hoping for a more cheerful bit of news, when my breakfast arrives. I wolf it down, order a coffee to take away and walk to a phone box near the travel agent's.

When Millie answers, I push a threepenny bit into the slot and she tells me that Joe is on board and agrees that the sooner she and the kids get away the better. I ask her if she can be ready to leave in the morning, she says she can and I go to the travel agent and buy three one-way tickets to Athens leaving from Gatwick tomorrow. I drive back to the house, Millie opens the door and I follow her into the lounge. Joe gets up off the sofa, holds out his hand and we shake. I give the wallet containing the tickets and the passports to Millie.

'That's you and the kids on the 9am flight to Athens from Gatwick tomorrow. You need to get there about 7 o'clock.'

Millie opens the wallet and when she's looked at the tickets I hand her another envelope. She opens it and takes out a wad of notes.

'What's this?' she asks.

'Something to help you get sorted over there.' I reply.

'Look at this,' she says, handing the wad to Joe who flicks through it.

'Must be a grand at least,' he says.

'One and a half,' I say.

'I can't take this from you,' says Millie.

'You can and you will.'

'But...'

I ignore her and turn to Joe, who's looking confused. 'We need to talk.'

'Right.'

Joe gives Millie a look and she picks up the tickets, passports and money and leaves the room.

'She's told you the score?'

'Yes.'

'And you're OK?'

'I've got to be, ain't I?'

'I reckon.'

'What I didn't tell your lady was that, for insurance, I need to be able to prove I've offed you.'

'How can you do that?'

'You drive a digger, don't you?'

'Yeah.'

'How wide is the bucket?'

'Four foot.'

'That'll do.'

'What for?'

'I need a photograph of you lying in it, with a bullet hole in your head, looking like you're about to be buried, that I can get to Jack Drake.'

'Blimey.'

'Where's your digger now?'

'On the site in Barking.'

'Can we get to it tonight?'

'The gates will be shut.'

'What kind of lock?'

'Padlock.'

'Not a problem. Night watchman?'

'No.'

'I'll pick you up here at two o'clock tomorrow morning.'

'Right.'

'What's essential is that you don't get seen by anyone who could know Jack and his merry men, between then and when you get on a plane.'

'Why can't I go with them tomorrow?'

'Chances are he'll have someone keeping tabs on them, which is how he knew about you and his missus. If he's told they were seen at the airport without you, he'll just think they're off on holiday.'

'Oh, right.'

'Is there anywhere you can go?'

'My brother's in Barking.'

'Family won't work.'

'I've got a caravan over Rainham Marshes.'

'Sounds good. I'll drop you there after we've done the business.'

'Can't I take the van?'

'It's got to stay here.'

'Right.'

I'll see you at two.'

I leave Joe slowly shaking his head and go to the kitchen where Millie is filling the kettle.

'Cup of tea?'

'No thanks.'

She turns to me and I can see she's been crying.

'I don't know how to thank you for what you're doing.'

'It's OK, really.'

'The money and…'

'Don't worry about it.'

'But it's so much.'

'Just make sure you and the kids get on that plane.'

'I will.'

'Where did you go in Greece when you went before?'

'It was a lovely island called Hydra.'

'Go there when you get off the plane and tell Joe, so he knows where to find you.'

'I will.'

I look into the front room on the way out and remind Joe to be ready to go later, then I let myself out and walk to the car.

The traffic's heavy in London and it's halfway through the afternoon by the time I get home. I knock on Lizzie's door and I'm just about to give up and go into mine when she opens it looking sleepy in that baby doll nightie that always gets me going. I put my arms around her, nuzzle into her lovely soft neck and kick the door shut behind me. When we've had a good hug and a cuddle she leads me along the corridor, 'I've got some of the new Guerlain bubble bath.'

'Mmm… Have you now?'

I go and start running the bath, turn on the radio and get Cream banging out 'Sunshine of your Love'. Lizzie comes in with two whiskies, puts them on the side of the bath, adds a big dollop of Guerlain and we have a shimmy along with the boys as we take our clothes off and then slip into the silky warm water, sip our drinks and relax.

'How was the club last night?' I ask.

'All good, apart from a couple of punters fighting over a girl.'

'Which girl?'

'Heather.'

Heather is a lass from Lancashire. She's only about nineteen but she doesn't stand any nonsense.

'One of them throws a drink in the other's face and they start prancing round the dance floor with their fists up looking right idiots. As I'm pressing the bell for Max to come down, Heather trips one of them up and he falls flat on his face. While he's trying to get up, she whips the other mug into the back room. Max comes down, gets hold of the loser, makes him settle his bill and chucks him out.'

'We should have a minder inside.'

'Terry normally sits at the bar, ever since that Murphy ruck, but he'd nipped out to take care of something.'

'Did Kelly come in?'

'Yes.'

'Is she all right?'

'She was once I told her Dave Priest was cold.'

'Will she know it was me?'

'I reckon she might.'

'We should have given her a story.'

'Kelly's no fool, her brothers are as wide as a barn door and she's no stranger to a bit of action.'

I finish my drink, lie back in the water and stroke Lizzie's ankle.

'Mmm... that's nice,' she says, closing her eyes and sinking further down into the water as my fingers wander on up her leg.

• • •

I wake as Lizzie gets out of bed. I watch her put on her silk dressing gown and marvel at her beauty and the graceful way she moves about the room as she chooses her look for the evening. When she opens the doors to the wardrobe, I get a glimpse of the studded leather suits she used to wear when she worked as a mistress. They're bunched up at the far end of the rail and some of the masks and whips and different scourges she used are poking out of a canvas bag underneath. Now she's the manager of a hostess club and all respectable and legit, she chooses a pale blue silk blouse and a tailored suit in a darker blue which she hangs on the wardrobe door while she puts on underwear and nylons. When she slips on the suit and blouse, a pair of four inch heels and does her make-up and hair, she looks every inch the cool businesswoman and I almost feel like I should ask permission to get out of bed.

'Bye, loveliness,' she says, giving me a peck on the forehead and picking up her Hermès handbag.

'Do you want a lift to the club?'

'Relax. I'll get a cab.'

'Have a good night.'

'I will. Stay hot.'

As she sweeps out of the door, I feel how lucky I am to have such a wonderful lover who's stayed by me through all kinds of rough stuff over the years, right back to when I was fifteen and we buried Georgie's rapist in the rubbish dump in Talbot Grove in the middle of the night after I'd cut his throat. We carried him down there in an old pram, with Mum and my mate Claire, and Mum had to deck a couple of blokes who tried to be funny with us on the way. I'm so glad I was able to buy the club for Lizzie so she doesn't have to do the mistressing and service people who like it strange any more.

I put my clothes on and go upstairs to my flat. I make myself a ham sandwich and a cup of coffee, take them into the lounge and turn on the television. 'The Avengers' is on

ITV and Diana Rigg's looking good in a tight pink dress although I want to see her in her black catsuit with a chain round her waist. I've missed the beginning but it seems to be all about cats anyway. A rich businessman and some other people have been killed and it looks like they've been mauled to death by a tiger or another big cat. Steed and Emma come across this mob from a cat protection charity who are turning cats into miniature tigers and using radio waves to make them maul and kill people. They go after them and Emma Peel gets captured and tied to a chair but she manages to escape and wreck the radio transmitter, which gets the cats purring and being normal cats again. It's all a bit daft but they get there in the end and open a bottle of champagne. 'It's a Knockout' is up next and I turn the volume down, lie back on the sofa and drift off to sleep again while one team of idiots in big foam rubber suits try to carry buckets of water over greasy poles and another team of idiots squirt them with water cannons and pelt them with custard pies.

I wake up to the Epilogue, turn off the boring vicar, go into the bedroom and change into the black jeans, T-shirt, jacket and boots. Joe seems like he's on the level but as I don't know him I'm not taking any chances so the blades go in the boots and the Smith & Wesson in my belt. I put a couple of lipsticks, some mascara and a brush in my pocket along with my lock picks, then I get my Polaroid camera from the top shelf of the wardrobe. I go to the kitchen, put the camera in a carrier bag along with a bottle of Heinz tomato ketchup and a sponge and head for the car.

The streets are quiet and I get to Romford in good time and tap on the door of the house. Joe's ready to go, with a bag packed, and we get in the car and drive to Barking. On the way I ask him how he's feeling but he just grunts, so I don't push it and we drive in silence. The building site is massive with tower blocks being built to replace run-down tenements and poor housing, like councils are doing all over the country. Joe directs me to the far end of the site and I park near a wooden gate and turn on the interior light.

'This is where I make you look the part,' I say reaching for the carrier bag.

'You what?'

'Turn to me and hold still.'

When he sees me take out the mascara and the brush, he gets the idea and holds his face up to the light. I paint a .38 calibre hole in his forehead with the mascara and mix some lipstick into it to look like blood's oozing out. When I'm satisfied it looks convincing, we get out of the car and I pick the padlock without any bother, open the gate and follow Joe to where his digger is parked. We've got a bit of moonlight and I can see that it's right next to a big foundation trench which is perfect. I get him into the bucket and make him lie on his side, with his head on the lip, as if he's been dumped in there after he's been shot, then I tell him to hold still while I squeeze some ketchup onto his forehead to look like it's blood dripping from the bullet hole.

I take out the camera, look through the lens and I reckon I've got it. I switch on the flash, take a photograph and after I've waited and peeled off the coating, I'm satisfied that it looks convincing, all the more so because it's black and white. I take a couple more shots, one close-up of Joe with his eyes open and one with them shut, then I take a wider one showing the foundation trench, as if that's where he's going to get buried. The one with his eyes open looks better so I show it to Joe, who looks a bit shocked, then I clean up his face as much as I can and we go back to the car. He doesn't speak, apart from directing me to Rainham Marshes and when I drop him off at his caravan and remind him to keep his head down and leave for Greece in a couple of days he just nods and gets out of the car. I watch while he unlocks the caravan and goes in, then I drive off.

When I come out the other side of Dagenham on the A13, the sun's rising and I know I'm being followed.

6

It looks like a Ford Corsair, which is nippy but lousy round corners. It's a built-up area and I could turn off the main road and lose him easy enough but after what's just gone on I need to know who it is and what they saw. I wait for a bit of open country, take a left turn onto a straight two-lane road through some farmland and put my foot down. The Corsair follows and when it gets up close behind I can see there's only the driver in there. I get the gun out of my belt, open the window, stamp on the brake and pull over. As the Corsair lunges past me I fire three shots at his back wheel. The tyre bursts and I follow him close as he skids left and right and then slams sideways into the gutter. The car tips up on two wheels and almost goes over, then it thumps back down onto the tarmac. I jump out of the Mini, rip the driver's door open, aim the gun at his face and pull back the hammer.

'Get out. Slowly.'

He raises his hands and steps out onto the road. It's a tall man in a pinstripe suit and a stiff collar and as he straightens up I recognise the toff who offered me a drink at the Astor. I back off a bit and keep him covered. 'What the fuck are you doing?'

'I could ask you the same question,' he says, massaging his elbow.

'Tell me why you're here or I'll put one in your leg.'

'I'd like to talk to you.'

'There are easier ways.'

I hear an engine, look round and see a car approaching. I open the passenger door of the Mini, make him get in and I sit next to him, pointing the gun. He's got a narrow, gaunt face and there's a cold, distant look in his eyes as he turns them on me.

'I have a proposition for you.'

'No fucking way.'

'Perhaps Mr Jack Drake would be interested to know what I've just seen.'

'How about if I kill you now and you've just died in a car crash?'

'My colleague who's watching us would be most disappointed.'

I hear the car slow down and I glance round as it stops a short distance away.

'Drive,' I say, opening the door. The toff shifts over while I get into the passenger seat and hold the gun in my lap.

'Is the Ford traceable?' I ask, as he pulls away.

'Not remotely. What about this?'

'Belongs to a dead fishmonger from Bridgnorth.'

'We're clear then.'

I look at his fine profile as he drives and wonder what his game is and how he knows about Jack Drake. He talked about a proposition and the last thing I want is more work at the moment but he's clearly a pro of some sort with back-up and he's got me for what he knows I've done with Joe, so I've got to keep on him.

'The breakfast at the Langham is quite presentable,' he says, as he turns the car back onto the A13.

'I'm not quite dressed for it.'

'A private room?'

There's a risk of him getting his "colleague" in and offing me if I'm alone in a room with him but I suppose he could have done it already if that was the plan and I'm starving hungry.

'Sounds all right,' I say, releasing the hammer.

The early morning rush is starting to build up as we go through Whitechapel but he knows his way to the West End and it's not long before he's parking the car in Portland Place. The doorman at the Langham tips his hat to him, opens the door for us and I follow him to the desk. I stand a short distance away while he exchanges a few words with the clerk and then heads for the lifts, ignoring a bellboy who presses the call button. We go up to the fourth floor and along the corridor. He takes a key out of his pocket, which I didn't see him get from the clerk, opens a door and ushers me inside. The room looks like an office, with a mahogany desk at one end with a couple of chairs in front of it. There are two filing cabinets and a table with drinks on it along one wall and a single bed opposite.

'It's Rina, isn't it?'

'It is.'

'I'm Jeremy,' he says, offering me a chair. As he's about to sit down behind the desk, there's a knock at the door and he opens it to a waiter who offers him a couple of menus. He passes one to me and turns to the waiter. 'Grapefruit, Eggs Benedict, toast, and lashings of coffee.'

'That'll do,' I say, wondering what Eggs Benedict is. I hand the menu to the waiter, who bows out of the door while Jeremy sits behind the desk.

'Quite a night,' he says, leaning back in his chair.

When I don't respond he leans forward with his elbows on the desk.

'You'll recall meeting Sir David Ashbury at the Astor when he suggested you might like to... entertain him.'

'I do.'

'Sir David, as you may know, is the Conservative member of Parliament for Basingstoke and also happens to be my father-in-law. He has always enjoyed a varied and eclectic social life and taken full advantage of the many carnal delights available in our great city. Unfortunately his behaviour of late has become increasingly erratic and he could become a considerable embarrassment to the party, which would not in itself present any great difficulty or be particularly unusual, but one of his erstwhile lovers has decided to blackmail him, and in spite of being paid handsomely, simply will not go away.'

'Why are you telling me this?'

'I know you have a certain form in removing the inconvenient and I would like to offer you the job.'

'Why don't you put him on a pension?'

'Believe me we have tried. He has been given all manner of inducements to stop this harassment but he simply will not be discouraged. He's an extremely vindictive and unsavoury character and it is high time to take action.'

'How do you know I've got form?'

'I believe you were once instrumental in dealing with an enemy agent in Berlin.'

This is beginning to make sense. I fell into doing a bit of work for Military Intelligence a few years ago that got a bit complicated. The bloke who hired me turned out to be a spy and defected to Moscow so I thought my account with them was closed, but clearly not. This one looks like a fit for MI6 and if he is, there could be more to this than saving the reputation of an MP. There's no way out of it for me without risking Jack Drake discovering what I've done with Joe so I decide to get on with it.

'What are you paying?'

'A thousand pounds?'

'Not less than two.'

'Very well.'

He goes to a filing cabinet, takes out a photograph and hands it to me.

'This is Mark Weston.'

I'm looking at a man of about thirty, longish dark hair, good-looking, average height. He's walking along a city street, looking a bit shifty, and doesn't know he's being photographed.

'Where do I find him?'

'We believe he's in the West Midlands,' he says, handing me a piece of paper with an address in Stourbridge written on it.

'I must insist on clear proof of completion on this one. A photograph, as you'll understand, will not do.'

'Where do I find you?'

He takes a card out of his waistcoat pocket and gives it to me. There's no name, just an address in Belgravia and two phone numbers. I put it in my back pocket.

'I'm Brenda Matthews.'

'Very well.'

'And I'll need expenses.'

He takes a cash box out of the other filing cabinet and counts twenty-five notes off a roll of tens. As he hands them to me there's a knock at the door. Jeremy opens it and the waiter pushes a trolley laden with silver domes into the middle of the room.

Benedict certainly knows how to turn an egg into a winner and I'm still tasting the delicious creamy sauce as I walk along Portland Place. As I get to the car I'm wondering if I should get rid of it after last night's fun and games. Jeremy will have it down to me so I really ought to let it go. I find a phone box and call my mate Tommy at the breakers yard in Kensal Green. He tells me he's got a good Hillman Imp van for sale so I drive to the yard and have a look. It's dark blue, quite discreet and nearly new. I take it up Harrow Road and round a few corners. It's lively and handles well and Tommy tells me the Imp won the Tulip Rally a couple of years ago so I reckon it'll do. He wants two hundred for it but accepts one fifty, if I give him the Mini to sell for parts. I clear my tools and blades out of the old car, stash them in the Imp and drive it home.

I ought to go straight to George, tell him the news, show him the photograph and get it done but after the night's work and breakfast at the Langham, I decide to get some kip and see him later. I know Lizzie will be asleep at this time so I go straight to my flat, take a hot shower to loosen up and get into bed.

• • •

The phone wakes me. I look at the clock and see that I've slept for the whole day. I stumble into the hall and pick up the receiver.

'Governor's wanting news,' says Bert.

'I've got something for him.'

'Shall I pick you up?'

'Where is he?'

'White City.'

'I'll get there. How will I find you?'

'You won't. It's packed. I'll meet you at the gate.'

I hear the crowd roar behind him. I'm not in the mood for dog racing but I might as well get the photo to George and be done with it.

'Give me half an hour.'

I put the phone down and dial Lizzie's number. There's no reply so she's probably at the club. I'm thinking I might go and have a look at this Weston bloke after I've seen George. I feel a need to clear the decks so that me and Lizzie can get away somewhere for a bit and relax, maybe go and see Georgie in Cambridge. I bought a little house for her to live in while she's doing her degree and she loves it so much she's staying there for the summer holidays. I do miss her but I'm glad she's well away from what I get up to.

I go into the bedroom and open the wardrobe. When I see my new Alexander Milnes trouser suit I want to wear it, but it's too nice to risk roughing up, so I get back into the black jeans, boots and leather jacket with a Mary Quant cotton blouse for a bit of variety. I put the gun, blades and picks in place, give myself a lick of make-up, drop the knuckle duster in my pocket and head for the car.

I park in Dunraven Road, walk round the corner to the stadium and I can see Bert by the main gate, smoking a fag. He says something to the ticket bloke as I arrive, he opens the gate for us and I follow Bert through the crowd. It's between races and the owners are walking round the track with their dogs on leads. There must be tens of thousands here and there's men studying their race cards and eyeballing the dogs as they go past. I can see George near the rail with a few of his firm, talking to a bookie. His tic-tac man is next to him, in his white gloves, waving his hands in the air and sending the odds to someone down the track. George hands the bookie a fold of fivers, turns round and sees me.

'You want to put one on?' he asks.

'No, I'm all right.'

I've always thought gambling a mug's game, unless you're a bookie.

The crowd start to roar and I follow George and Bert to the rail and stand behind them. Suddenly the lure streaks past and the dogs are pounding after it and blokes all around me are yelling at their mutts to get a move on. I'm being pressed into George's back by the weight of the crowd and deafened by the noise, then suddenly it's over and blokes around me are cursing and tearing up betting slips, apart from one winner who's smiling and approaching the bookie.

'Fucking useless bitch,' says George, turning round and treading his betting slip into the ground.

'I got a lousy third,' says Bert.

'It's all on Marigold in the last one.'

'I've got something for you,' I say.

George looks at his watch. 'There's a table booked at the Paddock Grill. Come on.'

We follow him up the terrace to a restaurant where there's some posh people in suits and dresses, in among the sportsmen. The doorman shows us to a table with a view of the track and I sit opposite George. When he's ordered drinks, I take the photographs out of my pocket and pass them to him. One is of Joe lying in the digger bucket and the other is a close shot of his head. He studies them for a moment.

'That'll do. Where is he?'

'Site in Barking.'

'Under?'

'Oh yeah.'

He hands the photos to Bert. 'That should give Jack a night's kip.'

'I'll say.'

'You done a real nice job girl, now you can have your dinner,' says George, handing me a menu.

'I'd like to but I've got to be somewhere,' I say.

As I get up from the table, the waiter arrives with the drinks and I take my whisky off the tray and down it.

'Nice one, Reen,' says George.

'Sure.'

'Bert'll sort your pocket money.'

I leave them looking at menus and walk to the gate while another team of greyhounds are paraded round the track. I've heard the breeders treat the racing greys really badly, keeping them in pens or crates all day and killing them if they get injured or don't win races.

7

Stourbridge is a couple of hours drive up the M1, on the other side of Birmingham. It's nearly eleven o'clock when I get there and the pubs in the High Street are emptying. When I stop and ask a couple of blokes where Ridge Street is, one of them says he'll take me there and tries to get into the van. I drive off and leave him staggering in the road with his mate guffawing with laughter. After I've rounded a few corners I see a group of younger lads coming out of a boozer called 'The Bull and Bladder', which sounds like what enough beer will do to you. I pull up beside them and get directions.

I find Ridge Street and the house I want is in the middle of a terrace about half-way along. I can see a light on as I drive past. I park the van where I can see the front door and think about what I'm going to do about this inconvenience to the Tory party. I decide that I've got nothing to lose by fronting up to him so I walk to the house and press the doorbell. The curtain in the front window twitches, then the door's opened by a grey-haired old lady in a faded pink dressing gown and slippers.

'I'm sorry to bother you so late, but is Mark in?'

'You've just missed him, love. He's on nights this week.'

'Of course he is. How stupid of me.'

'Who shall I say?'

'I'm Sheila.'

'OK love.'

'Is he still at… oh, I can never remember the name…'

'Kesgrove House.'

'That's it.'

'As far as I know.'

'Thanks. I'll leave you in peace.'

'All right, love,' she says, closing the door.

I drive towards the centre of town until I see a phone box and look up Kesgrove House in the directory. It's a care home, in a place called Wolverley. I find it in my road atlas and it's only about eight miles away so I drive until I see a road sign that tells me where I am on the map and work out how to get there.

Twenty minutes later I'm in a small village with just a pub and a post office. I see a sign for the road I want and drive up a hill until I see a grey Victorian house set back among some trees. The sign on the gate says Kesgrove House and there are two cars and a minibus parked at the end of the drive. I go on up the hill, leave the van by the side of the road, climb over a five-bar gate and approach the house through a field. There are lights in the windows on each side of the front door and in a couple of rooms on the ground floor. I walk along a tall hedge that runs round the back of the house until I get to a wooden gate that I can just reach the top of. I climb over, jump down onto a stone path and walk across a well kept lawn to the back of the house. The lit windows all have closed curtains or blinds and the back door is solid oak and even though I could do the lock, it looks like it could be bolted from the inside. I follow the path round the side and find a lighter door with one mortice lock which turns easy. As I step inside, I hear a woman laugh and flatten myself against the wall. A door opens and a girl in a dark blue raincoat comes out, throws a 'goodnight' over her shoulder, walks to the far end of the corridor and goes up some stairs. I wait a moment and then follow her. When I come to an open door, I look in and see a changing room with benches and rails with sports kit hanging up and football boots and plimsolls on the floor underneath. I go in, shine the pencil torch over the kit, and the size of the boots and the shorts tells me I'm in a boys' home.

I hear footsteps in the corridor and get to the door in time to see a figure that could well be Mark Weston heading for the stairs with a clipboard under his arm. I give it a moment, then I creep up after him and watch him go through a door just off the landing. I move along the corridor until I can see into the room, which is bathed in a faint glow from some kind of night light. Weston is walking between two rows of beds with small bodies in them. He looks left and right, writes something on his clipboard and I hide round a corner when he turns and comes back onto the landing.

I follow him up to the next floor and watch him enter another dormitory. This time the door is almost shut and when he doesn't come out, I creep forward and look through the gap. He's sitting on a bed leaning over a boy and whispering something to him. The boy turns onto his back and Weston keeps talking to him while he strokes his wrist. After a while he takes his hand, helps him out of bed and leads him towards the door. I retreat down the stairs to where I can see him taking the boy onto the landing. He puts his arm round him, walks him along the corridor and through a door at the far end. The boy can't be more than five or six years old and he barely comes up to Weston's waist. When I get to the door and put my ear against it, I can hear two male voices. I want to bust it open and see what's going on but there could be any number of people in this building. I wait while the voices go quiet then I bend down and look through the keyhole. I can just make out Weston, lying on his back on a kind of medical bed. The boy is naked and Weston's holding his head over his crotch while a man in a white coat works his hands between the boy's legs. I stand back, slip on the knuckle duster, take a run at the door and kick it open. The white-coated man turns and I grab him by the lapels and smash his head down onto an iron radiator. I pull the boy off Weston, put him in the corridor and shut the door. As Weston gets off the bed trying to cover his cock, I knock him out with a right hook and he lands on the floor with a thump. I make sure they're both out cold, pick up the boy's pyjamas and go to him in the corridor. The poor mite is standing with his thumb in his mouth looking confused and tearful. I pick him up in my arms, make soothing noises and take him back to the dormitory. I help him into his pyjamas, put him back in bed and moments later he's asleep. I can only hope he's not dreaming.

Weston is stirring when I get back. I take out my gun and stand over him while he comes to and sees me.

'Who the fuck...?'

'Move,' I say, pointing the gun at the door.

As he gets to his feet, the one in the white coat moans and rolls away from the radiator. I kick him hard in the face with the toe of my boot and smash his nose. Stepping over the pool of blood, I jab the gun into Weston's back, push him down the stairs, along the corridor and out the back door. On the way to the van he starts whimpering and weeping and trying to get me to talk but I've seen enough and I know I'm going to finish the bastard. I march him up the road and lean him against the van. I can't risk firing a shot so I open the back doors, sit him on the tail board and whack him round the head with the gun. He falls back and I take off my belt, put it round his neck and strangle him.

I lean against the van a moment while I get my breath, then I bundle the body into the back, shut the doors and drive through the village to the main road. As I get into Stourbridge I see a phone box and pull over. I take Jeremy's card out of my back pocket and dial the first of the phone numbers. There's no reply, so I try the second one.

'Menton Hall,' says a clipped voice.

'Can I speak to Jeremy?'

'Who may I say is calling?'

'Brenda Matthews.'

'One moment please.'

After a while Jeremy picks up.

'Brenda, my dear.'

'Is this phone clean?'

'As a whistle.'

'It's done.'

'The matter we discussed?'

'Yes.'

'Well, that's excellent.'

'You want a sight?'

'I do, but I'm in the country.'

'Where?'

'Menton Hall.'

'Where the fuck's that?'

'Near Shuttleworth. Bedfordshire. Are you in Stour-bridge?'

'Near enough.'

'If you drive east and come down the B658 you'll see the lodge on the left, after you pass through a village called Broom. Turn in there and come up to the house.'

'How long will it take?'

'Couple of hours?'

'On my way.'

'Very well, Brenda.'

I find Broom on the map and get going, wishing the pubs were still open so I could get a quick drink. I decide to stop at Newport Pagnell services on the M1 and when

I pull into the car park I nearly run into a group of mods having a lively debate about something. They're talking over one another in loud voices and looking like they're well pilled up. I walk past their fleet of Vespas and Lambrettas, with the multiple mirrors and lamps all over them, and get a cheese sandwich and a cup of coffee from the café to take away. When I get back in the van one of the mods comes over, taps on the window and asks me if I can give him a lift to Toddington services. I tell him I'm turning off at Milton Keynes and when he has a look in the back and sees the body, I tell him it's my husband who's had one too many.

An hour later I've found the B658 and when I get past Broom I see a lodge and a pair of gates on my left. I turn off the road and go along the drive. There's only a pale new moon so all I can see in the headlights are trees on each side and above, until they part suddenly and a big lump of a house with a pointed roof and chimneys on each side of it rears up in front of me. I drive across the gravel, park the car next to a black Humber Super Snipe, walk up some stone steps to the front door and give a pull on an iron rod that's hanging down beside it. I hear a distant chime and after a while the sound of bolts being released. The door opens and an old boy in a tailcoat appears.

'Miss Matthews?'

'Yes.'

'Please come this way.'

I step inside and he closes the door and slides the bolts home. I follow him across the hall and get disapproving looks from the ancestors on the wall as he leads me past the foot of a wide staircase and along a corridor where I hear classical music playing. My man knocks on a door and steps back when it opens.

'Thank you, Bamforth,' says Jeremy.

The old boy gives a quick bow and beetles off.

'Brenda. You made good time. Do come in and have a drink.'

I can see he's got a load on and I don't want to hang around.

'I'd rather do the business,' I say.

'OK. Fine.'

'Is that her, Jerry?' says a voice from inside the room.

'Yes, it is.'

Before I can leg it the door's opened wide by Sir David, the honourable member for Basingstoke.

'Good evening, my dear,' he says, holding out his hand.

I kick myself for not making Jeremy keep me bearded on the job but it's too late now so I shake his hand.

'I'm terribly grateful to you for taking care of this unpleasant business,' says the old boy.

'Brenda is a woman of many talents,' says Jeremy.

'And so very beautiful.'

'Shall we do this?' I say, turning to Jeremy.

'Certainly. Is your car at the front?'

I nod and follow him along the corridor, hoping Sir won't come with us, but he gets in step behind me.

I unlock the back doors of the van, take hold of Weston's body and turn it round so his head is on the edge of the tailboard. I take out the torch, shine it in his face and stand back to give them a view of the job.

'Serves the blighter right,' says Jeremy.

Sir David steps forward to get a better look. 'Oh. He's all blue.'

'Asphyxia,' says Jeremy.

'Ah. Yes. Shame really. He could be so gentle.'

I'm thinking how gentle he was with that little boy as I shut the van doors and turn to Jeremy.

'All right?'

'Very much so. If you'll come inside, we can settle up.'

'I'll wait in the van.'

'Won't you come and have a drink?' says Sir.

'Might be a good idea to get Mr Weston off your land,' I reply.

'Ah yes. Of course.'

Jeremy goes into the house and I get into the driver's seat. Sir loiters around a bit looking at me and then taps on the window. I ignore him but he taps again so I wind it down.

'Do you think I might have your phone number?'

'Whitehall 1212.'

'Ah. Scotland Yard. Yes, that's funny.'

He scrapes at the gravel with his toe for a bit. 'I just wondered if we might get together some time?'

As I'm thinking how unbelievably stupid some

STEALTH

members of the gentry can be, and this one a fucking MP, Jeremy comes out of the house and gives me an envelope. I open it, see that the wad looks like two large and start the engine. Jeremy comes to the window.

'Can I get a phone number?'

'Ask him,' I say, as I turn the van round and gun it down the drive.

83

8

The breakers yard is shut when I get there but the café across the road is just opening. I go in and order a cooked breakfast, then I go to the phone box on the corner and dial Tommy's number. I tell him I need the Imp crushed and there's a carpet in it for him if he'll get over sharpish and do the business. He knows the kind of work I do and that three hundred notes means there's more involved than getting rid of a perfectly good van. He says he's on his way and by the time I'm finishing my second piece of toast and draining my coffee cup, I can see him over the road unlocking the gates. I pay for breakfast, drive the Imp into the yard and position it under the crane. I give Tommy the bung and he gets underneath the van, knocks a hole in the petrol tank to drain it, then he does the same with the oil and the transmission fluid. When the car's dry, he climbs up into the cockpit of the crane and the engine roars into life. Its great claws rear up, like some horrible bird of prey, swing round towards the Imp and there's a crunch of splintering metal as the car's hoisted up and dropped into the jaws of the crusher. The crane's engine dies and Tommy gets down, goes behind the machine and a low rumbling sound starts. As the walls of the thing start to move slowly together, I walk towards the gate.

I stop a passing cab and tell the driver to take me home.

As we go down Scrubs Lane I start thinking about what I saw through that keyhole and I'm getting in such a rage that I'm almost ready to go back to that boys' home and finish the other bloke who had his hands on that poor lad. I know I won't rest if I go home so I tell the cabby to take me to All Saints Road.

I walk into the gym, knock on the office door and go in. Barry's pouring tea into a mug and when he looks up I tell him I want my strip. He takes a bag out of a cupboard, gives it to me and I make for the Ladies. I'm the only woman who trains here and the lads just about tolerate me. I convinced Barry to put a shower into the Ladies by telling him he'll get more women in that way but I'm the only one so far. I change into shorts, a singlet and running shoes, put my clothes in the bag and take it into the gym with me. There's a couple of blokes on the weights at the far end and another two sparring in the ring. I ignore their looks and whatever comments they're making, pick up a skipping rope and bounce up and down for a bit, then I pick up some hand weights, do some bicep curls, dead lifts and bench presses. Once I'm well warmed up, I put on a pair of 12 oz gloves and pummel the speed bag until I've got a bit of venom going, then I turn to the heavy bag, locate Weston's face dead centre and slam lefts and rights into it until my arms are aching and the sweat's pouring off me. When I've exhausted myself and I'm hanging on to the bag, I notice that the two sparring partners are both looking at me. One of them comes over and asks me if I want to go a round or two. He's just a whippet and from what I've seen of him in the ring I know I could put him down easily so I decide not to waste my time. His mate's smirking behind him and I'd quite like to show him what I can do and wipe that look off his face, but you never know what some trivial beef can lead to and it's best not to get involved in anything casual. I tell the boy I'm out of time and head for the shower.

I get a cab home and I'm in the bedroom taking my clothes off and looking forward to a good few hours under my new fluffy duvet from Habitat, that new shop in the King's Road, when the phone rings. I'm tempted to leave it and get into bed, but I go into the hall and pick up, in case it's Lizzie.

'You're in trouble,' says Bert.

'What?'

'The Warrington. Now.'

The phone goes dead. I get dressed again and walk to the pub. Bert is at a corner table in the saloon bar. I get myself a whisky and sit opposite him.

'Go on then.'

'Joe Mason's been seen.'

'Joe who?'

'You know fucking well who. Millie's bit of stuff you swore you'd put in a digger.'

'Oh Christ.'

'The governor's waiting for you and if you want to see next week you'd better have a yarn.'

I'm bang to rights here and no one crosses George Preston. Bert gets up from the table and I swallow my whisky, follow him out of the pub and get into the Jag. He swings it round the roundabout, down Sutherland Avenue and across Harrow Road, turns right into George's street and stops outside his house. The door's opened by Jackie Parr, one of my dad's old firm, who I normally have a flirt and a laugh with, but today he looks down at the floor when he sees me and stands back to let me pass. Bert opens the door to the lounge and George turns from the window looking mean and angry.

'What the fuck are you playing at?'

'I couldn't do it to them.'

'What are you, Mother fucking Teresa all of a sudden?'

'They're good people.'

'And you're about the hardest I've got and you go and take a diabolical fucking liberty that could put Jack Drake up my arse.'

'Have you told him it's done?'

'You're fucking lucky I haven't. I'm going to the Moor tomorrow.'

'I'll sort it.'

'You do that bastard right now or I'm marking Jack's card and he'll have you under the fucking Westway.'

'Where was he seen?' I ask.

'Somewhere round Purfleet way,' says Bert.

That's near Rainham where his caravan is. I'm thinking I can get over there now and decide if I'm going to kill him or put him on a plane. I'm turning to leave when there's a knock on the front door. Bert goes to answer it and Ray is there. George beckons him to join us.

'What's the news?' says George.

'Joe Mason's out of the way,' says Ray.

'How come?'

'Jack's son Ronnie done him.'

'What? He's only a kid isn't he?'

'Eighteen.'

'Fuck. Does Jack know?'

'He heard it from a screw.'

'Is he all right with it?'

'He's fucking proud of the kid, putting it all round the wing.'

'He's going off his chump in there.'

I don't know whether I'm sorry or relieved. I can't believe I took it for granted that the boy would go with the plan to get lost abroad with his mother. It was all those memories of me and my dad on Clacton beach making me lose my grip. Ronnie must have got news of the plan from Millie, followed me and Joe to the building site and figured my whole game out, which means I've got to find him and straighten him before he can go on a visit and tell his dad the full story.

George turns, gives me his cold stare and waves the other two out of the room. When they've gone he sits in his armchair, nods at the one opposite and I sit down.

'If you weren't family I'd fucking have you for this.'

'I'm sorry.'

'If Jack ever finds out you done it…'

'He won't.'

'You'd better hope he doesn't.'

'The kid never saw me.'

'You don't know that.'

George is mad enough without knowing how badly I've messed this one up so I keep quiet. He leans forward and points a finger at me.

'You ever fuck me again…'

'I've got it, George.'

He sits back and stares into the fireplace. Bert is waiting in the corridor and when he opens the front door for me, I look up and down the street before I follow him to his car. We drive in silence until we get to my place. He pulls up outside and turns to me.

'Anything you need, you call me. All right?'

'Thanks, Bert.'

'Be careful, eh?'

'I will,' I say, as I get out of the car.

I climb the stairs and knock on Lizzie's door. Just as I'm thinking she's not there she opens up, takes one look at me, pulls me inside and closes the door.

'What's the matter, darling?'

'I'm in a bit of bother.'

'Come and have a drink and tell me all,' she says, putting her arm round me and taking me into the lounge.

She pours us a whisky each and sits beside me on the sofa. When I've finished telling her what's gone on with Joe and Ronnie, she nods her head and refills our glasses.

'All because you tried to do the right thing.'

'I should've known better.'

'How could you know an eighteen year old kid was capable of that?'

'I was younger than him when I done Johnny.'

'That was different. You were protecting your little sister from an evil scumbag.'

'Ronnie thinks he's done the right thing by his dad.'

'I suppose.'

I take a long drink and she reaches for the bottle and tops me up.

'I think you need to get out of town for a bit.'

'He'll still be here when I get back.'

'I suppose.'

'I need to find him and get it sorted.'

'You're not going to off him are you?'

'Of course I'm not.'

'Just checking.'

I'm thinking there's a chance he might not tell his dad about me, so that he gets the respect for killing Joe off his own bat. There again he could have ideas about doing me as well and building his reputation that way. I'm feeling too tired to think straight and as the whisky relaxes me I let go and snuggle into Lizzie. After we've done some close work on the sofa and I've dropped off a couple of times, she takes me to her bedroom, lays me down and I lose the last thing she says as I drift off.

Kesgrove House stands four square and solid in the moonlight. I'm in a field and there's a cold wind whipping at my legs. I want to get away but I can't move. There's an angry rumble of thunder, a crack of forked lightening, and the house starts moving towards me. I tear away, jump a fence and run across a ploughed field. When I look back at the house, the pointed roof is growing taller, the walls are bulging out sideways and the whole thing starts lumbering after me, coming faster and faster. I trip over, hit the ground and twist onto my back. The massive house is craning over me and there are naked young boys falling from the windows. I try to catch some before they hit the ground but I'm knocked down and buried under a heap of whimpering flesh. Desperate for air, I force my way out of the writhing tangle of arms and legs and see Mark Weston walking to the house holding a boy by the neck in each hand. I try to shout his name but can only make a thin whining noise. I struggle after him and he turns, laughing through bloodstained fangs and swings a boy at me. I dive at his legs and we burst through the wall of the house into a cellar where I pull his laughing head off and throw it to the two boys who kick it back and forth between them. Weston comes at me, blood pouring from the hole in his neck. One of the boys flings the head at him and he goes down. The two lads leap on him and as they pull his arms and legs off, the house lifts up with a great groan, falls backwards and lands in a heap of broken masonry. I wake up half out of the bed and see I've knocked the alarm clock onto the floor.

I wait while the dream fades then I get up. It's gone eight o'clock so I reckon Lizzie will be at the club by now. I get dressed, take a quick look round the flat to make sure she's not there, go upstairs to my place and dial Ray's number. A woman answers and when I say I want to speak to Ray, she asks who wants him. I say my name and he comes on the phone.

'Where do I find the kid?'

'It'll cost you a bullseye.'

Because I've gone against George, the slimy cunt thinks he can twist my arm but I need to know where Ronnie is and Ray's the best sniffer around.

'All right.'

'The French House at ten.'

'OK.'

I take a long shower, put on make-up, then it's my black Nina Ricci flares with a white low-cut blouse and my Cardin jacket. I put the Smith & Wesson in my belt and a blade in my boot, then I go to the bathroom, unscrew the panel on the side of the bath and take fifty quid for Ray out of my stash and put it in my back pocket. I replace the panel, lock up the flat and walk to the cab rank in Warwick Avenue. The drivers are all in the shelter so I knock on the door and ask for a ride to Dean Street.

9

The French House is full of all sorts tonight. I elbow my way through a gaggle of beardy beatniks in black duffle coats, looking depressed and sucking on half pints. I move round a couple of arty-looking types who step in front of me and look me up and down as I make my way to the bar. While I'm waiting to be served, a very pissed Welshman with a baby face and ginger hair jumps off his stool and starts shouting at a tall bloke in a leather overcoat. He's ranting on about some money the man owes him and how he left him stranded in New York or something. He's in a right strop and looking like he might start swinging punches so I move along the bar to get out the way and see Ray in the far corner. He heads for the door and I follow him into the street.

'Who's the Welsh git?'

'Some writer. I saw him getting chucked out of the Coach and Horses earlier. He's always blowing his top when he's had a few.'

'So where do I find Ronnie?'

'Last seen pushing pills in Take Five.'

'When?'

'About an hour ago.'

I put Ray's money in his hand and head for Berwick Street. The Take Five has some good bands. Me and Lizzie saw John Lee Hooker there, and a great support band, that I can't remember the name of, with a really punchy female singer who kept us dancing until dawn. I walk up Dean Street past the girls standing outside the strip clubs and clip joints, beckoning to the passing punters and promising them a good time. A cop car crawls along the street and stops outside a dirty bookshop. A plainclothes gets out and goes into the shop, probably collecting his pension for the week and a few magazines for the boys. I go along Old Compton Street past the 2i's Coffee Bar, which is all dark and closed down now. It used to be such a great place to see bands down in the basement. Even though the stage was only tiny and made out of milk crates, with just the one mic, so many bands and solo artists that got a start there went on to be really big. We saw Cliff Richard there and Adam Faith, before anyone knew who they were.

I turn into Berwick Street and walk along until I see the Take Five on the left. There's one bouncer outside who I've seen around and I slip him a quid, tell him I'm checking on my boyfriend and ask him to walk into the club in front of me so I won't be seen. He waits while I pay six bob to the bloke on the door and as I follow the bouncer down the stairs I can hear 'Hey Girl' wafting up from below. Jimmy James and the Vagabonds are on the stage pumping out the soul and looking really cool so it's no wonder the club is packed. I melt into the crowd while 'Hey Girl' finishes and they get into 'Now is the Time', with the band giving the backing vocals and grooving along behind Jimmy. I have a look round for Ronnie and I'm thinking maybe I've missed him when I see him leaning against a wall at the back of the club smoking a fag. He's in a dark grey mod suit with a trilby hat and he's got his eye on a couple of other mods nearby. One of them takes money from a hippy looking lad, shakes a few pills out of a bottle and passes them to him. As soon as that's done, the other one's already selling to a couple of girls and business is looking brisk. Ronnie looks at his watch, says something to the dealers and I slip further back as he moves through the crowd towards the stairs. I wait a second, follow him up to the street and watch him walk along Berwick Street and turn into Tyler's Court. I go to the corner and see him talking to a young boy on a bike. They exchange a few words and then it starts to get heated with Ronnie snarling at the kid and poking him in the chest. He smacks the kid across the face, tips him off the bike onto the cobbles, rips open the saddlebag, pulls out a package and stuffs it in his inside pocket. He picks up the bike, throws it down on top of the kid and I pull back into a doorway as he strides past me and disappears into the club.

I go and lift the bike off the boy, lean it against a wall and help him up out of the gutter. His face is red from Ronnie's slap and there's a nasty gash on his neck where one of the pedals or the handlebars have caught him. I can see he's no more than twelve or thirteen and there are tears in his eyes as he sways in front of me clutching his shoulder.

'Are you going to be all right?' I ask.

'I've got to go.'

He moves towards his bike, trips on the kerb, lands on the pavement and cries out in pain. I kneel down beside him and sit him against the wall beside his bike. He struggles to stand again but falls back down. I put my hands on his shoulders, 'Take it easy for Chrissake.'

'If he finds me…'

'He won't.'

'He's just in the club.'

'Wait here a second.'

I get to the corner just as a cab goes past. I put four fingers in my mouth and whistle. The cab slows and I step into the road, where he can see me in his mirror and wave. He brakes, backs up and pulls down his nearside window. I lean in and give him the benefit of the low-cut blouse.

'Can you take two and a bike in the back?' I ask.

'As long as I'll get a ride off you, darlin',' he says, with a leer.

I open the passenger door and help the boy up off the pavement.

'What are you doing?' he says.

'Taking you home.'

'Who are you?'

'I'm no friend of Ronnie Drake.'

He looks at me for a moment, as if he's wondering whether to trust me, then he takes a step forward and lets me help him to the cab. I put him in the back seat and sit next to him. The cabby picks the bike up, turns the front wheel sideways and slides it in beside us.

'Where do you live?' I ask the boy.

'Hoxton.'

'What street?'

'Forston.'

I look at the driver. He nods, shuts the door, gets behind the wheel and turns the cab round. After we turn right onto Oxford Street, I take a tissue out of my pocket, press it against the cut on the boy's neck and he holds it in place.

'How's the shoulder?'

'Fucking hurts.'

I lean forward and close the glass partition. 'How long have you been running for Ronnie?'

He turns away and looks out of the window.

'I'm no danger to you,' I say.

He looks at me for a bit and then he lets out a long breath.

'A few months.'

'How did he get you into it?'

'I got caught nicking in the market. He give the stall keeper a few quid to let me go and he had me.'

'What was the aggravation about back there?'

'I was short on the delivery and he thought I'd stole some. I told him there was no one there when I went to the second house in Bethnal Green but he wouldn't have it.'

He goes quiet and I can see tears welling up. I put my

arm round him and after a moment he closes his eyes and I feel him let go. He looks so young and thin and frail next to me. Part of me wants to take him home, look after him and keep him safe but I know I've got things I need to do, or I won't be able to look after myself, let alone anyone else. When the cab pulls into Forston Street the cabby asks for the number and stops outside a small terraced house with paint peeling off the front door. He pulls the bike out of the cab and I tell him to wait for me. I wheel the bike towards the front door and when the boy opens it, I pass it to him. He pushes it inside, leans it against a wall and turns to me.

'Er… Thanks.'

'It's OK. You take care of yourself.'

As I turn away I hear a woman's voice.

'Peter? Is that you?'

Through the cab window I see a large lady in a nightgown appear in the hallway with a glass in her hand.

'Where the fuck have you been?' she calls after the boy, as he goes up the stairs.

I tell the driver to take me to Randolph Crescent and he heads off towards Old Street. As we go through Islington, I'm thinking what kind of future that kid's got in front of him. He's well in the game already and there won't be a way out unless he emigrates to Australia or somewhere, and the money he'll be getting already will probably keep him in the drug trade and caught up in the villainy that goes with it, now the heavy mob are well in there.

As we drive along Marylebone Road, I lean my head back, close my eyes and start to drift off. I wake up again as we motor up Edgware Road and pass a clock that says it's nearly 3am. After we've turned into Clifton Road there's a flash of headlights through the back window as a car comes up close behind us. As I turn to look, it pulls out, shoots past us and skids to a stop in front of the cab. The driver slams the brakes on, I'm thrown forward, my head smacks against the glass partition and I go out.

I come round as I'm being dragged out of the cab by two men. Ronnie Drake is at the driver's window pointing a gun. One man's holding me round the neck, the other's got my legs and I'm struggling with everything I've got until they lay me face down between the two motors and kneel on me. They take my gun and blade, tie my hands behind me, shove me into the boot of the car and slam the lid shut. I hear doors closing and I'm thrown against metal as the car powers away.

Just as I'm feeling like I'm about to pass out again from being tossed around in this tin can, the car stops, the boot lid opens and I'm looking at Ronnie holding a gun on me with a crane behind his head. There are two others, both about his age, standing behind him. Ronnie backs off while the other two pull me out of the boot and stand me up. We're in a dockyard among lorries and dumper trucks. I'm marched towards the quayside where a wooden day boat is moored. One of the lads gets on board, rolls back the canvas cover, turns on a lamp in the wheelhouse and angles it down towards the engine housing. I'm pushed forward onto the boat and sat down in the stern. Ronnie gets on board and keeps the gun on me while the other two go into the cabin.

'Not so fucking clever now, eh?' he says as his mates reappear holding weird looking lumps of metal and coils of rope. When they get closer I see that the metal things are stage weights and when they start tying them to my ankles and Ronnie starts the engine, I know what I'm in for. When I've got one on each ankle and two round my waist, Ronnie gives the gun to one of them and pulls at the weights to check they're secure.

'Right. You two bugger off. I'll catch you at The Scene.'

'You said we could fuck her first,' says one of them.

'Get out of here. Now!'

'Bye, love. Enjoy your swim,' says the other as they climb onto the quay, untie the mooring ropes, chuck them in the boat and disappear into the dark. Ronnie turns on the boat's headlight and navigation lights, pushes off from the side and eases open the throttle.

'Fancy drowning at Greenwich? It's good and deep there,' he says as we leave the dock and turn down river. It's a calm night and the boat glides easily across the water.

I twist my wrists against the ropes behind my back until I'm sure there's no hope there, then I try to raise one of my legs. I can just get the weight off the floor but it's too heavy to swing at him or get any movement.

'Thought you had it sewn up, didn't you?'

While he steers into the middle of the channel, I look around the boat for any possible way of getting control. There's an anchor lying near me which I could do something with if I wasn't trussed up so tight. I keep straining against the ropes round my wrists and edging along the seat in case there's any bare metal behind.

'No one takes a liberty with my dad. Or me, you fucking dyke bitch with your girlfriend up Little fucking Venice.'

After he's told me how strong and powerful his dad is about another twenty times and how chuffed he's going to be when he finds out how hard his son is, he eases back the throttle and kills the engine. He looks all around, gets off his seat, comes towards me, grabs me by the lapels of my jacket and leans in close. 'Say goodbye, slag.'

I nut him as hard as I can. Blood spurts out of his nose as he falls back, lands against the side of the boat and crumples onto the bench. I try to get up but the weights won't let me. He stands, lunges at me, gets his hands round my neck, plants his feet either side of me and he's pulling me up off the bench and forcing me backwards over the gunwale, until my spine feels like it's about to break. The boat's keeling over and my head's going in the water when I hear a siren wailing and the sound of an engine. Ronnie lets go of me and I slump back onto the bench. He leaps to the controls, starts the engine and a blinding light sweeps over the boat. As he opens the throttle, a police launch comes alongside, with the siren screaming, and three coppers climb into the boat. One of them kills the engine and the other two grab hold of Ronnie and cuff him. While the siren dies down, a man in a grey mac steps into the boat.

'Ronald Drake. I am arresting you for the murder of Joseph Mason. You do not have to say anything, unless you wish to do so, but what you do say may be given in evidence.'

10

They lift Ronnie over the side and into the police launch. I sit back against the gunwale, take a deep breath of river air and close my eyes. When I open them, Jeremy is standing in front of me.

'You've put on weight, Brenda.'

'What the fuck…?'

'Later.'

He bends down and unties the rope around my waist. While he frees my ankles and wrists, one of the uniforms collects up the weights and puts them in the cabin. Jeremy takes my arm and helps me into the police launch. Ronnie's taken below and we sit on a bench in the stern opposite the plainclothes. After the day boat has been tied to the back of the launch, we make a tight turn and set off up river at a fair clip.

We get to Wapping, moor up at the police station and when Ronnie's been taken inside we get off the boat. Jeremy has a quick word with the man in the grey mac, then he leads me round the side of the station, along Wapping High Street to a grey Rover 90 and opens the door for me. I get in and let the soft leather cradle my aching back. Jeremy sits beside me, starts the engine and we head west.

'Were you on him, or me?' I ask.

'When Ronnie killed Joe, I decided to track him, then tonight I saw that you'd had the same idea.'

'You were at Take Five?'

'Nearby. Ronnie saw you take the boy, so I followed.'

'Just as well.'

'He's a nasty little tyke.'

'Will he go down?'

'They've got a witness who saw him enter the caravan, heard sounds of a fight and saw him leave.'

'How did he kill him?'

'Knife.'

'How solid's the witness?'

'He's an old boy who was walking his dog. He knew Joe and liked him apparently.'

'Let's hope he holds up.'

'Ex-army. He should be all right.'

As we motor through the City I'm telling myself I've got to get better at looking behind me when I'm in a taxi. First Ronnie gets up my back without me clocking him and then Jeremy creeps up on me and I'm none the wiser. He glances across at me and smiles.

'There's something I'd like you to do for me.'

'I might have known there'd be a price.'

'I think one good turn deserves another, don't you?'

Ronnie is never going to tell his dad about what I did with Joe in case he finds out that his son made a mess of straightening me and got himself done for murder. The only person who's going to tip Jack off about me is Jeremy, so he's got me.

'Perhaps you'd like to discuss it over a drink?' he says.

'If you want.'

'At your club.'

'Why there?'

'It concerns a spy, currently in London, who has a penchant for young ladies. I have arranged for the doorman at his hotel to recommend Abigail's as a place where he will find them and your friend Elizabeth has informed me that he has arrived at the club.'

When he brings Lizzie into it I'm tempted to lay into the smug bastard and put a stop to this nonsense right now, but if he's MI6 he won't be working alone and it could get complicated, so I've got no choice but to play along.

'You want this spy done?'

'Yes.'

We drive in silence until we get to Soho. When we reach Frith Street Jeremy parks the Rover near the club.

'I believe there is a back entrance we can use so as not to be seen?' he says, switching off the engine.

I get out of the car, lead him along the alleyway to the back of the club, down the stairs to the kitchen and knock on the window. Rico sees me and opens the door.

'Can you ask Lizzie to come down?' I say.

He turns to a waitress who's loading up a tray. 'Katie. Tell Madam that Rina is here.'

He goes back to the stove and tends to whatever's

sizzling in the frying pan while I lead Jeremy into the dressing room. I look to where poor Rose was lying on the floor and hope she's in a better place. Lizzie opens the door and I hear the band rocking it with 'I Heard It Through the Grapevine'. I get a glimpse of the bandstand and I notice that Caesar still isn't back on guitar. The bloke who's replaced him looks more relaxed though and he's giving the song a pretty good feel.

'Your man's in a curtained booth and I've told the girl to keep him there while we go through to the office,' says Lizzie, turning and going into the club.

We follow her round the dance floor and past the tables, which are almost all occupied, to the back of the room, through a door marked 'Private' and into the office. I notice a glass panel set into the wall that I haven't seen before. Lizzie clocks me looking at it, turns off the light and I can see into the club.

'We've put one-way glass in the mirror on the other side so we can keep an eye on what's going on.'

'Good move,' I say.

'Where is the man we have come to see?' asks Jeremy.

'Second booth from the left,' says Lizzie.

'Does he have a name?' I ask.

'Tolka Saltik.'

'Drink?' says Lizzie, going to the cocktail cabinet.

'I'd love a gin and it,' says Jeremy.

Lizzie adds Vermouth to a large measure of gin and hands it to him. As she's pouring two whiskies, the curtains of the booth open and Kelly steps out, followed by a short man of about forty, in a grey suit with black slicked back hair, bushy eyebrows, dark brown eyes and a hooked nose. He buttons his jacket as he goes to the bar and gets his bill. When he's paid in cash, he follows Kelly up the stairs and out of the club. Lizzie hands me my drink.

'On their way to his hotel, I imagine,' says Jeremy.

'That's how it goes,' says Lizzie, pulling a blind down over the window and turning on the lights.

'Thank you, Elizabeth. That all worked out very well,' says Jeremy, taking a good drink of his gin and getting his wallet out of his back pocket. He counts out ten fivers and hands them to Lizzie.

'Cheers,' she says, dropping the notes into a desk drawer.

Jeremy turns to me. 'Now that you've laid eyes Mr Saltik, perhaps you'd come to the Langham tomorrow morning, so that we can discuss the matter further and agree terms.'

'Not too early.'

'Shall we say twelve?'

'What's the room number?'

'332. I shall leave your name at the desk, Brenda.'

Lizzie looks at me and smiles. Jeremy downs the rest of his gin, goes to the door and turns.

'You will also have the opportunity of meeting a colleague of mine who will be working with you. Goodnight.'

Lizzie refills my glass.

'So how do you know Jeremy?' I ask.

'I don't. He came in at opening time, slipped me a cockle, asked me if I knew the doormen at the Hyde Park and said there'd be fifty in it if I could get Saltik down here tonight, then he turns up with you. What is all this?'

'He followed me the night I fitted up Joe's death in the digger and he threatened to tell Jack Drake about it unless I took out a bloke who was putting the black on his father-in-law, who's an MP.'

'Did you off him?'

'He turned out to be a nonce, doing it to little boys in a kids' home, so I was glad to.'

'And what's this caper with Saltik?'

'He's a spy of some sort and I reckon Jeremy's MI6. He wants me to do him.'

'Are you going to?'

'I've no choice. If he tells Jack that his son's being done for Joe's murder because I faked his death, I'll have half his firm after me.'

'Do you think he would tell him?'

'Can I afford to risk it?'

Lizzie sits beside me on the sofa and puts her arm round me. I snuggle down into her and when the band go into 'Baby Please Don't Go' all I want to do is stay curled up here on this sofa with the woman I love and forget about spies and Istanbul and the rest of it.

When I open my eyes, I'm alone in the office. I sit up, look through the glass panel and I can see Lizzie at the bar talking to Jane. Rico and the waitresses are putting chairs on the tables and girls are leaving the dressing room and heading home. I go into the club and join Lizzie and Jane while they talk about how the night's gone and who's opening up tomorrow. Max comes down the stairs and hands the door money to Jane who puts it in the till and locks it. We're saying goodnight and about to leave when Kelly comes in looking flustered.

'You all right, Kel?' asks Lizzie.

'That Turk's been arrested.'

'Where?'

'In his room at the Hyde Park.'

'What happened?'

'We'd just got in there, sorted the money and we're about to do the business. The door opens, four of them charge in and grab hold of him. He has a go and one of them knocks him over. They land on him, cuff him, pick him up and march him out of there. One of them stays behind, tells me to fuck off and keep schtum or I'll get done. As I leave he's tipping the bloke's suitcase out on the bed and going through his stuff.'

'Was it Old Bill?' asks Lizzie.

'There was two squad cars outside when I come out.'

'Are you OK, love?'

'Yeah. It was just a bit of a surprise.'

'I'm sure.'

Jane pours a brandy and gives it to Kelly.

'At least you got your wedge,' says Max.

Kelly smiles and takes a drink of brandy. Lizzie gives her a kiss and tells Max to see her home. We say goodnight, head up the stairs, walk up Frith Street and flag down a cab in Soho Square.

'That's you off the hook then,' says Lizzie, after we get in.

'Maybe.'

'Will you still go tomorrow?'

'I reckon.'

Even if the Saltik job is off, Jeremy's still got me because of what he knows and I need to stay close until I can find a way out.

• • •

I try not to wake Lizzie as I slip out of bed, get dressed and go to my flat. I take a shower, wash my hair and put on a black Norman Hartnell pencil skirt and jacket, with a pair of high heels. Even though I'm never going to make it to the Langham by midday, I take my time with my hair and make-up, go into the kitchen and make myself a bacon sandwich which I munch on the way to the cab rank in Warwick Avenue.

When I get to the Langham, I tell the desk clerk I'm Brenda Matthews, take the lift to the fourth floor, find room 332 and knock on the door. It's opened by Sir David Ashbury, MP for Basingstoke.

'Hello my dear.'

'I've come to see Jeremy.'

'Ah. Right. Won't you come in?'

As I follow him into the room, I see that the drawers of the filing cabinet are open and there are files and paperwork piled up on the desk.

'Just having a bit of a clear out, you know.'

'Where's Jeremy?'

'You are looking very beautiful today, my dear,' he says, moving towards me. I back off but the desk is in the way. He puts his hands on my shoulders and leans in. Just as I'm about to introduce my knee to his withered bollocks, the door opens and a tall, blond, middle-aged woman walks in carrying two large suitcases. She sees what's happening and drops both cases on the floor.

'This is neither the time nor the place to be entertaining one of your sluts, Father!'

'Oh no… Nothing of the sort my dear. Just saying hello and all that,' he says, stepping back.

'This is Brenda Matthews, she came to see Jeremy… Allow me to introduce my daughter, Dorothy.'

She looks away and puts a hand on her hip and I realise she must be Jeremy's wife.

'Brenda was helpful to us in the matter of Mark Weston,' says Sir David.

'What?' she says, glancing at me.

'Very helpful.'

She considers me for a moment.

'This isn't the woman who…?'

'Yes, it is.'

'I see,' she says, looking at me now with some interest.

'Is Jeremy here?' I ask.

'I'm afraid not,' says Dorothy.

'Is he coming back?'

'He's been arrested.'

'What for?'

'What was your business with him?'

'He had a bit of work for me.'

'Tolka Saltik?'

'Yes.'

'They've both been arrested for passing secrets to the Russians.'

11

I leave Dorothy and her father filling the suitcases with the contents of Jeremy's desk and filing cabinet and head home, feeling mightily relieved. They told me he's gone on remand at Brixton and even though my doings with Joe will be the last thing on his mind, he won't be able to contact Jack Drake even if he tries. According to Dorothy they've got him on tape talking to a Russian and Saltik will stitch him up too, to get off lightly, so he's bang to rights and out of my hair for a good long while. As I get out of the tube at Warwick Avenue and walk along Clifton Road, I'm wondering how Dorothy knew so much about what the authorities have on him and why she was so cool about her old man being arrested for treason. I decide to forget about it and be glad the whole thing's out of the way.

When I get to the house I go to Lizzie's door, give it our special knock and she opens up.

'You're looking a bit chipper,' she says.

'Jeremy's had his collar felt.'

'You're kidding.'

'Being done for spying for the Russians, along with Saltik, and banged up in Brixton.'

'That's fantastic!' she says, dragging me inside, flinging her arms round me and planting a wet kiss on my lips.

'Bite of lunch to celebrate?' I say, when we come up for air.

'You bet.'

'Caprice?'

'Perfect. Give me two minutes.'

She disappears into her bedroom and I go to the lounge and have a look through the LPs beside the radiogram. I'm reading the sleeve notes of the Doors album when she comes in wearing a dark purple Givenchy sheath dress and four inch heels. She stands beside me in my black tailored suit and we look in the mirror.

'Pretty cool, eh?'

'I'll say.'

We take a cab to St James's. Lizzie knows the maître d' at Le Caprice and even though it's crowded and we haven't booked, he shows us to a good table in the main room. We ask for a bottle of Côtes du Rhône and look at the menu. I choose a crispy duck salad and steak tartare and Lizzie goes for Dorset crab and a rib eye. When we've ordered and the wine's been poured, we clink glasses, sit back and Lizzie catches me up with the gossip from the club. While she's telling me what's going on with the girls, I'm thinking how I never feel as good and safe as I do when I'm alone with my beautiful lover. We've been together since I was fifteen and I hope we still are when I'm fifty.

The waiter brings us our lunch and we're enjoying the delicious food and knocking back the wine when an idea occurs to me.

'I'd love it if we could get away for the weekend,' I say.

'Me too. It's so hot and sticky in town.'

'Do you reckon Jane and Max could handle the club without you?'

'I can ask. The weekend's normally light.'

'Punters at home with the wife.'

'Or on the golf course.'

'There might be a festival somewhere.'

'Have you got an *International Times* at the flat?'

'Only a couple of old ones.'

'We can get one on the way home.'

When we've done justice to the meal and finished off with coffee and brandy, I settle the bill and we walk round to St James's Street and hail a cab. We ask him to stop in Portobello Road on the way and I nip into Gandalf's Garden and buy an *IT*. The hippy behind the counter wants to show me a new water pipe that he's just got in but I tell him I don't smoke, take the paper, get back in the taxi and give it to Lizzie. She turns to the back and looks at the list of gigs and events.

'Hey, what about this? "Festival of the Flower Children", Woburn Abbey. It started today.'

'Who's playing?'

'The Kinks, Small Faces, Eric Burdon, Jeff Beck, The Move, Alan Price Set, Marmalade, The Dream and Dantalion's Chariot.'

'Great line up.'

'I'll say.'

'Dantalion's Chariot is Zoot Money's new lot, isn't it?'

'We saw them at the Tiles Club.'

'They were great. Where's Woburn Abbey?'

'Off the M1, near Milton Keynes. Only about an hour away.'

Lizzie often knows where the stately homes are. She's been to quite a few of them on business. The cab drops us off at home and we go up to Lizzie's flat. I wait while she phones Jane and Max and asks them how they feel about her taking the weekend off for a bit of extra handbag. She tells me they're fine with it so I go to my place to change. The phone rings while I'm looking through the wardrobe for something hippyish but I decide to ignore it, in case it's some new aggravation. I try on a yellow Biba frock which is loose and floppy and add some turquoise beads that I got from Indiacraft and put on a pair of moccasins. I frizz my hair up a bit, put on my sunglasses and I reckon I'd only need a flower in my hair to blend right into Haight Ashbury.

I go down to Lizzie's and she opens the door wearing bell bottom jeans, sandals and a floaty floral smock. She puts an old straw hat on her head and looks me up and down. 'Hey babe, you look kinda groovy.'

'You too. Shall we split?'

'Right on.'

We walk down to the street and round the corner into Randolph Avenue where Lizzie's Triumph Herald is parked and get a disapproving look from a gent in a pinstripe suit on the way. We put the roof down, turn on the radio and Lizzie drives through St John's Wood and up Edgware Road. When we get on to the M1, the sun's shining, the wind is warm and Roger Daltrey is 'Talking about my generation'.

We turn off the motorway past Toddington Services. I open the map and navigate along country roads until we see a sign for the festival and drive through a big stone archway and along a lane with grassy fields on each side. We can hear music wafting over from somewhere and there's tents and cars and caravans off to the right. We head towards them and I can hear the Kinks doing 'All Day and All of the Night'. We park the car behind a caravan and walk between the tents towards the stage.

We pay thirty bob each for a weekend ticket to a bloke in a tweed suit, sitting at a table with a golden retriever by his side. We walk past a row of stalls selling kaftans, beads, bells and paper flowers and on through the smell of incense and weed, until we're in among the crowd in front of the stage. As the Kinks go into 'Tired of Waiting for You', I sit down beside a girl with a flower in her hair and dark glasses with a yellow sun painted on one of the lenses. She sees me looking at her and offers me a joint. When I smile and shake my head she takes a long drag of it herself and lies back on the grass. Lizzie sits down next to me and we lean against each other and sway gently to the music. There are dancers near the stage making some lively moves with their arms in the air and a man with a film camera on his shoulder, getting pushed about among them but mostly people are standing or sitting around enjoying the music and taking it easy. I notice a group of mods among the hippies and I think of Ronnie Drake and feel glad he's banged up somewhere.

Lizzie nudges me and points at a hot air balloon in the sky that's coming towards us. Two people are waving from the basket hanging below and when the balloon comes directly above us, a big cloud of flowers float down all around us and people are clapping and whooping and cheering. I catch a couple, notice that they're red carnations and put one in my hair and the other one in the band of Lizzie's hat.

The Kinks come to the end of their set and Ray Davis waves to the crowd, says something I can't hear and there's lots of people throwing flowers and making peace signs as the band go off. Jeff Dexter comes on in a cowboy hat and sunglasses and tells us that Marmalade are next up. While the roadies are moving the gear behind him, he talks about life at sea on Radio Caroline and how he got seasick and nearly threw up over the mic when he got to the "hump" part of Engelbert Humperdinck. He gets a big laugh and goes on about how wonderful and peaceful the festival is and then Marmalade come on and go straight into 'Ob-La-Di, Ob-La-Da'. Lizzie gets up, pulls me to my feet and leads me towards the stage. As we get in among the dancers and start to shake it up, the music takes me and I blend in with the rippling bodies around me. The sun's on my face and I'm loving it and feeling free as a bird.

We dance on through the whole of Marmalade's set and after they finish with 'Best of My Love', we make our way through the crowd towards the food stalls over by the tents and caravans. I'm hoping there's a bar where we can get a drink but there's only hot dog and hamburger stands and one that's selling bowls of vegetarian stew. When I suggest that we find a pub and bring a bottle of whisky back, Lizzie says we don't need to because she's got one in the car, so we buy hot dogs and munch on them as we walk through the balmy night.

We're sitting in the car with the doors open drinking whisky when a searing guitar riff cuts through the darkness and a driving rhythm section gets in behind it. The beat gets hotter, the guitar gets faster and the bass drum's pounding through my chest as we hurry to the stage to see who's playing. The band are all facing upstage in white robes and rocking like there's no tomorrow. A singer I don't recognise bounds on to the stage, all in black, grabs the mic off the stand, screams something about love and death, leaps into the air, does the splits and lands in front of the drum kit. When he jumps up and screams some more, the band spin round to face us and I'm looking at Caesar, the Mexican guitarist from the club, playing lead. While the rest of the band start moving and jigging about behind the singer, Caesar moves off to the side, looking cool and relaxed, with his dark curls and his cute face, and cuts some scorching riffs into the night with a big distorted sound that he never used in the club.

The band power on, going straight from one song into another with the drummer giving the count on his sticks in between. The crowd are loving it and me and Lizzie are dancing up a storm and just when I'm feeling like I'm about to collapse, the set finishes, the singer mumbles something about the crowd being great, the band go off and Jeff Dexter is there telling us we've just seen Grim Reaper's first gig and saying the Small Faces will be on at midday tomorrow.

We go round the back of the stage hoping to get a word with Caesar. While a couple of security men stop us at the gate, I see him walking towards a long black car with the singer. Lizzie calls his name and he sees us, comes over and the men let us through.

'Hey, you were great,' I say.

He looks a bit embarrassed for a moment. 'I sorry not to tell you I was leaving club.'

'It's OK,' says Lizzie.

'Thank you for letting me play.'

Even though I know he's only eighteen, as we found out when Lizzie helped him get an extension on his visa, he looks even younger now and more vulnerable somehow.

'It was good to have you with us and we're glad you're doing so well,' says Lizzie.

I'm about to tell him how good he was tonight when, the door of the black car opens and Bobby Grant, the owner of the Astor, appears. 'You're not having him back, Liz. He's far too good for your crummy little shebeen.'

'Oh Christ. I might have known,' says Lizzie, when she sees who it is.

'Just kidding, eh?' says Bobby, as he joins us. 'Well, if it isn't Harry's gorgeous little girl, an' all.'

'Hello, Bobby,' says Lizzie.

'Wasn't he great?' he says, putting an arm round Caesar's neck.

'Not so good in 'Heart from Hell',' says Caesar.

'Fucking Denny cocked it up, not you. Stupid cunt come in with the verse instead of the chorus. Off his fucking nut, as per.'

'Still, I should have…'

'Forget it. You were great, my son.'

'I never noticed anything,' I say.

'There you are,' says Bobby, slapping Caesar on the arse. 'Do you want to come back to the hotel for a drink, ladies?'

I'm feeling quite buzzy after the last set so when Lizzie looks at me I nod.

'Cheers Bobby,' she says.

We go through the gate and past the crew, loading the band's gear into a truck. Bobby opens the back door of a black Austin Princess for us and I get in next to the singer who's spark out, with his mouth hanging open. Lizzie gets in beside me and Bobby sits in the front with Caesar between him and the driver. As we move off I look through the rear window and see a couple of roadies leading a group of girls towards the van.

12

The hotel is an old manor house on the outskirts of a village a couple of miles away. The Princess stops at the side of the building and the van pulls up behind us. The singer, who's been snoring beside me all the way, wakes up and sees me.

'Allo sweet,' he says, wrapping his arms round me and trying to kiss me. I put a hand on his chest and push him away. Bobby turns from the front seat.

'Leave it out Denny, that's a lady you're sitting next to.'

We get out of the car and Denny flops down on the seat again. The doors of the van open and the drummer, bass player, rhythm guitarist and some of the road crew get out. Caesar makes some quick introductions while Bobby leads the way round the side of the building to a stable block. He unlocks the door and we follow him along a corridor into an open area with sofas and chairs and rooms leading off it. While I'm wondering where we're going to get a drink, a bloke in a Grim Reaper T-shirt comes in and puts a case of bottles on a table. Another lad appears behind him with a similar case and a box of glasses. Drinks are poured, a radio's turned on to a blues station, joints are rolled, mirrors appear on tables and white powder is chopped and snorted. Lizzie and I aren't into drugs so we go and sit together on a sofa at the back of the room with a couple of large drinks while the band and the crew get stuck in. Denny lopes in, looking well past it, until he gets a couple of lines up his nose and starts rabbiting away to the drummer and jabbing him in the chest to make his point. Caesar comes over, sits next to Lizzie and they talk. Bobby's on the other side of the room having an intense conversation with a tall, slim bloke in a suit, who I didn't see come in. As I'm thinking we're the only women here, the door opens and a couple of roadies come in with the girls I saw them with behind the stage. They hover uncertainly for a moment but they're soon surrounded by the lads and being given all kinds of refreshment. I ask Lizzie and Caesar if they want another drink and as I take their glasses and get up from the sofa, I notice the man in the suit casting looks at Caesar while he talks to Bobby. I pass close to them on the way to the drinks and hear his American accent as they discuss whether they should record the band at A&R or Capital Studios in New York. Bobby prefers A&R because it's cheaper but the American says Capital is better because it's got linear faders and can do multi-track drop-ins, whatever they are. As I'm hovering to hear more, the bass player appears beside me, puts his arm round me and asks my name.

'Pat Boone,' I say, wriggling out of his grasp.

I step over a couple snogging on the floor and get the drinks. When I get back to the sofa Denny's sitting next to Lizzie, where Caesar was, and I feel a flash of anger as he puts his arm round her and starts kissing her ear. Lizzie turns and says something to him and he jumps up and walks away.

'What did you say?' I ask, as I sit down.

'Told him I'd got syph.'

While we're laughing, I notice Caesar going out of the door between Bobby and the American. I take a drink, sit back, close my eyes and listen to Howlin' Wolf singing about that spoonful. When the song ends I look round and see it's all getting a bit steamy. There's a couple getting down to it next to us, a naked girl lying in between two blokes on the other sofa and plenty of action on the floor. More coke's being chopped, the fug of dope smoke is getting to me and I reckon I've had enough.

'Want to make a move?' I ask.

Lizzie nods and we finish our drinks and head for the door, fending off a couple of suitors on the way.

As we reach the end of the corridor, I hear the American's voice and look through a half open door. He's got Caesar up against the wall with his hand between his legs and he's trying to kiss him on the lips. Caesar's turning his head away and struggling to get free but Bobby's right next to him, blocking his escape. I look at Lizzie, she nods and we go in.

'We're going now C, if you want a lift,' says Lizzie.

'He's not going anywhere, so you can fuck off!' says Bobby.

The American lets go of Caesar and backs off. 'Are these chicks press?'

'Nah. Just a couple of slags. Get the fuck out now, before you get a smack,' he says, striding towards us. When he makes a grab for Lizzie, I punch him on the jaw, kick him in the bollocks and as he folds up I give him a right hook to the temple. He hits the deck and the American scurries past us and out of the room. Lizzie takes Caesar's hand and I follow them along the corridor and out into the night. We go round the corner of the building to where I can keep an eye on the front door. Caesar is looking upset and confused. Lizzie puts her arm round him. 'Are you all right, love?'

'Yes, I am OK… I should go back,' says Caesar.

'I don't think so,' says Lizzie.

'He will beat me.'

'Bobby?'

'Yes.'

'Who's the American?' I ask.

'Is called Steve. He is from record company in New York.'

'Has he done that to you before?'

'Well…'

'And Bobby encourages it?'

'He says I have to, or he won't sign us.'

'Slimy sod,' says Lizzie.

I turn him round to face me. 'After what you did onstage tonight you don't need to be anyone's bum boy to get a deal.'

'You were fucking brilliant,' says Lizzie.

'It is not so simple.'

'Why?'

'He has my passport and visa. I have no money except for five pounds a week he pays us. He says he will get me arrested and sent to Mexico if I don't do what he tells me. I can't go back. There is trouble for me there.'

'What kind of trouble?'

'I had no money in Mexico. I wanted to come here and join a band, so only way was to bring cocaine inside guitar and in case with false part. I was meant to sell cocaine and send back money. I make stupid mistake when I get here and it was stolen from me. I need to make money and send it soon or they will have someone come and find me. Bobby says he will give us share of advance when we get signed and it will be enough for what I owe.'

'How much do you need?' I ask.

'Six thousand pounds.'

'That's a lot of cocaine.'

'It was packed very good.'

If it was half that amount I might be thinking of staking him the cash but six large is too much and I'm in bad enough trouble with Bobby without nicking his star guitarist.

'I should go back,' says Caesar.

'Are you sure?' asks Lizzie.

'It is the only way for me now.'

He could be right. If he scarpers and returns to the club, Bobby'll find him and do God knows what to him. He's probably best to get back in there, do what he has to do and hope he makes it big, which will give him the money to square it in Mexico and power over the vultures in the rock business. After what we saw on the stage tonight, I'm pretty sure he can do it, with or without Grim Reaper. I watch his elfin figure walking to the door and make a little prayer that he's going to be all right.

'Poor kid,' says Lizzie, when he's gone indoors.

'Bobby's such a bastard.'

'I've heard how bad he treats his girls up the Astor.'

'Now we know how bad he treats his bands.'

With no way of calling a cab, we start walking back to the festival through the moonlight. The night's warm, the air is soft and balmy and it feels good to be alone with nature. We bowl along, holding hands and swinging our arms, stopping for the odd snog and before long we can see the outline of the stage and the trailers up ahead. We walk through the camping ground, trying not to tread on the trusting souls sleeping under the stars. When we get to where the cars are parked, we find the Herald, put the roof up, get inside and ease the seats back. I take the flower out of my hair, put it on the dashboard, reach for Lizzie's hand and drift off to sleep.

I'm standing in front of the stage among the crowd who are leaping about and going crazy to some hard rock. I'm trying to see who's on the stage but I can't move. I'm frozen, like a pillar of salt. I get knocked to the ground and people are trampling on me and kicking me. I'm trying to roll out from under them when a massive wind whips up and the crowd are screaming and getting blown away and the stage comes crashing down and a helicopter is plunging out of the sky towards me and when I think it's about to crush me it stops, hovers above me and a rope lands on the ground. I try to reach for it and suddenly I can move and I'm strong again. I hold the rope and the chopper lifts off and I'm soaring up over the people running away and over the Abbey and off into the sun. I look up and Caesar's leaning out of the chopper and smiling at me. I start to climb towards him but as I get nearer the rope gets longer and the faster I climb the longer it gets and he's further and further away and he's waving desperately and getting smaller and smaller, then the rope breaks and I'm falling through the air for miles and miles until I see a massive balloon below me. I dive down, land on top of it, slide down the canvas, fall into the basket, land on a soft bed of red carnations. All at once I'm blissfully comfortable, time has stopped and I'm going to be there forever in heaven. Then the basket starts rocking up and down. I open my eyes and Lizzie's getting into the car with two cups of coffee.

'All right, sleepy head?'

'Mmm.'

I sit up, let the hot coffee chase the dream away and give Lizzie a kiss. She opens the window and the sound of the Small Faces doing 'Itchycoo Park' drifts over from the stage, which I'm glad to see is still standing. When Steve Marriot sings "I got high", the crowd give a big cheer.

'Do you want to have a look?' asks Lizzie.

'Not if Bobby's around.'

'It's all right. I just saw one of the crew, he told me Bobby and the band are gone. They're flying to New York today.'

'I hope Caesar won't be sitting next to Steve.'

We get out of the car and walk towards the stage, lingering for a moment by a yoga class that's happening in a clearing between the trailers. The bloke who's leading it has a great body and a perfect tan. He's sitting in a lotus pose talking to the group about how the right kind of breathing can stimulate your chakras and get you high. When he leans forward onto his hands, flicks his legs out behind him and goes into what he calls a cobra, I want to strip off and join in but then the Faces kick into 'Watcha Gonna Do About It' and the music wins.

We get near the front and have a bit of a shimmy while they rock along through a really tight set. They all look so young, you'd think they're bunking off school. When they slow it down with 'Lazy Sunday' we move back and sit down among the colourful people. The Faces finish up with 'Tin Soldier' as an encore and the crowd are still whooping and clapping when Tommy Vance walks on slowly and approaches the mic. He stands with his head bowed, then says he has some bad news. He tells us that Brian Epstein has died and the crowd goes silent.

Tommy stands with his head down for a bit, then he says there will be a break before Eric Burden and the Animals and walks off the stage. I feel sad about what I've just heard. He was only about thirty and without him we wouldn't have The Beatles and all that came after them. Lizzie says she wants to know more and she's going to try and talk to Tommy backstage. I don't feel like going with her so I stay on the grass. After a while a young bloke with long blond hair, in a paisley shirt and flared jeans, sits down beside me, looks at my tits and starts rolling a joint.

'Shame, eh?' he says.

'Yeah.'

'He made a pass at me once.'

I get the feeling he's going to be disrespectful, before the man's even cold.

'He was scraping the barrel then,' I say, as I get up and go in search of Lizzie.

I go round the back of the stage to the security gate and see her talking to Tommy Vance. I wait until they say goodbye and she comes and joins me.

'What's the news?'

'They found him dead in his bed in Belgravia. Overdose of sleeping pills.'

'Accidental?'

'They reckon. He'd been out clubbing so it could have been the sleepers on top of too much booze.'

'It's a real shame.'

'He was lovely.'

We go back to the front of the stage as the roadies are setting up the Animals' gear.

'They'll most likely do the same set they did at the 100 Club,' I say.

'Won't be much different.'

'Want to give it a miss and get something to eat?'

'Who's on after them?'

'Alan Price Set, to finish up I think.'

'Him with the dancing bear?'

'Yeah.'

'I wouldn't mind giving that a miss an' all.'

'Home?'

'I reckon.'

• • •

After stopping at Lotus House, the new Chinese restaurant on Edgware Road, to pick up a chop suey take-away, we leave the Herald in Randolph Avenue, go up to my place and settle down in front of the TV. Eric and Ernie are finishing up their show with a few gags and then they go off singing 'Bring me Sunshine' and doing the silly dance. Next is a film called 'Witness for the Prosecution,' with Marlene Dietrich and Charles Laughton, which looks like it could be good but after twenty minutes we're both having trouble staying awake, so we switch off the TV and go through to the bedroom. As we're getting undressed the phone rings. All I want to do is get between the sheets but I decide to answer it, in case it goes on ringing all night. I go into the hall, pick up the receiver and hear a posh woman's voice. When she asks for Brenda Matthews, I know it must be Jeremy's wife. I'm tempted to put the phone down but if she's been able to get hold of my number I need to find out how and what else she knows.

'Speaking,' I say.

'This is Dorothy Pargeter-Smythe. I was at the Langham.'

'Yes.'

'I was wondering if we might meet. There is something I'd like to discuss with you.'

'OK.'

'Are you free tomorrow morning?'

'I can be.'

'Could you meet me outside Green Park Tube Station, at eleven?'

I tell her I'll be there and put the phone down.

When I go into the bedroom I see that Lizzie's already asleep. I turn off the light and get in beside her.

13

It's another beautiful sunny day and I watch the people strolling in Hyde Park as the taxi takes me along Bayswater Road and down Park Lane. I'm a bit early for meeting Mrs Pargeter-Smythe, so when I've managed to interrupt the cabby's lecture on the evils of the Wilson government and how much better Enoch Powell would be at the job, I tell him to drop me at Hyde Park Corner and take a leisurely walk along Piccadilly.

Dorothy is standing outside the tube station, looking elegant in a cream-coloured pleated dress, a soft fedora and dark glasses. She sees me coming and walks towards me.

'Let's sit in the park, shall we?' she says.

'Why not?' I reply, following her through the gate.

She sets off across the grass at a fair old clip and I get in step beside her. We come to a clearing among some trees where there are benches set around an old iron street lamp. She heads for an unoccupied bench, sits down, folds her arms and offers me a tight smile as I take my place next to her.

'I have been appraised of your work in the Weston matter,' she says.

'Right.'

'Before we proceed, you should know that his colleague

at Kesgrove House, whose skull you fractured, is able and willing to identify you.'

'And if I don't do what you want, you'll introduce us and make sure he does.'

'You're very perceptive.'

Even with witness identification, they'd have a hard time making a case against me without Weston's body, but if there are any prints or traces that put me at the scene and no other reason for me to be there, it could get ugly and I can't risk it.

'What do I have to do?'

'Kill Tolka Saltik.'

'Why?'

'Much as I despise my husband and his infantile infatuation with communism, there is a fair chance that he will be executed if he is found guilty of the charges he is awaiting trial for.'

'I thought the death penalty was abolished a couple of years ago.'

'Only for murder. You can still hang for treason and espionage. Jeremy's death would cause me a great deal of inconvenience and without the testimony of Saltik, the case against him will be severely weakened.'

'I thought you said they had him on tape talking to a Russian.'

'The matter of the tape has become somewhat complicated. We will consider the issue once Saltik has been eliminated.'

'Where is he?'

'On remand in Wormwood Scrubs.'

'I'll never get to him in there.'

'You'll have to find a way.'

'There is no way.'

'Then I shall show your photograph to that nice man at Kesgrove House.'

'Fuck you.'

'I'm sure you'd like to, from what I know of your private life, but I need this man killed and if it means you extending your repertoire, so be it.'

She takes a card out of her pocket and puts it in my hand.

'I shall pay you two thousand pounds when the job is done and I expect to hear from you soon. Good day.'

I watch her stride off towards Piccadilly and wonder if I shouldn't do her instead. Then I remember her dad's still in the game and so I'm wide open there. I suppose I could take out the other nonce at Kesgrove House but I reckon there's a good chance that if I did, Madam would find some way of getting me done for that and still make me off Saltik. On the way to the park gate, I look at the card she gave me and memorise the Belgravia phone number, before I tear it up and put it in a litter bin.

I knock on Lizzie's door when I get home but she's not there so I go up to my place, make a cup of coffee and take it down to the communal garden. I sit on a bench near a family having a picnic on the grass. The parents are chatting away and two toddlers, a boy and a girl, are playing with a ball. The little boy throws it to the girl and when she tries to catch it she trips over and cries. I want to go and pick her up but her mother takes her in her arms and comforts her. Dad offers her an iced lolly from the picnic box and moments later she's fine again. The little boy looks a bit crestfallen until he gets his own lolly and then they sit next to each other on the grass and lick away contentedly. I sip my coffee and briefly nurse my regrets at the unlikelihood of ever having my own children, before returning to the question of how I'm going to save myself from a murder charge by getting at Saltik in the Scrubs. Just as I'm deciding that it's probably impossible, a young couple stroll past me arm in arm and sit on a nearby bench. When they share a kiss moments later, I get an idea.

I go back up to the flat and phone Bert. His wife Carol answers and tells me she thinks he's in the Walmer Castle.

On the way over there in a cab, I remind myself that I need to get a new car. Bert's sitting at a table with a couple of faces from George's firm. He clocks me as I walk past and sit on a stool at the far end of the bar. I order a whisky, have a chat with Ken, the landlord, who I've known a long time and then Bert's standing beside me.

'All right, Reen?'

'I need a word.'

'They'll be gone in a minute,' he says, nodding towards the table.

'I'll come.'

He goes back to his seat and when the two blokes leave, I go and join him.

'How's it going?' asks Bert.

'Not bad.'

'Ronnie Drake's got a trial date.'

'Yeah?'

'About a month away.'

'The case must be holding up.'

Bert nods and takes a long pull on his pint.

'Is there something you need?' he asks.

'You were in the Scrubs, right?'

'A while ago.'

'Remand?'

'Yeah.'

'How do I get a visit to a remand prisoner?'

'Phone up.'

'Simple as that?'

'You need his number and you have to give your name and address, date of birth, relationship to the prisoner and all that.'

'Does it have to be kosher?'

'I doubt they check.'

'Is the visit through the glass or open?'

'Open for remand.'

'Sitting at tables with them?'

'It was when I was there.'

'That's great, Bert. Thanks,' I say, finishing my drink.

'You want another?'

'I ought to go.'

Bert's known me since I was born and he has too much respect for me to ask who I'm visiting in the Scrubs or why. I give him a peck on the cheek and leave him to his pint.

As soon as I get home I call Dorothy's number and when her butler finally answers and brings her to the phone, I get Saltik's prisoner number from her and write it down. I look up H M Prison Wormwood Scrubs in the phone book and dial it. When I get through to the right department, a woman answers and tells me the next visiting day is tomorrow. I tell her I want to book one and give her Saltik's name and number. I give my name as Jane Greenwood, with an address in Pinner, tell her I'm twenty-seven and my date of birth in 1940. She tells me to be at the main gate in Du Cane Road at eleven o'clock in the morning to sign in.

My next call is to Ben Griffin down on Walworth Road. I tell him what I need, he says he can supply me with the necessary and I can pick it up from him anytime this afternoon. I decide I need a car for all this running around so I take a wad of notes from the back of my underwear drawer, walk to the rank in Warwick Avenue and get a cab to the used car lot in Harlesden where I bought a motor once before. As I'm walking between the rows of cars on the forecourt the owner comes out of the office, in the same brown trilby hat that he wore last time I saw him.

'Hello again,' he says, making his way towards me.

I stop by a dark blue Ford Anglia that looks like it might be all right.

'That is a very nice motor car,' says Trilby.

'Not great round corners.'

'True enough. There are cars that hold the road better.'

I look along the row and spot a black Mini Cooper at the far end. It looks like the same model as the red one that I got rid of.

'What about this?' I say, as I get to it.

'Lovely car. Just come in. Lady owner, low mileage, really well looked after.'

'Give us a drive then.'

'Yes ma'am.'

He trots over to his office and comes back with a pair of trade plates which he puts over the Mini's. After removing the £350 ticket from the windscreen and putting it on the back seat, he takes a large bunch of keys out of his pocket, selects one and opens the door for me. I get behind the wheel, he sits beside me and I drive up Scrubs Lane and onto the North Circular, where I can get up a bit of speed. The car feels good and fast and the brakes are solid so I turn back towards Harlesden while Trilby drones on about the Mini being the best car ever made, how they last forever and the rest of it.

'Three hundred cash,' I say, as I pull onto the forecourt.

'Three two five.'

'Three ten.'

'I wish I could but it's got to be three two five.'

'See you then,' I say, getting out of the car and heading for the road. Trilby runs after me and agrees to three ten and a full tank of petrol. I go to the office, count out the notes and he gives me a receipt and the log book.

As I get near Shepherd's Bush I decide I may as well go and collect what I need from Ben in Walworth Road and then I'll be all set for the Scrubs tomorrow. I drive along Holland Park Avenue to Marble Arch, down Park Lane, over Vauxhall Bridge and into Walworth Road. I park by a phone box, call Ben and tell him I'll be outside his place in two minutes. I roll along a bit further and see him standing on the pavement. I stop the car, he gets in and hands me an envelope.

'There's two in there,' he says.

'We said a bullseye, didn't we?'

'That's it.'

I take my wad out of my pocket, count off fifty quid and give it to him. He thanks me, gets out of the car and I put the envelope in my pocket and head back into town. I don't feel like going home and I'm wondering if there'll be anyone in the club at this time. I stop at a phone box by Elephant and Castle and try the number. Jane answers and tells me that Lizzie's on her way in early to sort out the accounts with her so I say I'll join them in an hour or so. As I'm going over Westminster Bridge I realise I haven't eaten all day and I'm starving. I drive to Charlotte Street, get a table for one at Bertorelli's and order calamari, chicken Milanese and half a bottle of Chianti.

The club isn't open when I get there so I ring the bell and wait until Max comes up the stairs and lets me in. We go down into the club and he returns to his seat at the end of the bar next to Terry. Most of the girls are in, sitting at tables and chatting. A couple are still in their street clothes but most of them have changed into their working outfits. I go through to the office where Lizzie and Jane are sitting at the desk with account books and a cash box in front of them.

'How are things?' I ask, as I sit down on the sofa.

'We're in really good shape,' says Lizzie. 'Bar takings are up and we made two and half grand clear last month.'

'That's great,' I say.

'August's looking good as well,' says Jane.

'How much are we bunging the Dirty Squad?' I ask.

'A ton a week.'

'Sounds about right.'

It's well worth it for the protection we get. If a punter gets the hump about something and goes to the law, the ones we're paying a pension to will make it go away. There was a ruck a while back and a punter tried to get Max done for GBH but the filth threatened to do him for rape of one of our girls and he dropped it.

'It's time we opened,' says Lizzie, closing up the account books and putting them in a drawer. Jane picks up the cash box, puts it in the wall safe, closes it and goes into the club. Lizzie sits beside me on the sofa and slips her arm round me. I relax into her and we kiss and cuddle for

a while until we can see through the glass panel that suits
are coming down the stairs and the night is beginning.

14

I park in Du Cane Road and walk towards the main gate
of the prison which sits between two solid brick and stone
columns. There's the bust of a woman halfway up the one
on the left and the same of a man on the other one. I see a
queue of people outside a door to the side and get on the end
of it, next to a woman holding a baby. After a few minutes
the door opens and we move forward slowly. Once inside,
I confirm my name, address, date of birth and relationship
to the prisoner Saltik, which I'd given as 'friend', to a
screw sitting behind a desk. He writes something in a big
ledger, swivels it round and offers me a pen. I sign it as
Jane Greenwood and get waved on to a female screw who
gives me a body search. When everyone's been signed in
and tickled, we're shown into a room with rows of tables
and chairs. The screws come in after us, two of them stand
in each corner of the room and we're told to take a seat. I go
to a table in the middle, to be as far away from the screws as
possible. The woman with the baby, who was in the queue,
is on one side of me and there's a teenage girl on the other.
I check my make-up in my powder compact mirror, open
the jacket of my dark blue Aquascutum suit and undo two
buttons of my blouse. After a couple of minutes, a door in
the corner opens and the prisoners come in. A big bloke
with tattoos and a pot belly comes over and sits down with

the woman and baby and a painfully thin young lad joins the teenage girl. Saltik's one of the last in and he's looking a bit confused as his eyes search the room. I stand up and give him a discreet wave. As he moves towards me I nod encouragingly and hold my hand out to him. He shakes it hesitantly, we sit down and I look into his eyes, give him a warm smile and get out my best smoky voice.

'It's Mr Saltik, isn't it?'

'Yes.'

'And you're from Turkey?'

Saltik nods. The woman next door passes the baby to the big bloke. He rocks it in his arms and kisses it.

'My name is Jane Greenwood and I work with a charity called Far from Home which caters for the needs of foreigners who have been arrested and detained in this country.'

The baby starts to cry. Saltik looks across as the big bloke passes it back to the woman, who soothes and quietens it. I smile at Saltik and I lean a little closer to him. 'We try to make sure that you have adequate legal representation and that you are fully aware of your rights under the law.'

'That is good,' he says, settling a little in his seat and lowering his eyes to my cleavage.

'My function is to ascertain whether you may need any assistance or advice and to arrange visits from appropriate professionals,' I say, taking a notebook and pencil out of my bag.

He's still got his eyes on the prize so I don't speak. I notice the young bloke on the other side of us reaching for the girl's hand. His head is down and he looks like he's about to cry as well.

'How are you being treated?' I ask Saltik.

'Not bad.'

'Do you share a cell?'

'Yes.'

'And your cell mate…?'

'He is an idiot.'

'I see.'

'We do not speak.'

The couple with the baby are now arguing about whether someone is going to appear in court or not and the man is telling the woman she's got to do something or other to stop it happening. She's saying she can't and when he starts shouting and pointing his finger at her, a screw comes forward and tells him to calm down or he'll go back to his cell. The man raises a hand in surrender and apologises. Saltik and I share a smile.

'Do you have any family in Turkey that you would like us to get in touch with?' I ask.

He leans forward and looks me in the eye.

'I would rather they did not know.'

'I can understand that but if you are convicted and have to serve a sentence…'

'I will not be convicted.'

'How can you know that?'

He leans forward and lowers his voice, 'I have deal.'

'Really?'

'Once I testify, I will be free.'

'If you are sure…'

'I am sure.'

'In that case I need not trouble you any further, Mr Saltik.'

'Thank you very much for coming to see me.'

'You're welcome.'

At that moment the young couple next to us lean forward and kiss. I let my fingers brush against Saltik's hand as I reach for the notebook. He looks at me and I smile.

'I did not expect a visit from such a beautiful lady.'

'It's been very nice to meet you,' I say, giving him a coy look and putting the notebook in my bag. 'I'll say goodbye now.'

'With a kiss, perhaps?'

He leans across the table towards me.

'Why not?' I say, taking a handkerchief out of my jacket pocket. I dab my lips with it and slip something into my mouth. As he comes closer, I lean forward and kiss him, forcing the cyanide capsule down his throat with my tongue. He pulls back and puts his hand to his neck.

'What the hell is that?'

'Just something to help you relax.'

'What?'

I put my hand on his. 'Don't worry, it'll just make you feel good for a while.'

I take a card out of my pocket with a random phone number on it. 'Feel free to call me if you need any assistance.'

I leave him looking bemused and walk through the tables to the door. When the screw's unlocked it and let me out, I go into the office, sign Jane out and walk to the main gate. Ben said the cyanide will kill him in twenty minutes and it'll look like a heart attack. The residue in the bloodstream will disappear quickly and should be untraceable by the time they get a sample to a lab, though in a case like this they probably won't even bother to test him.

I drive along Du Cane Road, across Wood Lane and Ladbroke Grove into Maida Vale and park by the Warrington. There are people sitting at the tables outside enjoying a lunchtime drink in the sun and I'm tempted to have one myself but I need to find out if Saltik's snuffed it before I can relax. I go to the phone box beside the pub and dial Ray's number. The same woman who answered before picks up and then Ray comes on.

'Have you got anyone in the Scrubs?' I ask.

'I might have. Why?'

'I need to find something out.'

'It'll cost you a ton.'

'How soon can you get it?'

'Depends what you want.'

'I need to know if a rat's been straightened.'

'Easy.'

'No blather, eh?'

'Agreed.'

I give him Saltik's name and number and he says he'll phone me as soon as he's got anything. When I get into the flat I suddenly feel hungry and remember that I didn't have any breakfast. I go to the kitchen but there's nothing but a couple of tins of beans and no bread. I don't want to go to the shops in case Ray gets back to me. I'm wondering if Lizzie might have something and I'm about to call her when the phone rings. I pick up the receiver and recognise Dorothy's clipped tones.

'That was fast,' she says.

'I…'

'Found in his cell.'

I feel relieved and I want to know more but I don't want to have this conversation on the phone.

'Can you come to the house?' she asks.

I tell her I can and she gives me an address in Belgrave Square. I go downstairs to the phone box and call Ray to tell him not to bother with the Scrubs. He says he's just tried to call me at the flat to tell me Saltik's gone. The prison doctor examined him and got a description of how he went from his cellmate. The doc told the governor he'd had a heart attack and certified natural causes, which puts a nice lid on the business. Ray wants his wages and I tell him to meet me at the club about ten o'clock tonight.

I get a cab to Belgrave Square and ring the bell of number fifty-four. A pretty young girl in a maid's uniform opens the door and I tell her I've come to see Mrs Pargeter-Smythe. She invites me in, asks me to wait, walks across the hall and goes up a wide staircase. I'm taking in the portraits on the walls and a bust of some Roman bloke with a frizzy hairdo and no arms, when Dorothy comes down the stairs, followed by the maid.

'Brenda. Come into the library. Will you have tea?'

'That would be nice,' I say.

Dorothy turns to the maid, 'Thank you Mary.'

Mary disappears downstairs and Dorothy leads me across the hall and into a book-lined room with a large desk under the window and two comfy looking velvet-covered sofas facing each other in the middle. She waves me to one of them and sits on the other.

'How on earth did you pull it off so quickly?' she asks.

'I never discuss my work.'

'You tell me it can't be done and the man's lying dead on the floor of his cell the following morning. Most impressive, I must say.'

'How did you find out?'

'As chance would have it, Saltik's defence counsel, who happens to be a friend of mine, was given the news when he tried to make an appointment to see him.'

And the first thing the honourable defence counsel does is tell the wife of the man in the dock that the witness who was going to shop him is dead. The way these upper class cunts look after each other makes me want to vomit. If this cow didn't have me over a barrel for doing Weston,

I'd give her a slap and get out of here. The door opens and Mary enters pushing a silver trolley. She motors it to the low table between the sofas and puts the teapot, cups and all the business on it. I'm glad to see ham and cucumber sandwiches going on the table next to the cake stand. Dorothy pours tea, passes me a cup and then offers me the milk jug. I pour some into my tea, add a couple of lumps of sugar and when she passes me a plate, I load up with sandwiches and get stuck in. Dorothy sips her tea, takes a macaroon from the cake stand, puts it on her plate, looks at it for bit and then clears her throat.

'When we spoke at the Langham, I mentioned an incriminating tape recording of Jeremy in conversation with a Russian agent.'

'I remember,' I say, swallowing my fourth sandwich and reaching for a cupcake.

'I want you to find and destroy it.'

'How about paying me for doing Saltik, before we talk about anything else?'

'Your money is in an envelope on the hall table.'

I nod and take a bite of the delicious cupcake.

'The tape is believed to be in the hands of a Soviet agent, who I'd like you to kill.'

I want to tell her to stuff it but she's a cold bitch and she'll shop me for Weston if I knock her back.

'Where do I find him?'

'Istanbul.'

Dorothy sits back and sips her tea while I think about

how close I came to getting killed in Berlin a few years ago, the first time I got caught up with spies and secrets and that.

'I'd be no good there.'

'Why do you say that?'

'I don't know the place, or the language...'

'But I do.'

I put my teacup down.

'Which is why I shall be coming with you.'

The way she's looking at me tells me she means it.

'I only work alone,' I say.

'What makes you think you have a choice in the matter... Rina?'

• • •

A chauffeur drives us over Westminster Bridge to a house the other side of Clapham Common where I get my photograph taken by an old bloke in shirtsleeves and braces. He asks me my age and when I tell him I'm twenty-seven, he goes down to the basement with Dorothy. Half an hour later they come back and he hands me a passport in the name of Brenda Matthews with my photograph in it and an address in Potters Bar.

'I thought our Brenda might like a trip abroad,' says Dorothy.

On the way back in the car she tells me to meet her at Heathrow at one o'clock tomorrow afternoon.

15

I pick up my new Mini in Belgrave Square and drive home. I'm pretty sure Lizzie will be at the club but I knock on her door just in case she hasn't left. When I get no answer, I go upstairs to my place and run myself a bath. I put 'Disraeli Gears' on the turntable in the lounge, hoping it will take my mind off Dorothy and her doings and pour myself a large whisky while the opening riff of 'Strange Brew' fills the air. I turn it up loud, go into the bathroom, take off all my clothes, put my hair up, pour a good dash of Softique oil into the bath, slide into the silky warm water and close my eyes.

By the time Eric and Jack are into 'Sunshine of your Love', I'm wide awake and thinking that if the trip to Istanbul only involved getting hold of the incriminating tape, Dorothy could probably do it herself, or pay someone there to take care of it and the reason she wants me there is because she's expecting aggravation. Getting caught up in a rampage in a place where I don't know anyone, or even how to get around, is about as unsafe as it gets. The only way out of it that I can see is to do her, which is a risk because Sir David probably knows the plan and would finger me for the job. I'd also have to take care of the nonce at Kesgrove House, which Sir may also know about and, even if he couldn't prove anything, I can do without that much attention from the law, so it looks like I've got no choice but to give it a go and hope for the best.

I give myself a rub all over with the loofah, get out of the bath and dry myself, then I go into the lounge, take the record off, pour myself another drink and I'm on my way into the bedroom when the phone rings. I pick up the receiver and it's Georgie.

'Can you talk?' she asks.

'Of course I can. How are you?'

'I'm OK. And you?'

'Fine thanks, except I've got to go to Istanbul tomorrow.'

'How come?'

'You don't want to know.'

'I see.'

Georgie knows what I do and we maintain a kind of Chinese wall between us about my work. The last thing I want is for her to get mixed up in anything.

'How did your exams go?' I ask.

'Not bad, thanks. The Shakespeare paper was a bit tough.'

If I know her, she will have sailed through them. 'When do you get the results?'

'Not until next term.'

'You're on holiday now, right?'

'That's what I wanted to talk to you about.'

'How do you mean?'

'I'd like to go away.'

'Good idea.'

'Abroad, maybe.'

'Great.'

'Only I'll need some money.'

'That's no trouble, I'll send you some.'

'Would that be all right?'

'Of course. Will you go with a friend?'

'Yes.'

'Did I meet her when I came up?'

'It's a him.'

'Oh. Is he nice?'

'Yes.'

I'm really excited to hear this. Georgie's never had a boyfriend as far as I know. She's always been so quiet and withdrawn, which I've put down to the rape and the killing that she's never talked about. I decide not to ask any more about the boy in case I embarrass her.

'I'll put some money in the post to you. You've got your passport, haven't you?'

'Yes.'

'Where do you think you'll go?'

'We haven't decided yet.'

'OK, well have a great time.'

'Thanks.'

'And send me a postcard.'

'I will,' she says, putting the phone down.

This is good news. Georgie going abroad on a holiday, with her boyfriend.

I go into the bedroom, look in the wardrobe and

decide on the Alexander Milnes trouser suit with a purple silk blouse. I hang them on the wardrobe door, sit at the dressing table and turn on the radio while I put on make-up. When I hear Herman's Hermits doing 'Mrs Brown you've got a lovely daughter', I start to feel nauseous and turn the dial. After a bit of static, I get to Radio 3 and some orchestra groaning away, and then Radio 4 where some posh bloke is explaining the rules of a new game where the people on the panel have to talk about something for a minute without repeating themselves, or something. I leave it on while I put on mascara and lipstick and by the time I'm getting dressed I'm laughing at Derek Nimmo having a go at Clement Freud because he's interrupted him and the posh bloke is trying to calm them down but they won't let him get a word in and they're still going at it when I brush my hair, put my heels on, turn off the radio and leave.

I drive into town and when I get to the club, I say hello to Max and Terry on the door and wait while a group of business types pay Jane at the desk and go in. I'm just about to follow them when Max gives me a nod and takes a couple of steps away from the door. I go and join him.

'How's your hand?' I ask.

'Pretty good, thanks.'

I wait while he has a quick look round.

'There was a geezer asking for you last night.'

'Do you know him?'

'No.'

'What does he look like?'

'Short, mean looking. Wears a mod suit and a pork pie hat on his bald head.'

'How old?'

'About thirty?'

I look round and see Terry talking to a couple of blokes who look like they're half pissed and trying to get into the club. As Terry raises his arms to stop them, the taller of the two takes a swing at him. Max strides over, grabs him by the collar, marches him a few yards up the street and chucks him against a wall, knocking the breath out of him. The man looks up, sees Max closing in and legs it along the street. The other one sees what's happened to his mate and hurries off after him. Max joins Terry back at the door and I give them a smile as I walk past them into the club.

The band are playing 'I was Made to Love Her' and even though Tim's not quite got Stevie's soul, he's getting pretty close and when I see Kelly walking past the bottom of the stairs I'm tempted to drag her onto the dance floor but a punter beats me to it and takes her to the bar. The club's really busy, all the tables are occupied and there'll be plenty of action going on in the curtained booths. I can't see Ray anywhere so I make my way through the tables to the back of the club. When I go through into the corridor, the door to the gents opens and a man in an expensive suit, with white powder on the lapel, walks past me wiping his nose on a silk handkerchief.

I put my head round the office door and see Lizzie at

the desk, talking on the phone. She looks up, waves me inside and I sit on the sofa and listen to her bargaining with someone about the price of something. She sticks to the fifty quid she's offering and finally gets the other party to agree.

'Fucking wanker,' she says, putting the phone down.

'Who was it?'

'Some drab who's collared a scotch whisky truck by mistake and wants to shift it quick.'

'How many cases are you buying?'

'Twelve. Ten for the club and one each for you and me.'

'You beautiful girl!' I say, putting my arms round her and giving her a kiss.

'Should last us a couple of weeks,' she says.

'Let's have one now.'

Lizzie goes to the drinks table, picks up a bottle of Bells and pours.

'There was a nasty little creep in earlier trying to vex me.'

'Pork pie hat?'

'How did you know?'

'Max said he was asking for me. When was he here?'

'About nine. I was behind the bar while Julie had her break and he sat at the end staring at me and making snide remarks.'

'Like what?'

'"This is a nice little club. Shame it won't be here much

longer"… Stuff like that. I was about to ring for Max when he slung his hook.'

'He could be one of Bobby's.'

'I know.'

The last thing I want is to be away when the club's being threatened. Bobby's got access to a lot of muscle if he wants to use it and Lizzie could be in danger. I'd give anything to be staying here with her but if I don't go with Dorothy and she grasses me for murder, I'll be even less able to protect my girl if I'm stuck in Holloway. She sits beside me on the sofa.

'I'm going to Istanbul tomorrow,' I say.

'I thought that was all over, with Jeremy inside.'

'His wife's got other ideas.'

'Like what?'

I refill our glasses and explain about Dorothy wanting the tape and what she'll do if I don't get it for her.

'How do you know she'll leave you alone once she's got the tape?' says Lizzie, when I've finished.

'I'm hoping I can get enough on her in Istanbul to even up the scales.'

'How will you do that?'

'Take my camera and hope for the best.'

'Good luck.'

'I'll ask Bert Davis to put three more minders in tomorrow. Another on the door and two in the club, tooled up at all times.'

'That'll help.'

I look through the one-way glass just as Ray comes down the stairs.

'There's someone I need to see,' I say, opening my handbag.

Lizzie clocks Ray as he walks to the bar.

'Got yourself a date?'

'Just paying the help,' I say, counting out a hundred notes. 'Have you got an envelope I can have?'

'Sure.'

She takes one out of a drawer and hands it to me. I can tell she wants to know what this is about and I'd like to tell her, because she knows about Jeremy and me taking care of Weston but there isn't time to go into it now. I leave Lizzie in the office, go into the club, join Ray at the bar and hand him the envelope. He takes a look inside, flicks through the notes and puts it in his back pocket.

'What'll you have?' I ask.

'Pint of Guinness.'

I catch Julie's eye, ask for Ray's pint and a whisky for me. When she's given us our drinks Ray takes a long pull of his Guinness and lights a cigarette.

'Who do you know who's short, bald, mean looking, wears a mod suit and a pork pie hat?' I ask.

'It'll cost you more than a pint of Guinness.'

'You've just had a ton for making a phone call!'

'But I'm the only one who knows the number.'

He's got a point. It's how he makes his living and he's the best sniffer I've ever known.

'How much?'

He smiles, takes a drink and a long drag on his fag. 'As you're on the firm, you can have this one on me.'

'Cheers,' I say, signalling to Julie for the same again.

'So who is he?'

'Sounds like Dave Green.'

'I've never heard of him.'

'Just out of Parkhurst. Done a ten for breaking a security guard's legs on a blag at Heathrow that went tits up.'

'Who's he with?'

'Anyone who wants him. He grassed Harry Trent years ago so most won't touch him. He hangs around the rock business, picking up a bit of enforcement here and there.'

Now I know he's come from Bobby.

'Where does he live?'

'It was Bethnal Green, before he went inside.'

I leave Ray at the bar and go back to the office. Lizzie's at the desk with the cash box and an account book in front of her.

'Busy?' I say.

'Just doing the wages.'

'Can I help?' I ask.

'It's OK, I'm nearly finished. Have you talked to Bert about the extra bodies?'

'I'll see if I can get him now,' I say, picking up the phone and dialling his number. Carol answers and tells me she thinks he's in the Elgin. I look at my watch and see that if I leave now I can just make it before closing time. I tell Lizzie where I'm going, give her a long kiss and say I'll see her at home later. I walk through the club, which is really full now. The band are playing 'The In Crowd' and giving Ramsey Lewis a run for his money. Ray is still at the bar, talking to a sharp-suited Italian bloke, who I've seen around Tony Farina's clubs. I go upstairs to the door and tell Max and Terry to watch out for the pork pie hat and to expect some more help to arrive soon. Max looks a bit concerned and wants to know who they'll be getting but when I tell him Bert'll be on the case he's all right with it.

I drive fast to Ladbroke Grove, park outside the Elgin and get in as the drink-up bell is clanging. Someone grabs my arse as I push through the crowd, gets a sharp elbow in the stomach and lets go. Bert's at a table in the corner with some of George's firm and a couple of girls. He sees me as I get near and when I turn and head for the door he follows me.

'Don't you want a drink?' he asks, when we're outside.

'I'm all right, thanks.'

'What's up?'

'I need three more minders at the club.'

'There's a couple in there I can put on to you.'

'Can they use a tool?'

'Course they can.'

'I need three.'

'No problem. What's occurring?'

'I don't know yet. Could be nothing.'

'But you want to play it safe.'

'You've got it.'

'When do you need them?'

'Tomorrow.'

'It'll cost you.'

'Tell George to up the pension and let me know.'

'All right.'

'Thanks Bert.'

He nods towards the pub. 'There's a lock-in tonight, if you want a good drink.'

'I ought to be going.'

'Take care of yourself, Reen.'

As Bert turns to the door, I see a short man in a hat standing on the corner of Westbourne Park Road. I say goodnight to Bert and walk up the Grove. When I'm sure he's following me, I go on past the car. There's quite a few people about so I turn into Elgin Mews, duck into an entry halfway along and watch him coming through the arch, taking a blade out of his pocket. When he's gone past me I step out behind him, grab him round the neck, knee him in the back and force him onto the floor. I kneel on his chest, take off a shoe and ram the heel into his eye. When he cries out I put a hand over his mouth and look round to make sure we're alone. His blade is on the ground where he dropped it. I pick it up and stick it between his ribs.

The pub is shut by the time I get there so I ring the bell and wait. The landlord opens the door, I ask for Bert Davis and he lets me into the bar. Bert comes out of a back room and I tell him what's gone on and ask him if he'll take care of the body. He says he'll do it because it's me, but he'll need a monkey for his mate. I say I can give him the five hundred notes in the morning and he agrees. I tell him the body is in the entry, where I dragged it to. He asks me how tall the bloke is and when I tell him he's short, he nods and goes into the back room. As I'm starting the car, I see Bert and another man walking towards the Mews, carrying a dustbin.

• • •

I drive up Westbourne Park Road with Aretha Franklin telling me to "try a little tenderness", but it's a bit late now. When I saw that blade, I knew he meant to kill or mark me so I had to take care of him in case he meant to do the same thing to Lizzie. Short men are often the most dangerous. If they're in the game, they need to make up for what they're lacking in weight and reach by being quick and dirty.

When I get into the flat I call the office number of the club.

'Abigail's. Can I help you?' says Lizzie.

'Pork pie followed me to the Elgin.'

'What happened?'

'He tried to get funny so I finished him.'

'Blimey. Did you get hurt?'

'No, I'm fine.'

'Are you at home?'

'Yeah.'

'I'm on my way.'

I go into the lounge, pour myself a drink, kick off my shoes and sit on the sofa. I normally feel good after I've put some creep away but tonight I feel so tired I can hardly keep my eyes open. When I've finished my drink I go into the bedroom. As I'm hanging my jacket in the wardrobe I hear the front door opening. I go into the hall, Lizzie drops her bag on the floor and puts her arms round me. She leads me into the bedroom, unbuttons my blouse and slips it off me while she kisses my neck and shoulders. My bra comes off, the kissing goes on, then it's my trousers and pants. She pulls back the duvet, lays me on the bed, whisks her dress and undies off, lies down beside me and then we're stroking and kissing and everything's beautiful.

16

The cab stops outside the Royal Oak and I tell the driver to wait while I go into the public bar and give Bert his money for last night. I tell him I saw them with the dustbin and ask if it went off all right. He's laughing as he tells me how they just managed to stuff Green into the bin and tie the lid on before they chucked it off Tower Bridge. He asks me if I still want the extra men at the club and I tell him I do. I need to make sure Lizzie's safe while I'm away and I'll take up the slack if George's extra pension is too much for the club.

I tell the driver to take me to the post office in Queensway, where I put five hundred quid in a registered envelope and send it to Georgie in Cambridge. Then it's on through Knightsbridge and along the A4 to Heathrow. Dorothy phoned this morning and told me to meet her at Building One and when the cab pulls up outside, I pay the driver, pick up my suitcase and go in through the glass door. Dorothy's waiting under the departures board and I go to join her. As I get close, I recognise the pretty young maid from Belgrave Square standing slightly behind her.

'Good afternoon, Brenda. Thank you for being punctual.'

'Afternoon,' I reply.

'I think you met Mary at the house.'

'I did. Hello again.'

'Afternoon, ma'am,' she says, bobbing a curtsy.

'My name's Brenda and I'm just like you, so you can call me by my name and you don't need to curtsy. OK?'

I've obviously startled them both. Mary is looking confused and Dorothy is regarding me with deep disapproval. I hold her gaze and after a moment her expression softens and an enigmatic smile appears. She puts a hand on Mary's shoulder.

'I believe Brenda is merely trying to be friendly and I think perhaps you should do as you're asked.'

I offer Mary my hand and she just manages a smile as we shake.

A loudspeaker crackles into life and calls passengers on a flight to Uganda to their departure gate.

'It's time we checked in,' says Dorothy, beckoning a porter who's leaning on his trolley by the door. She tells him we want the BOAC check-in and he loads up our cases and leads us across the hall. There's nobody behind the desk and no one waiting, so the porter takes our bags off the trolley, pockets his sixpence, tips his cap and trundles off. Dorothy stands tapping her foot impatiently for a few minutes, looks at her watch and then marches to the Aeroflot desk next door, goes to the head of the long queue of passengers and demands immediate attention from a meek looking official who's busy checking tickets and putting labels on luggage. He tells her that someone will be coming shortly but this doesn't satisfy Dorothy who goes on badgering the unfortunate man in a voice so loud that people in the queue start to tell her, in various languages, to shut up and get out of their way. I'm starting to find the whole thing funny and can't help giggling. I look at Mary and I can tell she thinks I shouldn't be laughing at her mistress but when I give her a nudge with my elbow she starts to smile. A large fat man with a red face and a fur hat steps out from the back of the Aeroflot queue and starts marching towards Dorothy, muttering something foreign. As he gets near her, a woman in uniform arrives at the BOAC desk. The Aeroflot clerk sees his colleague and hastily points her out to Dorothy, who turns and walks away just in time to evade capture by the Russian Bear.

We show our passport and tickets, get our boarding passes and I watch my suitcase disappear along the belt, hoping Istanbul customs won't decide to open it up and discover my spare Smith & Wesson and the tools I've packed. Dorothy marches off and we follow her to the departure lounge, where we're the first to arrive. We sit down and Dorothy takes a copy of *The Times* out of her coat pocket and disappears behind it. I take a seat beside her with Mary next to me as our fellow passengers start to arrive. They're mostly Turkish looking men in suits and women wearing headscarves, as well as a couple of groups of English who are dressed as if they might be going on holiday. I sit back, let the buzz of conversation wash over me and I'm wondering if I'll learn any Turkish while I'm there when a woman in uniform appears and calls for any first class passengers to come forward. Dorothy folds her paper, stands up, takes her boarding pass out of her pocket and beckons me to follow her. I look at my pass, see that I'm in first class and stand next to her in the line. I look back, see that Mary is still in her seat and turn to Dorothy.

'Mary's coming with us, isn't she?'

'Of course.'

'Well then…'

'She's in economy.'

I resist the temptation to kick Dorothy's arse and hand my passport and boarding pass to the attendant.

On the plane, Dorothy ignores the seats we've been given near the front of the cabin and once the other passengers are seated, she asks the very blond stewardess if we can sit in the back row. The girl gives us a sparkling white smile and says we may. Dorothy takes the window seat and buries her face in *The Times*. I sit next to her, lean back and feel the rumble of the engines. I've never been good at flying. I always get nervous when the bird takes off, although I'm usually all right once it stops climbing. I close my eyes, try to breathe evenly and relax, then the doors are being shut and the pilot comes on the speakers and tells us we're about to take off, we'll be arriving in Istanbul in four hours and ten minutes, it's eighty five degrees there and the sun's shining. Someone repeats what he's said, in what I presume is Turkish, the plane starts moving and the very blond stewardess stands in the aisle and shows us how to put on a life jacket and blow a whistle.

The engines roar and I grip the armrests and press my back into the seat as the plane surges along the runway and lifts off. Dorothy's lowered her paper and she's looking out of the window. I'm clenching my jaw and feeling as though I've left my stomach on the ground. I close my eyes and keep a firm hold on the armrest and my breakfast, until I finally hear the engines calm down and the plane levels off. Dorothy undoes her seatbelt and turns to me.

'Nervous flyer?'

'Just a bit.'

The stewardess arrives with a tray of drinks. 'Campari, Cinzano Bianco or champagne?'

I take a glass of champagne and Dorothy does the same. When the stewardess has gone and we've tasted the bubbly, she checks that there's no one in the row of seats in front of us, leans close to me and speaks in a hushed voice.

'The Consul General in Istanbul is a cousin of mine. His name is Geoffrey Bagshot and we will be staying at the consulate with him and his wife Charlotte.'

'I see.'

'In order for you to fully understand your mission over there, you should know a little about what that idiot husband of mine has been up to.'

'It might be handy.'

'When we were up at Cambridge, he fell under the influence of a coterie of overgrown schoolboys who decided that the way to get revenge on all those fathers and house masters and rugby captains who had bullied and beaten and abused them was to arrange for the Communist doctrine of Marx and Engels to be established throughout the world without delay. After they graduated, some of them, including Jeremy, joined the Intelligence Services and began spying for the Soviets. Over the next few years most of them bungled it in various ways, got exposed and beetled off to Moscow. I expect you were aware of that?'

'Philby and…'

'Exactly. Jeremy, although by no means the brightest of the bunch, somehow managed to remain undetected.'

'What was he doing?'

'The late Tolka Saltik was employed as a translator at Karamürsel US Air Base in Turkey, where the Americans monitor Soviet radio transmissions. Jeremy was paying him for information about US operations to subvert communism in Turkey and passing it on to a Soviet agent.'

'So why did he want me to off Saltik?'

'I believe he thought a colleague at MI6 had become suspicious after he went to Turkey with Jeremy as part of a delegation. I imagine he was trying to cover his tracks.'

'Where does the tape come into it?'

'The Soviet agent, a Turk named Omer Turan, recorded his conversations with Jeremy in which he received information from him and when Jeremy was arrested, Turan offered to sell the tapes to British Intelligence for fifty thousand Turkish lira, which is about ten thousand pounds.'

'So why didn't they buy it?' I ask.

'As soon as they arrested Saltik and he agreed to talk, they didn't need it but now that they've lost their only witness, thanks to you, they're negotiating with Turan for the tape as we speak, which is why it's imperative that you get hold of it and take Turan out immediately, so that he can't testify.'

'Where is he?'

'That I hope to discover when we get there.'

I sip champagne and appreciate the stewardess's delicious rear view as she walks up the aisle.

• • •

The heat wraps itself around me like a warm cloak as I walk down the steps onto the tarmac. The sun is about to dip behind the roof of the terminal building as Mary joins us from the rear of the plane and we follow a uniformed official towards the wide glass frontage. While we wait for a good while in a long queue for passport control and customs, I'm praying that Dorothy won't kick off like she did in London. Fortunately she stays calm and we get through without any bother and collect our suitcases. We walk along a corridor, make a couple of turns and come out into the main hall where a small crowd of people are waiting behind a cordon, some holding cards with names on. Dorothy makes a beeline for a man in a dark suit and tie who raises his hand in salute and relieves her of her suitcase.

'Evening, Jacobs.'

'Good evening, ma'am.'

'This is Brenda Matthews.'

'Ma'am,' says Jacobs, giving me a slight bow.

'And you'll remember Mary.'

'Indeed,' says Jacobs, giving the girl a brief nod before

summoning a porter and placing Dorothy's suitcase on his trolley. Mary and I put ours alongside it.

'The car is this way, ma'am.'

Jacobs turns and leads us on a long trek past airline desks, duty free shops and cafés, to a glass door at the far end of the building which he opens for us. Dorothy looks around and makes for a black Bentley parked among a line of mostly American cars. Jacobs gets to the Bentley first and opens the rear door for her. When she's settled in the back, he walks round the car, opens the door for me and I get in. Mary is placed in the front passenger seat and once our luggage is stowed in the boot and the porter's been tipped, Jacobs drives through the airport complex, makes a few quick turns and soon we're on a coast road with a beautiful blue sea stretching all the way to the horizon. I had a quick look at a map when I got in last night and I reckon that with the sun setting in front of us, it must be the Sea of Marmara which is one of the smallest seas in the world. After a while we turn away from the peaceful vista onto city streets with horns blaring and cars and motorbikes fighting for space between crowded pavements. A gap in the traffic opens up and a raggedy looking man pulling a cart full of melons tries to cross in front of us. Jacob puts his foot down, catches the side of the cart, tips it over and leaves the poor bloke scrabbling around in the gutter trying to pick up his melons.

After struggling through the traffic for a few more blocks, we turn into a quieter street and stop in front of a pair of iron gates set between two stone gatehouses. The door of one of them opens and two men in uniform step out, take a look at Jacobs and open the gates. We drive through and alongside a wide stretch of lawn towards an elegant, flat-fronted three-storey building with steps up to an arched front door and a Union Jack flying from a mast on the roof. Jacobs swings the Bentley round onto a paved courtyard behind the house and parks next to a grey Daimler. He opens the doors for us and after we get out, he asks us to wait a moment, goes into the house and returns with a young lad in a waistcoat and brown trousers. Jacobs opens the boot of the car, loads the boy up with all three suitcases and tells him to take Mary inside. While the lad staggers towards the back door with Mary behind him, Jacobs leads Dorothy and me round to the front of the house.

The heat's really getting to me as we climb the steps to the main door. We follow Jacobs across a wide hallway towards the foot of twin staircases which curve up and away from each other to meet again on a gallery above, in front of a large painting of a battle scene. Mounted soldiers go at each other with swords and lances, led by some general with a plumed hat and a big nose, mounted on a black horse. We go along a corridor past an open door and I get a glimpse of a long ballroom with arches round the sides and a bandstand at one end.

Jacobs stops outside a door near the end of the corridor and knocks. A deep male voice answers and he opens the door and steps inside.

'Mrs Pargeter-Smythe and Miss Matthews.'

As we enter the wood panelled room, a large white-haired man with a red face and handlebar moustache gets up from an armchair. 'Dorothy. How nice to see you. Do come and have a drink.'

A very thin lady with grey hair in a white brocade dress sways to her feet and approaches Dorothy, who takes her hand and kisses her lightly on the cheek.

'Hello Charlotte, my darling. What a wonderful dress that is.'

'Oh, this old thing. I should have thrown it out years ago.'

'Nonsense. You look lovely in it.'

Charlotte turns and looks at me.

Dorothy puts a hand under my elbow. 'May I introduce my secretary, Brenda Matthews.'

'How do you do,' says Charlotte.

As I return her greeting, I notice the red-faced man tugging on a bell pull by the mantlepiece.

'What will you have to drink, Dorothy?' he asks.

'I could murder a gin and tonic.'

'Coming up,' he says.

As he arrives with her drink, Dorothy turns to me.

'Geoffrey, this is Brenda Matthews.'

'Geoffrey Bagstock. Consul General. How do you do.'

As we shake, the door opens and Jacobs appears. The Consul General lets go of my hand and clears his throat.

'Perhaps you'd like to go with Jacobs. He can show you your room and so on,' he says, turning away.

I glance at Dorothy, who seems to be studying her gin and tonic. Jacobs looks at me, opens the door a little wider and I follow him back to the hallway, through a side door and down a passageway to the back of the building. We climb two flights of narrow stairs and he leads me along a corridor and shows me into a plain room with a single bed, a small wardrobe and a dressing table. My suitcase is on a wooden chest under the window.

'The bathroom is the last door on the right, at the end of the corridor,' says Jacobs, indicating the direction we came from.

'I'm afraid staff dinner has already been served but if you wish I will instruct cook to prepare a meal for yourself and Mary.'

'That would be good.'

'I shall send someone to fetch you when it is ready.'

'Thank you,' I say, as he backs out of the door.

When I've made a quick check of my suitcase to make sure my gun, blades and duster are still there, I lie on the bed and close my eyes. I'm glad I've been given the brush off by the toffs and sent to dine with the servants, although I could have done with a drink before I got my marching orders. All I want to do is get the job done and get out of here.

17

I'm woken by a knock on the door. I go and open it and Mary's there with her hands clasped in front of her.

'Supper's ready, if you want some.'

'I certainly do. I'm starving.'

'It's downstairs.'

'Just give me a sec.'

I close my suitcase, put it under the bed and join her in the corridor. We go all the way down the stairs to the basement. As we pass a busy kitchen, I can see a cook taking a big roast duck out of an oven, another one sets fire to something in a frying pan and I start looking forward to my dinner. Mary takes me into a room opposite the kitchen with a big round wooden table and chairs.

'Would you like some water?' she asks, crossing to a sideboard and picking up a china jug.

'Is there any chance of a real drink?'

'I can ask, I suppose.'

'Don't worry. Water's fine.'

'I don't mind.'

'It's all right, really.'

She pours two glasses, hands one to me and we sit at the end of the table. I can tell she's nervous and doesn't quite know how to place me in the pecking order.

'You've been here before, haven't you?' I say, after a silence.

'Yes.'

'Did you travel about at all?'

'Madam and the Consul went to Ankara one time and somewhere else as well but I had to stay here.'

'That's a shame.'

I hear footsteps, turn round and see the duck on a silver platter being carried past the open door towards the stairs, followed by several silver domes and dishes. As soon as the procession's gone by, a bloke in check trousers and a white jacket comes in and puts two bowls of soup in front of us. He takes spoons, knives and forks out of his pocket, puts them on the table and leaves. The soup smells strongly of garlic and it's kind of brown and fatty with chunks of gristly meat in it. I try a spoonful and although the garlic would take the roof off your mouth and it's a weird taste, I'm so hungry that I start to tuck into it. When the bloke in the check trousers comes back and puts a basket of bread on the table, I ask him what the soup is, in case he speaks English, but he looks at me blankly and leaves.

'Sheep's head,' says Mary.

'Sorry?'

'It's sheep's head soup.'

'Ah, right,' I say, putting down my spoon.

'I was helping them in the kitchen once and they were making some. It's got tripe in it too.'

'Really?'

177

I push the bowl to one side and reach for a piece of bread, hoping it will quell the nausea.

Mary seems to be enjoying her soup and when she finishes, our man reappears carrying plates of dark meat with tomatoes, carrots and cabbage. The duck is clearly for officer class only. I try a piece of meat and it tastes like beef, another bit tastes like lamb and I decide not to enquire any further. A bowl of rice and beans arrives beside me and I start to enjoy my dinner.

When we're sitting back with glasses of a pleasant fragrant tea and munching delicious almond cookies, I ask Mary where she's from.

'Menton.'

It takes me a moment to remember that Menton Hall was where I saw Jeremy and Sir David that night after I'd done Weston and I realise it'll be Dorothy's family estate.

'Were you born there?' I ask.

'My mother was the nursery maid.'

'Does she still work there?'

'She died last year.'

'I'm sorry.'

'She had the 'flu and then it got worse and she passed away.'

There are tears welling up in her eyes as she speaks and she looks so sad and frail that I want to go and put my arms round her. I pour her some more tea instead and she takes a sip and seems to calm down. I want to ask who her father is but I don't, in case that might be even more upsetting for her to think about.

'Have you been to any other places abroad?' I ask.

'We went to Washington last year.'

'How was that?'

'It was all right.'

'Did you see the White House?'

'I wasn't allowed out.'

I'm wondering what kind of person takes a young girl to a city like Washington and keeps her indoors, when Jacobs arrives.

'Madam would like to speak to you in your room, Miss Matthews.'

'I'm coming,' I say, draining my teacup and following him into the corridor. Jacobs heads for the kitchen and Mary and I climb the stairs. When we get to the top floor, we say goodnight and she goes into the room next to mine.

Dorothy is at the window looking at the night sky. She turns as I close the door.

'We're in luck. The Russian agent, Omer Turan owns a club in Bursa, which is a couple of hours' drive from here.'

She opens her handbag and hands me a small black and white photograph of a dark-haired man of about forty, walking in a busy street.

'The name of the club is 'Altin Kartal'- it means golden eagle,' she says, giving me a piece of paper with some squiggly writing on it. 'This is the address. It's in the old part of the town and it's open most of the night.'

'How do I get there?'

'You'll be driven to Bursa and taken to the club.'

'Do I come back here when I'm done?'

'Of course and you bring the tape to me. You can get a taxi. Just ask for the British Consulate, Istanbul, come to the side gate and give your name to the officer.'

She opens her bag, takes out a sheaf of notes and hands them to me.

'That's a thousand lira, about £200, which should see you through.'

'What if he's not at the club?'

'He is.'

'And if he's gone by the time I get there?'

'You find him.'

'What if he hasn't got the tape on him?'

'You find that as well.'

As she looks down her nose at me and turns back to the window, I wonder what a good right hook would do to that aristocratic profile.

'A car is waiting for you at the side door. You need to leave now.'

She sweeps out of the room and I get my suitcase from under the bed and look at the clothes I've brought. I take out a Balenciaga shift dress and a silk jacket that I reckon will do for the night's work. I step out of the navy blue trouser suit that I travelled in, take the wide elastic belt out of the suitcase and put it round my waist. I check the chamber of the Smith & Wesson is full and nudge it in between the elastic and the small of my back and slide the wad of lira and my lock picks in beside it. I change my bra for the Triumph, put a blade in my suspender belt and slip the dress over my head. I put on the jacket, step into a pair of low heeled shoes with a solid toe and do a couple of turns in front of the mirror to make sure the gun can't be seen.

Jacobs is waiting for me in the corridor and I follow him downstairs to the ground floor and along the length of the building to a lobby where a couple of uniformed guards are smoking fags and talking to a young bloke with a lot of black hair, wearing jeans and a white T-shirt. The guards nod to Jacobs, he says a few words in Turkish and the young bloke steps forward.

'This is Hakan, your driver.'

'Hi Madam,' he says.

'Evening, Hakan,' I reply, handing him the piece of paper with the address of the club on it. He reads it and nods. Jacobs says something to him in Turkish, one of the guards opens the door and I follow Hakan to a dark grey Chevrolet Impala that's got a good few dents and bruises. He slips behind the wheel and I get in beside him. He fires up the engine, slews the car round the courtyard and motors along the drive. Two guards open the iron gates as we approach and Hakan returns their salutes as we go through. He drives fast through busy streets where people are selling drinks and corn on the cob, chestnuts and different pastries and shouting out about what they've got. When we stop at traffic lights they come up to the car windows offering us their stuff. Hakan ignores them and looks straight ahead. I quite fancy a pastry but I don't want to slow us down. The lights change, we drive through the town to a dockside and before I know it, we're rolling on board a ferryboat.

Hakan looks round at me and smiles. He says something in Turkish and I shake my head to show I don't understand.

'We go seaside.'

'Good,' I reply.

'Then Bursa.'

I've no idea where Bursa is but I'm assuming we're crossing the Bosphorus and going further into Turkey. The boat pulls away from the dock and a man in uniform appears at Hakan's window. He pays him some money and gets a ticket which he drops on the floor as he sits back and lights a fag. After inhaling a lungful of Turkish tobacco smoke, I get out of the car, walk to the back of the boat and look at the lights of Istanbul and the domes and tall towers of its beautiful mosques.

We get to the other side, the car rolls off the ramp and we drive through a small town and onto a straight road. We pass a couple of builders yards and warehouses and then we're on the open road and Hakan puts his foot down and turns on the radio. When he manages to find a music station, I'm not sure what I'm hearing. It sounds like

'Downtown' by Petula Clarke but the words are in Turkish and it's a bit faster than Pet does it. When it's finished, a hysterical disc jockey waffles on for a bit, then it's 'I Got You Babe', also in Turkish and definitely not featuring Sonny and Cher. The whole effect is weird, although I suppose there's no reason why they shouldn't cover British and American stuff and make it their own. The next couple of tracks are songs I don't recognise and they sound like they could be original Turkish numbers. Then we get Chuck Berry 'Riding Along in My Automobile', which is much more like it and really suits the car. I lean back, shut my eyes and let Chuck take it away.

After about an hour's fast drive and another ferry crossing we come into the outskirts of an old city and Hakan tells me we've arrived at Bursa. As we get near the centre we pass a huge mosque with two really tall towers on the corners and rows of domes on the roof. There are steps up to the main door, with people going in and out and it makes me want to look inside. I'm hoping I'll have a chance to go into a mosque in Istanbul before I leave. Hakan sees me looking and says the name of it, which sounds like hula hoop and tells me that it's the biggest one in Bursa. We drive into an area of narrow streets with bars and restaurants and small hotels with plenty of food and drink sellers on the cobblestones, calling out their wares. We go past the end of a street that has lots of stalls with beautiful silks and satins and I'm about to tell Hakan to stop so I can get out and buy some when he turns into a dark street, stops the car, points through the windscreen and says the name of the club. There's an orange light above the door and a couple of blokes leaning on the wall beside it.

'You want I come with you?' asks Hakan.

'No thanks. I'll be all right.'

One of the men outside the club is looking at the car so I put my head down and tell Hakan to drive on past. He seems like a nice boy and I don't want him to be seen with me in case it goes sideways. After a couple of blocks I ask him to stop and I take out the paper that Dorothy gave me, check Omer Turan's name, show it to Hakan and ask him to say it for me. When I reckon I've got it, I say goodbye to Hakan and get out of the car. As I'm walking back towards the club, three young American men come round a corner in front of me, talking and laughing and I remember Hakan pointing out Karamürsel Air Base, where Saltik worked, after we made the second ferry crossing. I walk a short way behind and hear them arguing about where they're going to go. One of them, tall with a crew cut, is talking about a place called the Compound. When they get to a corner he stops and points along a narrow street to where some men are gathered in front of a gate, manned by two uniformed guards.

'That's it, right there,' he says.

'Is it a whorehouse?' asks the big man next to him.

'Kind of.'

'What the fuck does that mean?'

'It's a jail also. The women are inmates who get a little off their sentence if they put out for money.'

'That's fucking crazy.'

'Prostitution's legal here. The government run the whorehouses. It's how they control it.'

'Yeah?'

'The hookers even get health checks.'

'Cool. Let's go. Joey, you in?'

'Nah, I just want a drink,' says a younger one, hanging back.

'Come on. It's only a buck a ride,' urges the tall one.

'A buck?'

'Sure.'

'What are they, grotesque?'

'Some are OK.'

'I just want a drink.'

'You said you wanted to get laid.'

'Maybe later.'

The big one puts an arm round the young one's neck. 'Come on Joey, you and me gonna see some nice Turkey ladies and you gonna to get your little dickee sucked.'

I follow at a distance as the young one is dragged forward. At the gate, they're stopped by a couple of guards who pat them down and let them through into a short cobbled street, walled off at the far end, with a couple of dim streetlights throwing a murky glow over a row of two-storey houses on each side. The doors are open and men are wandering up and down, surveying the women on display in the lit windows.

18

The Golden Eagle stinks of Turkish fags and booze and I can hardly see across the dimly lit basement but I'm glad to hear Stevie Wonder's 'Uptight' coming out of the speakers. When my eyes have adjusted to the gloom, I move to the back of the club and stand in a dark corner. Most of the tables are occupied by girls with their marks and there are a few couples on the dance floor strutting it with Stevie. I don't see anyone who looks like Omer Turan, so I decide to get a drink. As I get to the bar, a row starts up between the barman and a middle-aged English type in a cream linen suit, who's sat on a bar stool with a girl up close to him. The barman is pointing to two empty champagne bottles on the bar, then at a bill he's holding and asking him for money. The Englishman tells him the bill is outrageous and when he appeals to a Turkish-looking bloke sitting on the next bar stool, also with a girl on his arm, the man just smiles and says he's paid his half of it. As the Englishman starts shouting at him and demanding to know why the fuck he brought him to a place like this, one of the minders from the door arrives. The girls melt away as the minder grips the Englishman by the arm, lifts him nearly off his feet, takes the bill from the barman, holds it in front of his face and whispers something in his ear. The man nods, the minder lets him down and he reaches into his pocket, takes out some notes, chucks them on the bar, gives the Turkish bloke a filthy look and stomps off towards the stairs, followed by the minder. When they're gone, the barman counts the money, smiles at the Turk, gives him a few notes and he knocks back his drink and goes upstairs.

I get a large whisky and ignore the barman when he asks me my name. I'm on my way to the back of the room when lights go up on the dance floor and a beautiful dark-haired girl in a glittery blue dress with a bare midriff slithers on and starts swinging her hips and belly dancing to a fast rhythmic number with guitars strumming and lots of high voices chirruping and yodelling away. She's waving a blue silk veil in the air as she dances and then she wraps it round a punter's neck, sidles up close to him until his chin's almost touching her naval then she whips it away and pirouettes really fast round the edge of the dance floor with the veil flowing behind her. She comes to the front, the rhythm builds, she shakes herself into a frenzy and then the music stops dead and she freezes with her arms in the air, hips slung sideways, her head on one side and a hot look in her eye.

She gets a good round of applause and I'm hoping she'll do some more but she takes a bow and goes off as a line of topless girls shimmy on, link arms, shake their hips and get into a steamy routine. As I'm moving forward to get a better view I see Omer Turan come through a door behind the bar. He's taller and broader than he looked in the photograph. I move closer but once he's exchanged a few words with the barman he goes back into the room he came out of. I buy another drink, sit at the end of the bar and while I'm watching the girls working their snaky moves and winding up the punters, the three American servicemen, that I last saw going into the Compound, come down the stairs.

'Y'all want Bourbon?' says the big guy as they get to the bar.

'Sure,' says the tall one, sitting on a bar stool.

'And a beer,' says the younger one.

'Gimme a bottle of Jim Beam and three beers.'

While the drinks are coming they light cigarettes.

'Oh boy! Did I get a load off in there,' says the big guy, inhaling and blowing out a long stream of smoke.

'You got the best one,' says the tall one.

'Yours OK, Pete?'

'For a fat-assed pig.'

'Why d'you go with her?'

'She knows how to move it.'

'Well there you go. How d'you do, Joey?'

'I didn't.'

'Why the fuck not? You were all up for it back at base.'

'They look like trash.'

'You expect to find a prom queen in a fuckin' hole like that?'

'And dirty.'

'They get inspected, like I said,' says the tall one.

'You're more likely to get a little clam chowder from the chicks in here.'

The barman puts a bottle of Bourbon, shot glasses and three beers on the bar. 'Our ladies very clean, sir.'

'Who the fuck asked you?' says the big one.

'Just saying, sir.'

'Well don't.'

He pours three slugs of Bourbon, knocks one back, takes a swig of beer, stands back from the bar and looks at me. 'Hey Joey, how about this nice lady? She sure don't look like trash.'

He puts his arm round Joey and stands him in front of me.

'You speak English, lady?'

'Not to you,' I reply.

'So what the fuck you doing here?'

'Leave it, Ed,' says Joey.

'You know what a fuckin' pain in the ass you are, kid?' he says, shoving Joey away from him.

'Cool it, Ed,' says the tall one, moving beside him.

'We come out to have a good time and this momma's boy's gotta bring it all down with the whinin' and moanin',' says Ed, pouring more whisky.

'Just shut up! All right?'

'Fuck you!'

Ed chucks his drink in the tall one's face and gets a punch in the mouth in return. Joey tries to get between them and gets thrown against a table for his trouble. The table collapses and two men who were sitting at it get up off the floor, shout something in Turkish and wade into the Americans. As the barman crouches behind the bar, Omer Turan comes out of the back room with a baseball bat, opens a hatch at the other end of the bar, steps through and starts swinging. The music stops, feet pound down the stairs and the minders appear and get stuck in. I sit on the bar, swing my legs over and disappear into the room that Omer Turan came from.

Shouts and crashes and bangs are coming from the club as I rifle through the drawers of a desk that's wedged between two racks of bottles. I check a filing cabinet on the opposite wall and by the time I've delved through some boxes on the floor, I know Omer doesn't keep his tapes at work, although he's got a nice little Beretta 950 in his desk. The noise from the club has died down so I go to the door and ease it open. Omer is leaning on the bar with the bat in his hand watching the minders carrying the big American, who's out cold, towards the stairs. Joey and his tall friend are slumped at a table, bloody and bruised, and one of the Turkish gents who got in the ruck is lying passed out on the floor with his mate holding his head and slapping his cheeks. There are no punters to be seen from where I am but there are girls sitting at tables by the dance floor, sipping drinks and looking like they've seen it all before.

I close the door and look at a pair of small windows above the wine racks. I stand on the desk, climb up one of the racks and crawl along the top. The windows don't open but there's a bit of light coming from somewhere above and I can just make out a stone wall opposite, with steps cut into it and a yard a few feet below. I reach down, take a bottle out of the rack, smash the window with it and use my blade to scrape the glass out of the frame. I get my legs through the window, turn onto my stomach and lower myself into the yard. I shake a few bits of glass off my dress and climb the steps onto a narrow cobbled street between tall buildings. I go to the end, turn the corner and walk along a line of cars until I come to a dark green Fiat 500. I look around to make sure I'm alone, pick up a sharp stone from the gutter, smack it hard against the window and the glass shatters. I reach inside, open the door, sit in the driving seat and use my blade to prise off the panel under the steering wheel. I cut the wires at the back of the ignition barrel, connect the red ones, touch the brown ones together and the engine starts. I check that I've got fuel, drive round the corner and park where I can see the front door of the club.

There are three cabs parked outside, the minders are back on the door and I watch them turning away a few punters. After a while some girls come out, followed by the two Turkish men. One of them is limping badly and has to be helped to one of the cabs. The tall American is next up, holding his side and moving slowly. Joey appears behind him with a napkin wrapped round his head. They get into the next cab and it whooshes past me.

After a while, one of the minders looks at his watch,

nods to his mate and walks off along the street. The one that's left leans on the wall and lights up a fag. I put the radio on very quietly and turn the dial past some talking and then some twiddly Arab music, until I get the 'Four Tops' telling me to 'Reach Out' and I'm tapping the wheel and wishing I could turn it up loud when the barman comes out of the club, crosses the road and walks towards me. I kill the music and put my head down as he goes past, then I catch him in the mirror as he unlocks an Oldsmobile parked along the street and drives off. A short while later Omer Turan comes out of the club, locks the door, sends the minder on his way and gets into the remaining cab. When it's gone past, I fire up the Fiat and turn it round just in time to see the cab make a right turn at the end of the street. I put my foot down, get round the corner after it and manage to keep up as it weaves through a maze of streets and then cruises along a main road. When it turns into a quiet street with two storey terraced houses on each side, I stop the Fiat at the corner and watch the cab pull up towards the far end. Omer gets out, walks to a front door and goes in.

I wait for a bit and then ease the car forward along the dark street, until I've got a view of the house that Omer went into. It's at the end of the terrace and there's a yard with an old bike and bits of rubbish between it and the next row of houses. The window on the ground floor of the house goes dark and then a light comes on upstairs. When it goes off, I look at my watch, wait ten minutes, then I get out of the car, cross the road and pick my way over the rubbish, to a brick wall that runs along the side of the yard. As the moon comes out from behind a cloud, I climb over the wall and drop down onto a concrete patio at the back of Omer's house.

I wait until I'm sure all's quiet and I haven't woken any neighbours, then I go to the back door. There's just one cylinder lock so I kneel down, take the wallet of picks out of my belt and open it. I put the cut down key in the lock, slide the pick in above it, feel around for the levers and lift them one by one with the pick. When I've got all five, I turn the key and open the lock.

The wallet goes back in my belt and I ease the door open. The moon's shining through the window as I creep inside and spot a box of matches on the window sill. I take one out, turn my back to the window, light it and shade it with my hand as I look round. I'm in a kitchen with a big iron stove and a mangle next to it. There's a cabinet, a small fridge, a table and one chair. I cross to a door and put my ear to it. All seems quiet so I open it and by the light of the dying match I can see along the hallway to the front door and a room off to the left. I'm tempted to go in there and start looking for the tape but I need to deal with the man who owns it first.

I drop the dead match, take out my gun, release the safety and move towards the stairs. As I put my foot on the bottom step I hear a noise behind me. I spin round, the gun's ripped out of my hand, I'm grabbed by the hair, my head's forced back and I hit the deck. A wet cloth covers my face. I smell chloroform and pass out.

19

I'm clinging to the rail as the prow of the boat rears way up towards the sky and hangs motionless in space before crashing down into the boiling sea. A massive wave towers over the boat then a ton of freezing water hits me and I hurtle along the deck until a hand grabs hold of me and the big American serviceman pulls me to him, wraps his arms round me and starts slobbering over me and kissing me. I dig my nails into his face and he screams, flings me over the side and I'm fighting to stay afloat among the angry waves and the boat is bucking up and down and I'm trying to swim towards it but it's moving away from me, faster and faster and getting smaller and smaller until it disappears into a wave in the distance. I'm sinking under the water and going down and down past coral reefs with glowing caves where skulls and skeletons stare out at me as I plunge past them into a shoal of massive black fish and I'm sliding off their slimy backs and they snap and snarl at me and I fight my way through them and on down out of their reach to a bed of ferns on the ocean floor where I lie still and close my eyes. I'm peaceful for a minute until I feel hands all over me and I try to get up and the hands hold me down but when I open my eyes the hands turn into crabs and lobsters and they're eating at my flesh and I'm trying to get up and pulling them off me and someone's swimming towards me and he swipes the creatures off me and his arms go round me and he's carrying me up through the water, faster and faster and I can see the sun above us and we break the surface and I take a huge breath and open my eyes...

I'm lying on a hard floor. The dream fades and I sit up and take in the bare room. A naked bulb hanging from a low ceiling, concrete walls and no windows tell me I'm in a cellar. I look at my watch and it says eight o'clock. My body tells me I've been out for a long time so it must be the evening after I followed Omer from the club. I crawl to the door and see it's a single mortice lock. I sit against the wall and wonder how I got rumbled. Two of them put me down so I reckon someone must have followed from me the club, got into the house before me and warned Omer. As I'm wondering who it could have been, a key turns in the lock. I stand and flatten myself against the wall. The door opens and Hakan, my driver, walks in with a gun in his hand.

I can't believe I've been so stupid. Trusting Dorothy to have a kosher team in a foreign country when I hardly know anything about her. Hakan walks to the middle of the room and I weigh up the chances of getting the better of him. His gun hand looks steady and even though he's young he might just shoot me if I make a move. He takes a step towards me.

'You one of those MI6 trash, try to stop us make communism in Turkey.'

'I'm not with MI6.'

'You liar too?'

I sink to the floor, sit cross legged and keep my head down.

'We find out all right. When Omer come, we burn your titties until you tell us who you are and why you here.'

I'm about to go for his legs, when he walks out of the door and slams it behind him.

I take a few deep breaths and try to figure out how I can get out of here. The only way is through the door and my picks are gone, along with my gun, blade and money. I have another look at the door to make sure he's locked it, then I lie down on the floor and try to relax. Suddenly Hakan's torture plans come back to me. I stand up, take off my jacket, pull my dress over my head, unbutton the Triumph bra and start tearing at the fabric with my teeth. The material's really tough but I finally manage to bite a hole in it and pull out the length of wire that goes along the bottom under the cups. I sit on the floor and bend the wire back and forth until it breaks in two. I make a right angle at the end of each piece, slide one into the keyhole, feel for the lever and turn it until I get some tension on the bolt. I put in the other pick, lift the lever, slide the bolt over and open the lock.

I put my clothes back on, pocket the wire picks and put my ear to the door. When I hear nothing, I turn the handle and open it slowly. There are stone steps leading up to the back yard of the house and the starry sky beyond. I step out and see light in the upper floor window but the one below is dark. I close the door, creep up the stairs into the back yard and I'm looking around to see if there's anything that I could use as a weapon when a light goes on in the kitchen. I move to the end of the yard and lie down behind a row of plant pots. The back door opens, Hakan appears, makes for the cellar and goes down the steps. I move to where I can see him putting his key in the mortice and turning it back and forth. When he opens the door and draws his gun, I jump off the top step onto his back, get my hands round his throat to stop him squealing, push him into the cellar and kick him against the far wall. He crumples into a heap and his gun spins across the floor towards me. I pick it up, stand over him and point it at his head.

'Where's Omer?'

'Fucking bitch!'

I swipe the gun across his face, press the barrel into his forehead and pull back the hammer.

'Where?'

He looks up at me with tears in his eyes and I see how young he is.

'In house.'

'The key.'

He sits up against the wall, takes a key out of his pocket, tosses it onto the floor and I pick it up.

'The back door?'

'Open.'

'If you shout, I will come and kill you.'

I step outside, lock the door behind me and hope he isn't wearing an underwired bra. I go up to the yard and see the light is still on in the upstairs room. The kitchen looks empty so I ease the door open and go in. As I walk past the table and into the hall, I hear footsteps on the stairs. I go back to the kitchen, turn off the light and stand behind the door. Omer walks in, I slam the door shut and he turns to me. I point the gun at his head, pull the trigger and it jams. He takes the Beretta out of his belt, I kick the table at him, he falls on his back and I land on him and go for the gun. He throws it aside, gets an arm round my neck, pulls me over and rolls on top of me so I'm face down on the floor. I sink my teeth into the inside of his wrist and tear the flesh away. Blood spurts and he yells, grips the wound and I get out from under him and dive for his gun in the corner. When I turn back with it, he's on his feet and coming at me. He aims a kick at my head. I drop the gun, catch his foot in both hands and twist. Bone splinters and he screams and collapses on the floor. I take a tangerine off the sideboard, sit on his chest, stuff the fruit in his mouth, hold his nose and wait until he suffocates.

I need to find the tape. The room next to the kitchen has a TV, a couple of sofas and not much else. I pull a row of books out of a bookcase and check behind them, then I go upstairs. The bedroom is at the front and there's a room at the back with a desk, a filing cabinet and a cupboard alongside it. I look in the desk drawers and the filing cabinet but it's mostly paper, apart from a wad of notes which I stuff in my pocket and a file of photographs of what looks like a US military base. There are a couple of aerial shots of the whole place and the rest are taken from the ground, showing the barracks and different buildings and servicemen and officers walking around or driving jeeps. In a different file there's a bunch of photos of a big ring of radio masts, taken from different angles, with 'Elephant Cage' written along the bottom and I suppose it's what they use to listen in to the Russians' communications.

I open the cupboard, hoping to find a tape recorder but there's only a shelf of notebooks full of Turkish handwriting and a pile of Playboy magazines, along with Rogue, Sultry and the like. I pull it all out onto the floor and check behind the desk and the filing cabinet. When I've gone round the room once more, I go into the bedroom, throw the mattress off the bed and look underneath. I go through the wardrobe, pull it out from the wall and check behind. By the time I've done the bathroom and had another look round the ground floor, I'm pretty sure there's no tapes in the house. I go into the kitchen, step over Omer and head for the fridge, in search of a beer I can drink before I start pulling up floorboards. I open the fridge door and there are six spools of tape in a polythene bag, on the top shelf.

I remember an empty briefcase in the study upstairs. I get it and put the tapes and Omer's Beretta into it. I find a bottle of beer in the door of the fridge, knock off the cap, sit at the table and drink it while I try and work out how I'm going to get back to Istanbul. If I nick a car I'll need a map and even if I can get one, I probably won't be able to understand it. I'm a good way from the centre of town, where the cabs are, and I don't fancy a long walk after the exercise I've already had tonight. I go into the front room and look through the window. Hakan's Chevrolet is parked up the street.

I finish the beer, take out the Beretta, check it's got a full chamber, go down to the basement and unlock the door. Hakan is crouched against the far wall.

'Give me your car keys,' I say, pointing the gun at him.

He stands up, takes them out of his pocket and hands them to me.

'Come on.'

'Where we go?'

'To the car. Go,' I say, pulling back the hammer.

I stand aside and follow him up the stairs and into the kitchen. He stops when he sees Omer's body. I give him a moment to get the idea then I poke him towards the front door with the gun. When we get to the car, I unlock the front door, put him in the driving seat, give him the keys and get in the back.

'Istanbul,' I say.

He looks round, sees the gun and nods.

'Are the ferries running now?'

'For the fishermans, yes. You have to pay.'

'OK. Go.'

• • •

About an hour later we pass the US base that Omer had the photographs of and I notice Hakan looking at it. I ask him what he knows about it and he starts talking about the US spying on the Soviets. I draw him out and he tells me how the Americans kidnapped and tortured his brother because he was a member of the Workers and Peasants Party and how much he wants Russia to invade Turkey and make it a communist state so everyone will be equal and the country can be at peace. When we've come off the second ferry and are on our way into Istanbul and he's told me about the cruel things the government and something he calls *Counter Guerrilla* have done to put down resistance from the left, I'm almost singing the Red Flag myself.

By the time we get near the consulate I'm convinced he's a good kid who's been badly hurt. It's made him passionate about creating a better world and I want to let him go. I count the odds of him being a danger to me and I reckon he'll know he's blown his cover with the British and he's got nothing to lose by coming after me, so I've got to kill him. I tell him to drive past the consulate and stop in the next street. I check there's no one around, lean over the front seat, raise the gun and pull back the hammer. He turns and looks at me with tears in his eyes and when his lips start trembling, I know I can't do it.

'You disappear,' I say, lowering the gun.

'Yes.'

'Now.'

I get out of the car and watch him drive away.

20

The guards let me into the consulate without any bother and I go upstairs to my room. It's nearly four in the morning but after rolling around in that dirty cellar I could do with a shower before I turn in. I put the tapes, the Beretta and the money I nicked from Omer's in my suitcase and chuck the briefcase under the bed. I change into my dressing gown, take the towel off the rail by the window, grab my wash bag and go along to the bathroom. There's no shower so I turn on the taps of the old bath and clean my teeth while it fills. I sink into the water and lie back. As the tension in my body eases I think about Lizzie and wish she was in here with me. The job's done and with any luck I should be on my way home tomorrow so we should be together soon enough. I'm hoping there's been no more aggravation at the club from Bobby Grant and his merry men. The warm water's making me sleepy so I get out, dry myself, put on my dressing gown and head back along the corridor. As I'm going into my room I think I can hear Mary crying next door. I turn the handle slowly and look in.

She's on her back on the floor and there's a large man in a purple robe on top of her. His arse is moving up and down as he mouths words into her ear... 'You dirty little whore… nasty little bitch… you need to be taught a lesson, don't you, you slimy little slut…'

I grab a poker from beside the fire, crack him on the back of the neck, kick him off her and the Consul General scrambles to his feet. 'What the…?'

I kick him hard in the balls and give him a straight right to the point of his jaw. He falls back against the bed and slithers onto the floor. As he groans and tries to get up I drop the poker, take a heavy metal vase off the mantlepiece, whack him on the head with it and stand over him until I'm sure he's out cold.

Mary's sitting cross-legged on the floor wiping her eyes. I take her suitcase from under the bed, open the wardrobe, gather up her clothes and fling them into it.

'What are you doing?' she says.

'We're leaving.'

'What?'

'Get dressed.'

Even though she's bruised and confused she takes off her nightie, puts on a dress and some shoes that I hand to her.

'Where's the rest of your stuff?'

'Er…'

'Where?'

'In that drawer.'

'Put it in the bag.'

'But…'

'Just do it!'

She goes to the dressing table, opens the drawer, scoops up her underwear and puts it in the case. I grab her hairbrush and her passport from the nightstand by her bed and throw them in on top. I check the Consul's still unconscious, close the case, pick it up, take Mary by the arm and lead her into my room. I put on my black trouser suit and throw the rest of my stuff into my case, on top of the Beretta and the tapes. I take out Omer's money and put it in my pocket. Mary sits on the bed with a hand between her legs.

'Where are you taking me?' she asks.

'Away from these fucking monsters.'

'But…'

'Do you want to spend the rest of your life with them?'

She looks at me for a moment, then something in her expression changes.

'I don't.'

'Good. Let's go.'

We go along the corridor, down the stairs to the ground floor. The lobby with the guards is at the end of the corridor. Explaining why we're leaving at this time in the morning could be difficult, so I lead Mary down to the basement and into the kitchen. I switch on a light, take a hefty carving knife from a row of blades by the cooker, turn off the light and go back up to the ground floor. We take a right turn off the main drag, go along a dark passageway and get into a narrow corridor that runs along the back of the building. I see a door marked Ladies and go in. There are two cubicles with a high frosted glass window behind them. It's got a casement latch but the handle's missing. I stand on the toilet, stab the carving knife in above the latch, force the tongue down and pull the window open. I can just make out the stone wall of the consulate fifty yards away and it's a short drop to the grass below. I get Mary up beside me, help her through the window, pass the cases to her and climb down next to her. The sky's just beginning to lighten beyond the wall and I hear the rumble of a lorry going past as we reach it. I make a stirrup with my hands, Mary puts her foot in it and just manages to reach the top of the wall. I push her up higher and she sits astride the top. I pass the cases to her, she drops them over the other side and then disappears herself. I jump up and try to reach the top of the wall but I can't. I've been so busy getting Mary over it I haven't thought about how I'm going to do it. I look round in the gloom for something to stand on but there's nothing. I walk along for a bit until I see a gash in the stone that I can just get my foot in. After a couple of attempts I manage to scramble up and over and I go along to where Mary's waiting. We cross the road and walk past the gates of the consulate in the direction that Hakan took towards Bursa in the Chevy. The city's waking up, a few cars and vans are buzzing about and after a while a cab comes past. I flag it down and tell him to take us to the airport.

We drive across a long bridge with the sun rising in front of us and then we're on the coast road we came along with Dorothy. Mary's looking out of the window and I want to ask her if she's all right but she seems to be in her own little world, so I leave her alone and think about what I'm going to do about this mess. Dorothy's going to find out me and Mary are gone pretty soon. If she gets the story from the Consul, she'll have a good idea that we've gone to the airport and she might well get him to send a team after us. I need to talk to her.

We get to the airport, the cab driver asks where we're going to and when I say London, he stops outside the same terminal we arrived at. I take a note off Omer's wad and give it to him. He offers me change and I take it and give him a ten lira tip. He gives me a broad smile, jumps out of the car, gets our cases out of the boot and hands them to us. We go into the terminal and I tell Mary to get her passport out of her case while I do the same. The BOAC desk is along the hall to our left and I can see a bank of phones beyond it. We walk to the desk where the uniformed girl tells us there's a flight to Heathrow in an hour and we're just in time to get the last two tickets. I do the business and when she's checked our cases, I ask her if there are public phones in the departure area. She says there are and when I ask her if she can give me the number for the British Consulate, she looks it up in a book that she takes from under her desk and writes it down for me. I show her the change I got from the cab driver and she points out which coins I can use in a payphone.

We go through passport control to the departure

lounge, which is close by a bar that has a couple of phones next to it. I get Mary settled in a seat and ask her if she wants a drink. She says she'd like some orange juice and I go and buy a large whisky, a bottle of Fanta and a bag of crisps. Once I've knocked back the whisky and bought another one, I take Mary's drink to her, give her the crisps and tell her I'm going to make a phone call.

I lift the receiver, dial the consulate number and after a good few rings a man answers. I stuff a coin in the slot, ask for Dorothy Pargeter-Smythe and give my name as Brenda Matthews. He tells me to hold on.

I look over at Mary sitting in the departure lounge, all neat and demure, showing no sign of having been pummelled and mauled by a twenty stone bully a couple of hours ago and I wonder if it might not be the first time. Dorothy comes on the line.

'What the fuck are you doing?'

'Going home.'

'Have you got the tape?'

'Yes.'

'What have you done with my maid?'

'She's with me and if anyone comes after us, or meets us at Heathrow, the tape gets cut to ribbons.'

'You've got a bloody nerve, young lady.'

'Take it up with the fat cunt you're staying with.'

'I want that tape.'

'I need to know you're going to leave that girl alone before you get it.'

'I don't give a damn about her. You can throw her out of the plane as far as I'm concerned.'

'You won't go after her?'

'She's a maid. Why the fuck would I?'

'All right.'

'Is Omer…?'

'Yes.'

'Very well. I'll be back tomorrow. Come to Belgrave Square at five pm.'

The phone goes dead. I can tell by the way she didn't argue that she knows what the Consul got up to and I bet he would have got away with it if I hadn't turned up when I did.

I go and sit next to Mary. She's looking a bit nervous and she hasn't touched her crisps.

'Have you got anywhere you can stay when we get back?' I ask.

'Only Menton.'

'You're not going back there.'

'I've nowhere else to go.'

'You can be at mine for a bit, if you like.'

'Do you need a maid?'

'Of course not, silly.'

I laugh and she looks confused, as if she's not quite sure what's happening.

'Why don't you stay with me in London while you decide what you're going to do?'

'Would that be all right?'

'Of course.'

'I would like to.'

'Good.'

'Thank you.'

'Don't forget your crisps.'

She smiles, opens the packet and puts one in her mouth.

• • •

I'm woken by the pilot announcing that we're about to land and telling the cabin crew to put the doors to manual. The seat belt sign has come on but I've been wearing mine all the way anyway. Mary's still asleep next to me and I check hers is fastened too. When I squeeze her hand to wake her, she gives a little cry, opens her eyes and looks around as if she doesn't know where she is.

'We're just coming in to land at London,' I say.

Her eyes focus on me and her breathing slows.

'You've been asleep.'

'Oh.'

'We'll get a cup of coffee when we land.'

She's still staring at me and looking confused.

'Is it all right?'

'What do you mean?'

'Coming away like this… Leaving Madam and…'

'What that man did to you was horrible.'

'But…'

'Has it happened before?'

'Well…'

'I thought so.'

'But…'

'You're nobody's creature, to be bullied and battered, just because you were born to a nursery maid on a posh country estate. You've got a right to have your own life and do what you want.'

She turns away and I know she's taking in what I said. I reckon she's got some spirit in there and with a bit of time and maybe meeting some new people, she won't be going back. I look out of the window at the neat rows of streets and houses down below and think about all the little people who live in them, going through their lives and having their ups and downs and their problems and I'm thinking about how much heartache and aggravation there is in the world. All at once I feel my stomach tighten as the ground starts coming up to meet us. I press my back against the seat and close my eyes as the plane bounces on the runway and then settles.

21

I change my Turkish lira at the airport, come away with a couple of hundred quid and we get a taxi into London. I noticed that Mary didn't eat anything on the plane, so when we reach Little Venice, I tell the driver to drop us at the end of Formosa Street and I go to the shop and buy some bread, eggs, ham, a tin of salmon and one of baked beans. I ask Mary if there's anything she fancies but she just shakes her head, so it's over the road to the greengrocers for some fruit and veg. I must be the world's worst cook and I know the meals I make are awful but at least I try. Lizzie's not much better, which is why we eat out so much.

We walk to Randolph Crescent and go up to the flat. I give Mary a quick tour, show her into Georgie's room and ask her if she'd like some tea. She says she would and I tell her to unpack her clothes while I put the kettle on. I go into my room, take the tapes and the Beretta out of my case, put them under the loose floorboard in the corner and remind myself to get some rounds for the Beretta from Bert. I'll need to get those tapes copied as well before I give them to Dorothy tomorrow, so that I've got a bit of insurance in case she decides to get that nonce at Kesgrove House to identify me for killing Weston. When I've made the tea I take Mary a cup, tell her I'm nipping out but I'll be back soon. Something tells me to lock the door before I go downstairs. I knock on Lizzie's and wait until she opens up, wearing that nightie.

'That was quick, wasn't it?'

'It went a bit strange over there.'

'Shall I run a bath?' she says, pulling me into her arms.

'I wish I could,' I say, after we've had a cuddle.

'What's up?'

'I've got a visitor.'

'Istanbul?'

'Kind of.'

I step into the hall and tell her all that went on in Turkey and why I've brought Mary back with me.

'Bring her down and let me have a look at her,' she says, when I've finished.

'Are you sure?'

'She needs a job and somewhere to live, so she doesn't lose her bottle and go back to the estate, right?'

'Well… yeah.'

'I might have something at the club.'

'She's too young to…'

'Not that, you daft thing.'

'What then?'

'Rico needs someone in the kitchen.'

'What happened to Anita?'

'She flounced out last night, he won't say why.'

'Mary did tell me she'd helped in the kitchen at the consulate.'

'There you are then. Go and get her, while I put some clothes on.'

I go upstairs, into Georgie's room and find Mary lying on the bed, staring at the ceiling. I sit beside her and see that she's been crying.

'Everything's going to be fine, I promise you,' I say, putting a hand on her arm.

She turns and looks at me. 'Have I done wrong?'

'Of course you haven't.'

'I feel...'

'What that man did to you was wrong and cruel and you're right to get away from those people.'

'What if she finds me?'

'She won't and even if she does, she'll have to get past me.'

I put my fists up, throw a couple of punches and she smiles and seems to relax. I look at her, lying there so small and fragile, and I'm thinking that always having lived within that world of privilege and pecking orders must have left her open to bullying and abuse, but it might also have given her a sense of being protected, in a way that she might be missing now.

'Do you want to come downstairs and say hello to a friend of mine?' I ask.

'Er...'

'Come on, she's lovely and we'll have a drink.'

She gets up off the bed and as we go into the hall the

phone starts ringing. I decide to leave it in case it's Dorothy or some other kind of trouble.

I use my key to get into Lizzie's and she's in the lounge with The Temptations on the radiogram and the whisky bottle in her hand.

'Aren't you a dishy little thing?' she says as we walk in. 'I'm Lizzie. Long suffering mate of Miss Walker here. Scotch?'

'Oh. I've never…'

'Well it's about time you did then,' says Lizzie, pouring a glass and giving it to her.

'Reen?'

'Please.'

We settle back with our drinks and let the boys soothe us with 'My Girl'.

Lizzie turns to Mary, 'Do you like a bit of soul music?'

Mary nods and smiles.

'How old are you, darling?' asks Lizzie.

'I'm seventeen.'

'Has Rina told you about our club?'

'No.'

'It's up the West End. We'll be going in later. You might want to come and have a listen to the band?'

'I'd like that.'

'But say you're eighteen, if anyone asks you.'

'OK.'

After another drink and a Supremes album, Mary's laughing and joking with Lizzie and looking a lot better.

Lizzie announces that she's got to change for the club and Mary and I go upstairs to do the same. Mary's worried that she's not got a nice dress to wear and I have a look through her clothes and realise she's right. It's far too late for the shops, so I look in Georgie's wardrobe, take out a green Biba dress I bought her when she was younger, that she never wore, hold it up against Mary and see that it's just about the right size. I can tell by the look on her face that she's never worn a dress so short but I tell her it'll look great and she puts it on. I feel a bit strange about giving her Georgie's clothes but I reckon she'd be fine with it if she knew. I take Mary into my room, put some make-up on her and brush her hair. When she stands in front of the mirror, she looks a bit surprised at what she sees but I think she's pleased as well. She sits on the bed while I have a look in the wardrobe, take out my dark red Emilio Pucci shift dress and put it on with sheer nylons and a pair of black Delman heels. We go downstairs, pick up Lizzie, elegant in her dark blue suit, and when we get to the street I try to remember where I parked the Mini. Lizzie spots it on the corner of Randolph Avenue and we get into it and drive into town.

I park in Frith Street and we walk through the warm evening air to the club. Max and Terry are on the door with another face that I've seen around with Bert. Lizzie takes Mary downstairs while Max introduces me to the new bloke who's called Kevin. I ask how the extra security is working out and Max tells me that there are two men downstairs in the club at all times and there hasn't been any trouble since I left. That could mean that Bobby Grant's decided to leave off, but I doubt it. If little Dave Green was his man and he finds out he ended up in a dustbin, he's going to want satisfaction.

The band are into 'Dock of the Bay' as I walk downstairs into the warm glow of the club. The tables are mostly occupied and a few people are moving slow on the dance floor. I can see one of the minders sitting by himself at a table in the far corner and the other one is walking towards the dressing room. Lizzie and Mary are at the bar with Kelly and as I join them I see Mary's eyes widening as she listens to Kelly telling them how she went to a hotel the night before with a punter who put on a dog collar, gave her a nun's habit to wear, told her to clasp her hands together and recite the Lord's prayer, while he wanked himself off. As we're having a good laugh and Lizzie's saying she hopes Kelly got a good collection, a man in an expensive suit approaches with his eye on Mary and offers to buy her a drink. I take her arm, tell the mark she's not available and lead Mary to a table beside the bandstand. Lizzie introduces the man to Kelly and has a word with Jane behind the bar before joining us, as the band go into 'The Midnight Hour'.

'Whisky all right for you, Mary?' says Lizzie, as a waitress arrives with a bottle of Glenfiddich and three glasses.

'Mmm, yes, thank you.'

There's a warm glow in her eyes as she nods her head to the music and I believe she's beginning to feel safe.

When the song finishes, Tim the keyboard player tells us the band are taking a short break and the boys put down their instruments and head for the dressing room. When Tim puts a cassette in the machine and The Supremes come on the speakers with 'Baby Love', I remember I need to get those tapes copied and I've no idea where I can get it done. It occurs to me that Tim will probably know how to do it, so I tell Lizzie and Mary I'll be back in a minute and follow him to the dressing room. The boys are through in the kitchen eating hotdogs and drinking cans of beer and for a moment I'm reminded of the frankfurters and rolls that I found in the freezer when I put Rose's body in there, a while back. I say hello to the lads, tell them they're sounding great and beckon Tim into the dressing room.

'Caesar never came back,' he says.

'He's in America.'

'Yeah?'

'With a band called Grim Reaper.'

'Were they at that Woburn Abbey gig?'

'That's right. They're recording in New York.'

'With Bobby Grant, right?'

'Yes.'

'Good luck with that.'

'How do you mean?'

'He's robbed every band he's ever had.'

He finishes his beer, crushes the can and chucks it in a bin.

'Talking of recording, I need to get some tapes copied and I don't know where to get it done.'

'I'd do it for you but my Revox has gone on the blink, so I've only got the Grundig for now. You can do it at a studio, if you don't mind paying.'

'I don't.'

'I've got a mate at Chappell Studios who'll do it for a few notes.'

'Great.'

'Shall I give him a call?'

'If you don't mind.'

'I've got to speak to him anyway about a session I'm doing on Friday.'

'Who are you playing for?'

'Al Martino.'

The door opens and Lizzie and Mary come in.

'I'll see if I can get him now,' says Tim, going into the club.

'We want a word with Rico,' says Lizzie.

I follow them into the kitchen where the band are still munching hotdogs and drinking beer.

Rico is working away at the stove and there's an older woman at the sink washing dishes. Rico looks round and sees Lizzie, wipes his hands on his apron and comes over to us.

'Good evening, ladies. What can I do for you?'

'Do you still need someone in here?' asks Lizzie.

'Certainly.'

Lizzie looks over at the woman at the sink. 'What about..?'

'My mother. She is just helping out.'

'That's good of her,' says Lizzie.

Rico's mum looks over at us, smiles and goes on with her washing up.

Lizzie turns to Rico. 'This is Mary. She's done kitchen work and she's looking for a job,' says Lizzie.

Rico looks her up and down, 'It is washing up, as you can see, food preparation, chopping, make salad. You can do that?'

'Yes,' says Mary.

'Can you come tomorrow?'

Mary looks at me and I give her a nod of encouragement.

'Yes, I can,' she says.

'Seven o'clock.'

Rico turns back to the stove, picks up a frying pan that's starting to smoke and we go back through the dressing room. As we go into the club, Tim appears beside me.

'He's just finishing a session and he can do it in an hour if you want.'

'That'll do fine.'

'His name's Clarke and he's in Studio 2.'

'Where's Chappell Studios?'

'Maddox Street.'

'Perfect. Thanks Tim.'

'Anytime,' he says, going into the dressing room.

Lizzie and Mary are back at the bar talking to Kelly. I take Lizzie aside, tell her I've got the chance to get the tapes copied and ask her if she'll look after Mary. She says she will and I give her a quick kiss and tell her I'll see her at home later.

I drive to the flat, get the tapes from under the floorboard and head along Oxford Street, down Regent Street and turn into Maddox Street. The studio is on the right hand side just before New Bond Street. I park the car, ring the bell and tell the voice that answers that I'm there to see Clarke in Studio 2. He tells me it's on the second floor, buzzes me in and I head for the lift. When I step out on the second floor, I see a sign pointing to Studio 2 and walk along a corridor with a thick grey carpet. A door opens and I hear a sweet reggae beat as three West Indian girls in very short skirts walk past me.

The door to Studio 2 is a very solid piece of oak so I ease it open and go in, without knocking. There's a young bloke in headphones, who I reckon will be Clarke, leaning over the desk in the control room and roadies working in the studio, unplugging amps and humping speakers onto a trolley. One of them picks up the bass drum and when he turns round I see that I've just missed the Bee Gees. I knock on the glass door of the control room and Clarke sees me, takes off his headphones and beckons me to go in.

'Rina, right?'

'Thanks for doing this.'

'It's OK. Have a seat.'

He indicates a sofa against the back wall and I sit.

'I've just got to check an edit, then I'll be right with you,' he says, putting on his headphones and turning back to the desk.

'Can I have a listen?'

'Sure.'

He presses a button, slides some faders up and after the violins have brought him in, Barry Gibb tells me he's going to Massachusetts, then the brothers blend their sweet voices in with the harmonies and I'm swaying along with a lovely song.

When it gets to the end, Clarke takes of his headphones and swivels round on his chair. 'Like it?'

'I love it.'

'They're really nice to work with.'

'Australian, aren't they?'

'That's what I thought but they were born here in actual fact, on the Isle of Man. They formed a band in Manchester then their family moved down under and after they got in the charts there, they came back here and Robert Stigwood took them on.'

I take the tapes out of my handbag and offer them to Clarke. He goes across the room to a row of machines and laces up the first one.

'Do you want the whole lot copied?'

'I'm not sure. Would you mind if we listen to some?'

'No problem.'

He presses a button and we hear Turkish voices having a conversation for a few minutes and then it stops and there's some eastern music which fades out. He winds forward and there's nothing more. I explain that I'm looking for a section with English voices so he puts on the next tape but it sounds like the same Turks again. They talk for longer but there's nothing else. I'm beginning to think I may have blown it when Clarke puts on the third one and after some more Turkish, Omer is suddenly speaking English and being told that the American Military at Karamürsel are about to raid the headquarters of the Workers and Peasants Party in Istanbul and given the time and date of the operation, but it's not Jeremy who's giving him the intelligence, it's Dorothy.

22

I get the original tape and two copies from Clarke, give him a score and tell him to bin the others. On the way home I'm marvelling at the neck of the woman. Not only is she spying for the Russians but when she feels a bit of heat, she frames her husband for it. She got me to do Saltik because he was her contact at Karamürsel Air Base and he was about to shop her. She's some piece of work and I need to get her banged up, before she can get that nonce at Kesgrove House to grass me for offing Weston. The trouble is, I've no idea how to do it. If I walk into MI6 and give them the tape, I'm going to be asked all kind of questions about my own involvement and Dorothy's such an operator she might well get me done for killing Saltik, or Omer, or both.

I need Lizzie's advice but when I get home and knock on her door she's not there so I go up to my place and phone the club. Jane answers and tells me that Lizzie left twenty minutes ago. I put the tapes under the floorboard, go into the lounge, pour myself a drink and put 'Aretha Arrives' on the Dansette. As Aretha gets stuck into 'Satisfaction', I hear a knock at the door. I go and open it and Lizzie's there.

'Where's Mary?' I ask, as she walks past me into the lounge.

'She's staying with Kelly.'

'How come?'

'Turns out Kel's given her boyfriend the elbow and she's got a spare room at her place in Meard Street. She and Mary were chatting away all night and she knew she was looking for somewhere. When we closed the club, Kelly said she'd show her the room and she could stay the night if she wanted. Mary asked me if it was all right and as I didn't know what you were up to, I gave her our phone numbers, just in case, and told her to go ahead.'

I pour a large one and give it to her. 'So you've got her a job and a place to live, all in one night.'

'Looks like it.'

'That's wonderful. Thank you, my darling.' I put my arms round her and we kiss.

'Did you get your tapes copied? she asks, when we come up for air.

'I'll say.'

'So you're covered if she comes after the little one.'

'She's not coming after anyone.'

'How come?'

'It's her who's the traitor.'

'You're kidding.'

'She's on the tape giving secrets to the Russian spy, clear as a bell.'

'What about Jeremy?'

'He's not on there at all.'

'So she was fitting him up.'

'That's right.'

'Rotten bitch.'

'All I need now is a way of getting her busted without putting myself in for offing those Turks.'

'You need a reporter.'

'What?'

'To put it on the front page and keep you clean.'

'That's brilliant.'

'She's an MP's daughter, isn't she?'

'Yeah.'

'Then it's a great story and I know just the man.'

'Can you reach him?'

'I think I've got his number.'

She reaches for her handbag, takes out her address book and flicks through it.

'His name's John Mayfield, he mostly works for the Sun.'

'How do you know him?'

'He was always lurking around and trying to get names off me when I was doing the mistressing.'

'Did you ever give him any?'

'Not likely. I would have been out of business in five minutes if I had... Here he is. I've got his office and his home number.'

'Great.'

'You want me to give it a go?'

'Sure.'

We go into the hall. Lizzie picks up the phone and dials but there's no answer.

'It is nearly four in the morning,' I say.

'I may as well try the office.'

She does get an answer but it's just a night manager who tells her that Mayfield will be in at about nine o'clock and to call back then. We go into the bedroom, I set the alarm clock for eight thirty while Lizzie sits beside me on the bed.

'I don't know what I'd do without you,' I say, slipping my arm round her and kissing her beautiful soft neck. She turns to me, strokes my cheek and looks into my eyes.

'You're my lovely girl.'

She takes the glass out of my hand, puts it on the bedside table and we slowly undress each other.

• • •

The plane's coming in to land and Dorothy's in the seat next to me and when I look round at her she's getting bigger and bigger like she's being pumped up and her face is bulging and she's turning purple and then she's so big that she's filling up the whole cabin and people are being squashed against the sides and the floor and there's a great bang and the roof's blown off the cabin and the plane crashes onto the runway and skids along with the sound of tearing metal and Dorothy's oozing out through the hole in the roof and flying up into the sky and getting bigger and bigger until she blots out the sun and it's getting darker and darker, then she reaches down into the cabin and grabs hold of me, lifts me up through the air, puts me in her great gaping mouth and swallows me. I'm sliding down her throat and down and down into her stomach and then I'm swimming in mucky champagne with old food floating in it, then it drains away and I'm being sucked down a slimy tunnel and I take out my knife, slash at the walls, make a hole and climb through it and I'm cutting my way through gloopy horrible muck until I tear through her skin and I'm out of her body and breathing fresh air. I'm falling towards the earth and I see the runway and the airport and the wrecked plane and fire engines rushing towards it and I land on the roof of an ambulance and it skids to a stop and the bell starts jangling right by my ear...

The phone's ringing. I sit up and Lizzie stirs next to me. The bedside clock says six-thirty. I get out of bed, go into the hall and pick up the receiver.

'Governor wants you,' says Bert Davis.

'I'll be round later.'

'Now.'

'It's half six in the morning.'

'Now.'

His voice has a hard edge to it and I know I've got to go.

'I'll pick you up,' he says.

'Don't bother.'

I put the phone down and go back into the bedroom.

'What is it?' says Lizzie.

'I've been summoned.'

'His Highness?'

'Yeah.'

'Something going off?'

'Sounds like it,' I say, taking a clean pair of pants out of the drawer.

'Let me try John Mayfield at home,' she says, wrapping a sheet round her and going into the hall. I carry on getting dressed while I hear her talking on the phone. By the time I'm tucking my silk blouse into my Jacquard pencil skirt, she's calling through from the hall, 'Can you meet him at El Vino in Fleet Street at eleven?'

'Yes,' I say, stepping into a pair of heels.

'What will you be wearing?'

'Suede jacket.'

Lizzie comes back in and I take her over to the bed, lie her down and cover her with the sheet and the eiderdown.

'What does he look like?'

'Small, fat, nearly bald.'

'Now you get some sleep. All right?'

'Mmm,' she murmurs, closing her eyes. I tuck her in and kiss her on the forehead.

I have a quick wash, brush my hair, put on a lick of make-up, grab an apple from the bowl on the kitchen table and chew it on the way down the stairs. There's a light rain falling as I drive along Elgin Avenue and across Harrow Road. By the time I get to George's, it's stopped and the sun's come out. I park outside and knock on the front door. Bert lets me in, leads me along the passage and opens the door to the lounge. George Preston is standing by the fireplace. His arms are folded and there's a steely look in his eye.

'Jack Drake's gone over the wall,' he says.

'From Broadmoor?'

'I've just had it from Ray that he's mad as fucking hell and coming after me.'

'Why?'

'He knows you took a liberty, didn't do Joe Mason and caused Ronnie to kill him and get on a murder charge. He's blaming me for it, as the one who had the work, and putting it about that I lost it over a bit of skirt and need straightening.'

'What are you going to do?'

'It's what you're going to do.'

'You want me to get to him first?'

'You took a right fucking liberty not doing Mason but I let it go. This is where you make it right.'

The last thing I need is more work but I can see that this is down to me. By the code, Jack Drake has got to get satisfaction for Ronnie and it's George he has to come after.

'Where is he?' I ask.

Before George can answer there's a knock on the door. Bert opens it and Ray comes in.

'What have you got?' asks George.

'Drake's taken it on his toes to Greece, he's after Millie and the girl.'

'Do you know where they are?'

'No.'

George turns and his eyes bore into me, 'Don't come back until he's cold.'

• • •

On the way home, I stop at the French café in Clifton Road, and buy some croissants. It's nearly eight o'clock when I get to the flat so I go into the bedroom, take off my clothes, set the alarm for ten and slide into bed beside Lizzie. She stirs in her sleep, puts an arm round me and I snuggle up to her and close my eyes, hoping to put a couple of hours kip in the bank before I have to go and meet the reporter. Even though I try to relax, I can't stop thinking that if Jack Drake's really lost his marbles inside, Millie and her daughter could be in real danger and I owe it to them to get after him as soon as I can, but I've got to make sure Dorothy's busted first so she can't get me done for Weston. I only hope this reporter can take care of it quickly so I can go to Greece.

I give up on sleep and get out of bed. It's warm and sunny now so I put my clothes on, wake Lizzie and suggest we have coffee and croissants in the garden. When she finally surfaces and sees the sunshine coming in the window, she agrees it's a good idea so I make a flask while she has a wash and gets dressed. When we get downstairs and are settled on a south facing bench, she asks me what George wanted and I tell her the score and how I've got to go after Jack.

'You've only just got back.'

'I know.'

'I can't bear that you're in so much danger.'

'I'll be all right,' I say, pouring her a cup of coffee and giving her a croissant.

'Do you want me to come with you?'

There's nothing I'd like better but I'll never put her in danger if I can avoid it.

'I need you here looking after the club.'

'To hell with the club.'

'I'll be fine, honestly.'

'Promise me you'll be careful.'

'Promise,' I say, kissing her on the cheek.

She seems a little bit reassured and we sit back and nibble our croissants while the gardener fires up the lawnmower and chugs along the far side of the grass.

'Will you keep an eye on Mary while I'm gone?'

'Of course I will.'

After we've drained the flask and eaten another croissant, we go back upstairs and I leave Lizzie at hers and go and get one of the tapes from my bedroom.

I drive along Marylebone Road, down Southampton Row, round the Aldwych and into Fleet Street. I've never been to El Vino but I know it's where a lot of reporters hang out. As I'm nearly at the end of Fleet Street, I see it on my right hand side and park the car.

23

There are only a few men in suits in the place and I get a few looks as I walk in. The barman is an older bloke in a flowery waistcoat. As I approach, he frowns and crosses his arms.

'You can't be at the bar,' he says.

'What?'

'Ladies aren't served here.'

'Why not?'

'It's the rules.'

'I'm meeting someone.'

'Go to a table in there and wait for him and he can come and get you a drink, or you can get one from the waitress,' he says, pointing to a room at the back of the bar.

For two pins I'd stick one on him but I need to see this Mayfield geezer so I walk past the men who are clearly enjoying this little drama and go into the back room. There are two women at a table in the corner, both with briefcases. One of them is writing in a notebook, the other one smiles at me as I take a seat.

'Old Frank Bower knock you back?' she asks.

'He wouldn't let me buy a drink.'

'We're not allowed to stand at the bar either. Crazy, isn't it?'

'What's it about?'

'Doesn't like women. He reckons he'll have brasses looking for business if he lets us mix with the men in the bar. He's a stupid old fossil who needs to wake up.'

'We're working on it,' says her friend, looking up from her notebook. 'There's a protest next week. We've got women from all different papers taking part and we're going to march into the bar mob-handed, Saturday lunchtime, and demand to be served.'

'Good luck,' I say.

'Join us, if you want. We're gathering outside at midday.'

'I'd like to but I think I might be away.'

'Come if you can, eh?'

'I will.'

The waitress appears beside me and as I'm ordering a large scotch, I notice a short, fat figure with a shiny bald head, entering the bar from the street. He looks into the room and clocks my suede jacket. I smile at him and he comes in and holds out his hand.

'Liz Jensen's friend?'

'That's me.'

'I'm Johnny Mayfield. What can I get you?'

'I've got one coming, thanks.'

'I'll be right back,' he says, putting his briefcase down and waddling off towards the bar.

I watch him order a drink and chat away to a couple of men while the old badger in the waistcoat pours him a brandy and takes his money. He says something and leaves them laughing before he walks back to the table and sits opposite me.

'So. Lizzie said you might have something for me,' he says, taking a handkerchief from his top pocket and mopping his brow.

'I've got a tape of someone giving US military secrets to a Turkish Soviet agent.'

'Have you now?' he says, folding the handkerchief and putting it away.

The waitress arrives with my drink. When she stands waiting, I realise she wants paying so I open my handbag but before I can get my purse open, Mayfield takes some change out of his pocket and gives it to her.

'Thanks,' I say, taking a sip of a good whisky.

Mayfield takes a swig of his brandy, 'Two more, love.'

The waitress nods and goes to the women's table in the corner. Mayfield watches her walk away and leans forward.

'So what do you want to do with this tape then?' he says.

'I want her done for spying.'

'Her?'

'Yes.'

'Does she have a name?'

'I need to know if you can do it before I tell you.'

'It was me who offered Blunt up to MI5 a couple of years ago. I made sure they had him bang to rights but the fuckers gave him immunity if he confessed and put others in the frame.'

'I think I read about that.'

'I hate those fucking traitors and I know the right people to go to. You give me this slag you've got on tape and I'll do everything I can to get her nailed.'

The way he's sweating as he talks tells me I've got the right man.

'Her name's Dorothy Pargeter-Smythe.'

'David Ashford's daughter? Married to Jeremy Pargeter-Smythe?'

'That's her.'

'But Jeremy's awaiting trial for spying himself.'

'He's clean. She's fitted him up.'

'You're kidding.'

'I'm not.'

'Can we prove it?'

'She's on the tape, doing the business.'

'Have you got it with you?'

'Yes.'

'Can you come with me now?'

'Sure.'

The waitress arrives with our drinks. Mayfield pays for them and drains his glass. I do the same, give the girls a wave and follow him out of the door.

He hurries along Fleet Street as fast as his little legs will carry him, turns into an alleyway next to an office block and I follow him round to the back of the building. He rings a bell beside a metal door and the uniformed man who opens it recognises him and lets us in. We walk along a corridor, Mayfield knocks on a door at the far end and when there's no response, he opens the door to a small room with three tape recorders on a shelf above a desk that has two mics and three phones on it. He offers me a chair and I sit down and give him the tape. He puts it on one of the machines, laces it through the slot thing in the middle and loops it onto the empty spool. When he presses the play button, Omer says a few words and then Dorothy's posh tones fill the room. When the conversation comes to an end, he switches off the machine and sits back in his chair.

'That is fucking great, except for one thing,' he says.

'What do you mean?'

'The Turk doesn't say her name.'

'He calls her Dorothy at the beginning.'

'It's not enough.'

'Is there anything we can do?'

'Maybe,' he says, sitting back in his chair, taking a packet of Players out of his pocket and offering me one. When I shake my head, he lights one up and takes a long drag.

'What are you thinking?' I ask.

'If I can get her to identify herself on tape, and the two

are played side by side in court, a jury might buy it and convict.'

'Why wouldn't they?'

'Depends how good the defence brief is. Reasonable doubt and all that shit. It's well worth a try though. I'll need her phone number.'

'I know it.'

'You're a fucking diamond, you are,' he says, pulling one of the phones towards him and plugging a lead from the back of it into a socket on one of the tape recorders. He positions a mic in front of a speaker next to it, asks me for Dorothy's number, takes a notebook from his pocket and writes it down.

'Dead schtum now, eh?' he says, dialling the number and switching on the tape recorder.

After a few rings a male voice comes through the speaker.

'Belgravia 4219.'

'Mrs Pargeter-Smythe, please,' says Mayfield, suddenly sounding posher then the Queen Mother.

'Who may I say is calling?'

'Pip Boyland.'

'One moment please.'

Mayfield pauses the tape recorder until Dorothy comes on.

'Hello,' she says.

'Is that Dorothy Pargeter-Smythe?'

'Speaking.'

'Name's Pip Boyland, we met briefly at a ball you gave at Menton.'

'Oh yes?'

'Binky Sutcliffe asked me to telephone you. Silly blighter's fallen off his horse down at Crampton and he's laid up for a few days but he's having a wee a gathering of the clans next week at Eaton Square and he'd love you to come.'

'Which day is that?'

'Friday the nineteenth.'

'I'm not sure I can but I'll put it in the diary and hope for the best.'

'Jolly good. How's Jeremy holding up?'

'Are you…?'

'We were in the Blues and Royals together.'

'Ah… He's as well as can be expected.'

'Any light at the end of the tunnel?'

'Things are in hand. Now if you'll excuse me I have to…'

'Yes of course. I hope to see you at Eaton Square.'

'Good day.'

The line goes dead and Mayfield unplugs the phone and the mic. He rewinds the tape recorder, presses a button and we hear the conversation. When it finishes, he plays the Istanbul tape on the other machine.

'Pretty good match,' he says, reverting to his East London accent.

'What happens now?' I ask.

'I talk to a man I know at Special Branch and the lads pay her a visit. Belgrave Square isn't it?'

'How did you know?'

'I've been after her old man for years.'

'Is it true he's a homo?' I say, hoping to sound like a tourist.

'He'll fuck anything, animal, vegetable or mineral.'

I might have known a gun dog like him would be on to Sir David's doings. I only hope he doesn't find out what happened to Weston.

'Good luck with that one,' I say.

'He's a slippery cunt.'

'How soon can you put it on Dorothy?' I say, as I stand up.

'No time like the present,' he says, pulling one of the phones towards him and dialling a number.

'Inspector Corbett,' he says, after a pause. He has a look at my legs while he's waiting.

'Dave? I've got one. Meet me at the drinker.'

He puts down the phone, rewinds the tapes, takes them off the machines and puts them in his briefcase.

'Keep me up to speed, will you?' I say as he gets up.

'Of course I will. Give me your number.'

'Can we do it through Lizzie?'

'If you want.'

He opens the door for me and we walk back the way we came and along the alleyway to Fleet Street. We say goodbye and when I get to the car, I look back and see him go into El Vino.

As I drive round the Aldwych, I think about the old prune who won't have a woman at his bar but who's got a warm welcome for a sleazebag like Mayfield and the way those suits smirked when the old sod gave me the elbow. When I start thinking how I would have waded into them and notice how hard I'm gripping the wheel, I reckon I need to lose a bit of energy and head for All Saints Road.

At the gym, I collect my kit from Barry, who's making tea in the office as usual, and go into the Ladies. As I'm changing into my singlet, shorts and gym shoes, I notice there are clothes on the next hook to mine and I wonder if there's another female member at last. When I go into the hall, I see her right away on the heavy bag and giving it some punishment. She's tall, well muscled, wearing a black catsuit and getting a lot of looks from the men. I get a skipping rope off one of the hooks by the door, walk past her to the back of the room and warm up. She's still pounding the bag when I go to the weights and pick up a sixty pound barbell. I start with squats and dead lifts then I lie on a bench and do some presses. By the time I've done ten I'm exhausted and I know I've got to come here more often if I'm going to stay in shape. A couple of the lads lift the barbell off me and I rest for a bit and watch Cat Woman reach the end of her session on the bag. She looks over and returns my smile as she walks towards the ring and climbs in. A bloke wearing sparring gloves gets in with her and she sets about him with a lot of dodging and weaving and some great footwork. I smack the speed bag for a bit, then I'm on the heavy one and giving it as much as I can muster.

While I'm lathering up in the shower, it occurs to me that if Dorothy thinks I've listened to the tape and rumbled her as a spy, she'll try to get rid of me, like she did Saltik, but she'll want to get her hands on the tape first. If I don't give it to her now she's bound to send someone after me and I'm going to have enough trouble in Greece without some gamekeeper up my arse. My best chance is to offer her the tape at five o'clock, all innocent, and hope she thinks I haven't heard it.

As I step out and reach for my towel, Cat Woman comes in and starts taking off her suit.

'Good to see another woman training here, I thought I was the only one.'

'Just passing through,' she says, in an American accent.

'Have you been fighting here?'

'Touring Europe with a carnival.'

'How was that?'

'Funny mostly, but well paid.'

'When do you go back?'

'Tomorrow. I have a fight in Florida, Saturday.'

'Good luck.'

'Thanks. You fight?'

'Not in the ring.'

She laughs as she steps into the shower.

I'd like to stay and talk but when I look at my watch I see that I need to get a move on if I'm going to go home, get the tape and be at Belgrave Square by five o'clock. I put my clothes on and say goodbye to Cat Woman. When I go into the office to leave my kit, her sparring partner is there with Barry.

'Hey, you were looking good out there,' he says.

'Thanks.'

'Harry Schneider, Joanne's manager,' he says, shaking my hand.

'Hello.'

'We just toured Europe with Joanne in the booth punching out the locals.'

'I pity the locals.'

'Right. Would you be interested in that kind of thing?'

'No thanks.'

'There's good money in it.'

'I can't leave my hairdressing business.'

'Oh, right.'

The door opens and Joanne looks in. 'Harry?'

'Coming,' he says, picking up a kit bag.

'Good meeting you both.'

He swings the bag over his shoulder and leaves.

Barry chuckles, 'I don't think I'd risk a short back and sides from you.'

• • •

I want to tell Lizzie how it went with Mayfield when I get back but she's not there. I'm a bit knackered from the workout and I need a cup of coffee before I can face Dorothy, even though I'm a bit late, so I go into the kitchen, put the kettle on and switch on the radio. The news is on and the man's talking about the daring escape from Broadmoor and how the authorities don't yet know how it was done. I'm wondering if I can get a flight to Greece this evening when the phone rings. I switch off the gas and go and answer it. It's Dorothy.

'I have a photograph of you on the table in front of me, Miss Walker, next to the name and telephone number of the man who's skull you fractured at Kesgrove House. If you do not return my property immediately, I shall contact him, arrange to show him your photograph and invite him to identify you as the murderer of his friend and colleague.'

'I'll be there in twenty minutes,' I say, putting the phone down.

I go back into the kitchen wondering why some members of the upper classes have to speak like they're in a West End play and where the fuck she got that photograph. The news has finished so I switch off the radio and make a lukewarm cup of Nescafé with the nearly boiled water. I drink half of it, tip the rest down the sink, go into the bedroom and get a tape from under the floorboard, leaving the other one there for insurance.

I drive to Belgrave Square, park in Halkin Street and walk to the house. A crusty looking butler lets me in and shows me into the drawing room. I sit on the end of a

Regency sofa and when Dorothy enters I take the tape out of my pocket and put it on the coffee table. She picks it up.

'Wait here,' she says, and goes out of the door.

I pick up a copy of the *Daily Telegraph* and I'm reading an article about a scandal at Ely Hospital in Wales and how the staff have been mistreating the mental patients and stealing money when Dorothy comes in.

'I think that concludes our business. As you've stolen my maid, I shan't be paying your fee. Kindly leave my house.'

'I want that photograph.'

'Get out of here now.'

'Not without the photograph.'

'You've asked for it, you little bitch.'

She goes to the door, flings it open and two men come at me. I pick up the coffee table and throw it at them. One of them catches it full in the face and goes down, the other one grabs me round the neck and chucks me on the floor. I twist onto my back and kick him under his kneecap. He staggers back and falls. The other one gets onto all fours. I stand up, stomp on his hand, knee him in the face and he goes down. The other one tries to get up. I take hold of a standard lamp, lift it up high and smash the base plate down on his head.

I grab the photograph, run past Dorothy, out the front door and along the street. When I get to the end of the square and look back to check I'm not being followed, I see a patrol car stopping outside the house and an unmarked pulling in behind it. The uniforms stay in the car while three plainclothes get out and go to the front door. I hurry to the Mini, turn it round and park at a discreet distance from the house, where I can see the front door. After a while, two uniforms get out of the patrol car and go into the house. More time passes and then Dorothy emerges, surrounded by officers and is driven away in the unmarked car.

24

I drive back to Randolph Crescent with one hand on the wheel and the other massaging my neck. It's a good job they were only a couple of amateurs and I was able to get out before Special Branch arrived. Inspector Corbett certainly jumped to it and I only hope they don't give her bail. I reckon Mayfield will get the story in the paper tomorrow which should keep her behind the door. I park the Mini and go into the house. I ought to get on with booking a flight to Greece but I can't resist knocking on Lizzie's door and then she's there in her silky dressing gown and my arms are round her and we're kissing, then she pulls back, looking at my neck.

'You're hurt, my darling.'

'Dorothy set the dogs on me.'

'What happened?'

'It's all done. Your man Mayfield did the business and she's been arrested.'

'So you're in the clear.'

'I couldn't have done it without you.'

'You would have found a way, you always do.'

'I need to find a way to a Greek island called Hydra now, before that psycho gets to his wife and kid.'

'You're not going tonight?'

'I should if I can.'

'Do you want to come in and I'll phone the travel agent?'

'They'll be shut now, won't they?'

'I've got a tame one.'

'Of course you have.'

'Used to like being smeared with Marmite and...'

'That'll do, thanks.'

Lizzie laughs and goes to the phone.

'Pour us a drink,' she says, as she dials.

I go into the lounge and do as I'm told. I look at the comfy sofa opposite the TV and all I want to do is settle down with a bottle of whisky and my beautiful girl for the evening. She puts her head round the door.

'There's a ten o'clock charter flight to Athens, if you want it. You have to get a boat from there to Hydra.'

'That'll do fine.'

She disappears and I put The Dave Brubeck Quartet on the record player, count the tracks, place the needle on Take Five and Paul Desmond is just easing into his delicious solo, when Lizzie comes in.

'Your ticket will be at the Thomas Cook desk in Building One at half past eight.'

'I'll call a cab for eight then.'

'I'd take you but I need to be at the club.'

'Is everything all right?'

'There was a bit of bother after you left last night.'

'What happened?'

'Nothing much. A punter got pissed and started a fight

with a German bloke, something about the war. The boys had him out in seconds but Maisy got an elbow in the face and I need to make sure she's all right.'

'She's new, isn't she?'

'Been with us a couple of weeks. She's good.'

'Looks good.'

'Down girl.'

'Just saying.'

'You're far too sweaty to go to Greece, Miss Walker. I'm putting you in the bath.'

• • •

An hour later I've said goodbye to Lizzie and I'm upstairs putting on Levis, a white T-shirt, ankle boots and my leather jacket. I throw my holdall on the bed and stuff it with all the flares and floaty tops I've got, sunglasses, sandals, a couple of light dresses and my swimsuit. I'd like to take Omer's Beretta but I've only got the six rounds in the chamber, so I wrap my other Smith & Wesson in underwear and put it in the bottom of the holdall with some extra rounds, a blade and my lock pick wallet. I go into the bathroom and use a nail file to unscrew the panel on the side of the bath. I take a wad of notes from the stash I keep in there and replace the panel. I pick up my toothbrush, go back into the bedroom, take some make-up off the dressing table and put it in the holdall with the money. I'm zipping it up when the doorbell rings and it's my cab. I take my passport from the shelf at the top of the wardrobe, put the bag over my shoulder and go downstairs.

The driver's a leery old boy and he's got a peeping mirror stuck on the dashboard, below the regular one, so he can get an eyeful of any canoodling couples he gets in the back. He has a quick look at me as we move off but he's out of luck as I'm wearing jeans and there's no skirt to look up. He drones on about the hot weather and the traffic and how badly Arsenal are playing, until I'm losing the will to live. When he asks me where I'm going, I tell him I'm visiting my husband who's stationed in Aden and he shuts up.

He drops me at Building One and I go to the Thomas Cook desk, show the uniformed woman my passport and she finds my ticket and gives it to me. I pay her eighteen quid and see that it's one-way only to Athens. I ask the woman if she knows where I get the boat to Hydra and she tells me it leaves from the port of Piraeus which is about a half hour drive up the coast from the airport. She checks my bag in, gives me a boarding pass and tells me the flight's on time. I walk the length of the building to Departures, show my passport at security and go into where the bars and duty free shops are. The boarding gate for my flight isn't showing yet so I buy a large scotch from a bar called the Britannic, take it to a payphone and dial Ray's number. The woman who always answers picks up and I give her my name, ask to speak to Ray and she tells me to hold on.

'Evening,' he says.

'Does that man that we both know have any idea whereabouts his missus is?'

'I don't reckon so.'

'Is he alone?'

'No.'

'How many?'

'One, could be two.'

'Do you know how he got out?'

'They threatened a screw's kids and he got a grappling hook in to him and let him into the yard at midnight. His boys chucked a rope over the wall, he tied the hook on and got over.'

At that moment, my flight is announced over the speakers.

'I'll buy you a drink when I get back.'

'Better make it two,' he says, as I put the phone down.

I walk the long trek to the boarding gate and find the lounge filling up with passengers. There are lots of shorts and T-shirts and straw hats and a buzzy, holiday atmosphere and I might not be the only one who's had a drink. As I take a seat, next to a couple holding hands, a group of young blokes bowl in joshing and laughing and when they can't find seats together they sit in a group on the floor.

After a while we're called to go onboard and there's a bit of pushing and shoving as the lads try to get into the front of the queue. The airline staff intervene, remind everyone that the seats are numbered and we'll all get on in good time. They send the lads to the back of the queue, tell us to come forward and check our passes as we go through the gate and down the walkway to the plane.

I'm sat by the window towards the back of the plane with a middle-aged couple next to me. The man unfolds a copy of the *Daily Mirror* and disappears behind it while his missus takes her knitting out of her bag and gets stuck in. I reach for the Thomas Cook magazine in the pocket of the seat in front, flick through it and stop at a picture of Warren Beatty and Faye Dunaway arriving at Heathrow for the premiere of *Bonnie and Clyde,* one of the best films I've ever seen. Such a shame they got killed at the end. The cabin fills up and the loud boys bounce into the two empty rows in front of me. There's the sound of seatbelts clicking and beer cans opening as the pilot comes on and tells us we'll be landing in Athens at two thirty in the morning. I'm thinking I'll need to find a place to stay and then get a boat to Hydra first thing tomorrow. The engines rumble and the plane moves off towards the runway while the ladies do the life jacket dance in the aisles. When they sit and strap themselves in, I grit my teeth and press my back against the seat as the engines roar, the brakes go off and we pound along the runway and up into the sky.

When we reach cruising height and level off, I relax, sit back, close my eyes and listen to the lad in the seat in front telling his neighbour about his girlfriend shagging his best mate and how he's got to straighten him for it but his mate's bigger and harder than him and he doesn't want to get hurt but he's got to do it. I think about how much aggravation there is over people cheating and two-timing and why everyone gets so steamed up about it when it doesn't really matter that much. Lizzie's had it away with God know how many men and women and I don't give a stuff because I know she loves me and I love her and that's all that matters.

Apart from a bit of shouting from the lads when the stewardesses try to stop them drinking their own duty free booze instead of buying it off the trolley, the flight goes off peacefully and I'm almost asleep when the pilot comes on and tells us we're landing in ten minutes. I put on my seatbelt and look at the perfume ads and the tasty models in the magazine. There's an article at the back about how to cut down on carbs and lose weight and it makes me think of tubby Johnny Mayfield and when he'll get Dorothy's story in the paper.

We get off the plane and walk across the tarmac to the terminal. Even though it's nearly three in the morning the air is hot and humid and I slip my jacket off while the man in the booth studies my passport. I wait in the baggage hall for a bit and then lift my holdall off the carousel and pass through customs without any problems. I go to a kiosk on the far side of the terminal, change a hundred quid into eight thousand drachmas, stuff them in my back pocket and walk out of the main door. As I join the queue for a taxi, I notice the boys from the plane climbing into the back of an open lorry at the side of the building while a man with a clipboard ticks them off a list. I'm wondering what their hotel will be like when a Fiat 124 stops in front of me and I get in.

I ask the driver if he knows somewhere I can stay the night in Piraeus, where I'm getting the boat from in the morning. He tells me that his cousin has a small hotel beside the port and I tell him to take me there.

There's moonlight reflecting off the sea when we turn onto the coast road and I wind down the window, sit back and let the warm air bathe my face. The driver's asking me where I've come from and where I'm going. When I tell him I'm bound for Hydra, he says I can get a boat in the morning and his cousin's place is a short walk from where it leaves. He puts the radio on and instead of some nice bouzouki music to put me in the mood, we get my least favourite track of the year: Engelbert Humperdinck singing 'Please Release Me'.

The car turns off the quayside, drives along a row of low buildings, past a café and a couple of shops and stops in front of a small hotel with a battered sign above the door. The driver gets out of the car and I see he's a big man of about fifty, as he takes my bag out of the boot and opens the door for me. I pay him the thirty drachmas he asks for and he knocks at the door of the hotel. When there's no response, he knocks again and a light goes on. There's the sound of movement inside and then an older woman in a dressing gown opens the door. The driver introduces his cousin, talks to her in Greek and she nods at me and shows me inside. I thank the driver, pick up my holdall and follow her to a small desk where she offers me a pen and tells me to write my name in a ledger. When I've obliged, she has a quick look at the book before closing it, then she takes a towel out from under the desk, leads me along a narrow passageway to the back of the building, opens the door of a small room with a single bed and turns on the light. She looks at me for approval and when I nod she hands me the towel, steps into the passage, opens another door and shows me the bathroom. As she walks back to the desk, I can see the driver is still there. They exchange a few words, the driver leaves and she locks up and goes upstairs. I close the door, take my clothes off, open the holdall and when I find my nightie, I slip into it, turn the light off and get into bed. I'm instantly too hot, so I go to the window, open the sash from the top, take the cover off the bed and lie down. I pull the sheet up to my waist, let the tension melt away and drift into sleep.

There's a scratching sound. I open my eyes and turn on my back. A hand's clamped over my mouth and a body lands on top of me. I struggle to move but I can't. My arms are pinned down and there's a knee between my thighs, forcing them apart. I go completely limp. When he gets his cock into me and starts thrusting, he loosens his grip on my mouth. I get my teeth round his little finger and bite it off. He cries out and rears up. I spit out the finger, throw him on the floor and kneel on his chest. It's the driver. I pound his face with my fists until I've broken his nose, smashed his cheeks and knocked him out. I stand up and get dressed. When I've pulled on my boots, I chuck my stuff into the holdall, put three hard kicks into his bollocks and climb out of the window.

25

I walk past the taxi and resist the temptation to pick up a stone and do the windows. I don't want to draw attention to myself and I reckon that bastard will have enough trouble driving with the state he's in and that's before his cousin gets to him. The sun's rising in a clear blue sky and I can feel the heat building as I walk along the street, round the corner and onto the road that runs along the quayside. There are some boats that look like ferries moored up some distance away and I need to find out which one goes to Hydra. I can see a building that could be an office at the far end of the quay. As I get near it, a van pulls up outside and a man in uniform steps out, unlocks the door and goes in. I approach a window on the side and he sees me, slides it open and I ask for a ticket to Hydra. He tells me it'll cost fifteen drachmas and I give him the money.

'You go holiday?' he asks, handing me the ticket.

'Yes,' I reply.

'First time?'

'Yes.'

'Beautiful island.'

'So I'm told.'

'Too many hippy.'

'Oh?'

'No spend.'

'Ah.'

A tiny old woman in a black dress and hat, leading two goats, appears beside me and takes a purse out of her pocket. I ask the attendant which boat I need to get and he points to the middle one of three moored on the quay and says it leaves at eight o'clock. I look at my watch, see that I've got almost an hour and make my way past the goats to a café that's opening up along the quay. I wait at the counter behind a Greek family who are taking their time making up their mind between the different breads and pastries on the counter. Dad lifts each child up in turn so they can choose and when they're sorted and sat down with orange juice, Mum and Dad order from the menu on the wall and go and join them. The menu's in Greek and means nothing to me but when the man in the apron puts eggs and tomatoes in a frying pan and asks me what I want, I say I'll have the same with coffee and he seems to get it.

I go to sit outside where I can see the ferry but when I feel how strong the sun is, I move into the shade. I need to get myself a sun hat if I'm going to survive the heat. The waitress brings a small brass pot and a cup and I pour my first Greek coffee. It's really good, smoother than Turkish, and when my breakfast arrives I ask for another one as I take a mouthful of egg and tomato. There's feta cheese in the mix, which I've had in Greek salads before and never been sure about. I've always found a hint of feet in there but mixed with the tomatoes and plenty of olive oil, it tastes good.

I hear the Greek family laughing and I look over and see the little boy swinging a cuddly bear round his head. When he lets go by mistake and it hits Dad in the face and lands in his breakfast, the laughing stops. Dad lifts the bear up in the silence, wipes it on his napkin and the little boy is looking like he's going to catch it, but then Dad walks the bear across the table to him, making squeaky noises, ruffles his hair and they all laugh again.

Over on the ferry, a member of the crew is opening a gate at the top of the gangplank and letting people on board. I finish my coffee, pay the man at the counter and go to the Ladies. I take the Smith & Wesson out of the holdall, put it in the back of my belt and slip the blade into my boot. There's still a half hour before the boat leaves and I really want to get a sun hat so I don't have to spend the whole journey in the cabin. I walk up the quayside, looking into the side streets and see something in one of them that could be a clothes shop. As I'm about to go there, a bloke pushing a barrow, covered with hats, silk scarves and sunglasses, comes round the corner and nearly knocks me over. He bowls past me and stops on the quayside by the ferryboats. He's still unfolding the legs of his barrow and laying out his stuff when I get to him and start trying on hats. I settle on a white straw number with a wide brim and have a look at his sunglasses. I've got a pair in my bag but they're a bit straight and boring and I'm tempted by a pair of heart shaped Lolita ones but when I put them on and look in the mirror, I reckon it might be asking for trouble, so I choose a nice pair of round ones with dark red frames.

A hooter sounds behind me and there's a deep rumble as the boat's engine starts up. I pay the stallholder, put my hat and glasses on, show my ticket to the ferryman and walk down the gangplank. The little old lady with the goats is right behind me and when I go to the front of the boat and sit on a bench, she follows and takes a seat opposite. One of the goats comes over and has a sniff at my knees and she pulls it away and says something in Greek. It seems like a nice goat and when it comes back for another sniff I pat it on the head and stoke its neck. The lady smiles as it settles down on the floor beside me. The hooter sounds again and the crew carry the gangplank onboard, untie the mooring ropes and the boat moves away from the quay and gathers speed.

The sun is glistening on a perfectly calm sea of the purest blue as we leave the harbour. The sky is clear, the mountains of the coast are moving slowly past us and I feel more and more calm and relaxed as I let the foulness of the night drain away, witness the beauty all around me and feel my nice goat licking my hand. After we've sailed the open sea for a while, we pass an island on the right and I remember dipping into a book of Georgie's about Greek mythology. When I look at the little island standing alone in the sea under the big sky, I can really imagine how they could feel the presence of the gods in ancient times. When the captain makes an announcement that contains the word Hydra, I'm jolted back into the present and reminded that I'm here to find Millie and her daughter and get them to safety before that maniac of a husband turns up and there'll be plenty of time for dreaming about the gods when that's done.

As we approach the island I make out a small town of white houses with tiled roofs clustered round a horseshoe-shaped harbour and rising up through a valley between rugged hills. The boat docks and I shoulder my bag, say goodbye to my goat and the old lady and walk up the gangplank and onto the quayside. A group of people who get off with me seem to know where they're going and they turn up the cobbled street that runs up the hill between the houses. There are a few cafés and bars along the front and the atmosphere seems quiet and relaxed. I walk to the one at the far end, sit at a table and order a whisky from an attractive young waitress in shorts and a halter top. The clientele are all ages and I'm aware of some American voices. A boy with long dark hair is strumming a guitar quietly at a table nearby. When he starts singing 'Colours' by Donovan he gets moans of disapproval from his friends and I share their relief when he switches to 'Mr Tambourine Man'.

I have another drink and decide I'd better have a look round. I realise that I've no idea where Millie and Wendy might be or whether they're even on the island. My only chance is to start searching and hope I get lucky. I need to leave my bag somewhere and I haven't seen anything that looks like a hotel, so when the singer finishes 'Masters of War' and goes back to strumming, I turn towards a girl near him.

'Sorry to bother you but do you know where I could find somewhere to stay?'

'We just arrived a couple of days ago, don't really know anything.'

'OK.'

'We're in his parents' house,' she says, nodding to the guitar player. 'Where's your folk's place, Benji?'

'Vlychos,' he says.

'It's along the coast. Great beach.'

'That's nice.'

'Is there a hotel there, Benji?'

'No.'

'Sorry.'

'It's all right, I'll find somewhere,' I say, picking up my bag.

'See you around,' says the girl as I go to the bar where the waitress is washing glasses. I pay for my drink and ask her the same question.

'There's a room where I am,' she says, with a soft American lilt in her voice.

'Is that near?'

'Just up the hill.'

'Sounds good.'

'I'm off in an hour. I could take you there.'

'That'd be great. Could I leave my bag here?'

'Sure.'

'Thanks,' I say, passing it over the counter to her. 'I'll have a wander and come back.'

'Cool.'

'I'm Rina, by the way.'

'Celeste.'

I leave the café and walk along the port past an old church with a tall clock tower and monastery beside it. There are stalls in front selling fruit, vegetables and cheese and quite a few people milling about but no one looking like Millie or Wendy. I walk back along the port, take a left turn up a narrow road and pass a donkey, overladen with onions, that's being prodded with a stick as it skitters on the cobbles and tries to climb the hill. An old man with a shopping bag comes towards me muttering darkly as he overtakes a young couple carrying a beach bag and a bottle of wine. I go on up the road which winds between white houses of different shapes and sizes, set at various angles to the thoroughfare. When I reach a fork near the top of the hill, I see that it's time to go and meet Celeste so I retrace my steps, passing the onion laden donkey on the way, and take a seat at the café. Celeste is talking to a bearded man in a baseball cap behind the bar. She sees me, picks up my bag and comes over.

'This is really good of you,' I say, taking the holdall from her.

'It's OK, really. I only hope you like the room, it's kinda basic.'

'I'm not looking for luxury.'

'It's right this way,' she says, leading me back up the road I've just come down.

'It's called Donkey Shit Lane, by the way.'

'Really?'

'By the locals too.'

'How appropriate.'

'Right.'

'I haven't seen a single car.'

'They're not allowed on the island. It's all donkeys.'

As if to prove her point, we have to dodge sideways as four examples of the breed come clattering out of an alley on the right, roped together and driven by a teenage boy who stares at Celeste's legs as he passes.

We climb some steps onto a verandah and pass under a stone arch. Celeste opens a wooden door and leads me into a dark hallway with four rooms off it.

'Let me see if Donald is in,' she says, approaching a door at the end of the hall and knocking.

'Gimme a second,' says an American voice. I hear the sound of a typewriter and then someone sighing and moving about. The door finally opens and a tall, dark-haired, thin-faced man of about thirty, with a gloomy look, appears. Behind him I can see a desk piled with books and papers with a guitar leaning against it.

'Hi Don, how's it going?' says Celeste.

'Slow. How're you doing?'

'Not bad. This is Rina.'

'Hi Rina.'

'She needs a room.'

'Uh huh?'

He looks a little more closely at me.

'How about next to mine?' says Celeste.

'That's cool.'

'You sure?'

'If you want... I... have to...' He waves over his shoulder towards the desk.

'Didn't mean to disturb you,'

'That's OK... See you later Rina,' he says, closing the door behind him.

The typing resumes and I share a smile with Celeste as we turn away from the door.

'Donald is a poet.'

'I see.'

'He can be a little... far away, sometimes.'

'Yes.'

'I think his songs are better than his poems actually,' she says, as she moves along the hallway and opens another door. 'Here's the room.'

It's small with a single bed, a chest of drawers and an

abstract painting with yellow blobby bits and red stripes on the wall.

'This'll do nicely,' I say, dumping my holdall on the bed.

'Great. Are you here on vacation?'

I instinctively trust this girl and I can't be bothered to lie. 'I'm actually looking for a friend of mine.'

'Oh.'

'Something's happened in London and she needs to know about it.'

'She lives here?'

'Arrived recently, with her daughter.'

'Do you know where they live?'

'I don't.'

'Oh well, it's a small island and this is the only town so it shouldn't be that difficult to locate her. She's not a writer is she?'

'Er, no.'

'Only I know most of them here.'

'Are you one yourself?'

'Afraid so.'

'Poetry?'

'I'm writing a novel.'

'That's great.'

'Talking of which… I ought to be working,' she says, indicating her room.

'I ought to be looking for my friend.'

'What's her name, in case I hear anything?'

'Millie Drake.'

'I'll be on the beach around five-thirty. Make a left at the port, if you want to cool out for a while.'

'Sounds good.'

'Maybe see you later.'

26

I put my gun and blade back in the holdall, change into shorts and a loose blouse, put on my sandals and head out to start looking for the girls. By four o'clock I've been up and down nearly every lane and alleyway in the town and I'm knackered and about to head for the beach to check it out when I see a blond figure come out of a shop in front of me. I go past her, turn round and take off my hat and sunglasses.

'Hello, Millie.'

She stops and grips the bag she's holding, a look of alarm on her face.

'Rina?'

'I didn't mean to scare you.'

'No, I just didn't expect…'

'Shall we get a drink?'

'Er, yeah, all right.'

We walk to the nearest café and take a table outside.

'Why are you here?' she asks.

'I'm afraid I've got a bit of bad news.'

'What is it?'

'Jack's out.'

'Oh my Christ.'

'I think you need to move on.'

'Does he know where we are?'

'I'm not sure, but he's in Greece. You should get out of the country fast.'

'Fucking right.'

'When's the last boat out?'

'Six o'clock.'

'Can you make it?'

'As long as I can find Wendy.'

'Where is she?'

'On the beach, I think.'

'Shall we go?'

I can feel Millie's determination as I walk beside her along the front and I'm so glad I found her.

'I suppose you know about Ronnie,' I say.

'I know they've dropped the charge.'

'What?'

'I managed to get on the phone to my sister from the post office yesterday. She said the witness withdrew his statement.'

'They put the frighteners on him.'

'Course they did.'

'You must be relieved.'

'In a way I am. But if he did a long one inside he might come to his senses and work out that villainy's a mug's game.'

'Most of them don't.'

'True enough. It's all Jack's fault. Raising him like he did.'

Millie falls silent and I can feel her anger.

'Did you come all this way to warn us?' she says, after a while.

'Partly.'

She looks at me. 'Is he after you an' all?'

'Oh yeah.'

'Well don't hold back on my account.'

We round the headland and climb over rocks onto the golden sand. I follow Millie as she strides among the sunbathers and looks around for her daughter.

'Does Wendy know the score?' I ask.

'I've told her everything.'

'Good.'

'She's going to be so pissed off. She loves it here. She's just got herself a job looking after goats on a farm and she really likes it.'

'You've got to go though.'

'Course we have.'

As we get down to the sea, she spies Wendy treading water a good way out, shouts her name and waves. Wendy turns, sees her mother and starts a fast crawl to the shore. When she reaches Millie, I walk away while they talk and I see how angry and distressed Wendy becomes as she's given the news. Once she's changed into her clothes, they set off and I get in step behind the two of them as they head back up the beach. I keep a distance while they talk and consider how it must be for a girl of fifteen to know her father's coming after her mother with God knows what evil intent. I only hope that Millie can give her the love she'll need to get through the whole nasty business.

'Have you got your passports?' I ask, as we reach the top of the beach.

'They're at the farmhouse.'

'Where's that?'

'Up there,' she says, pointing to the road ahead of us that winds up the hill.

'Can you get there and be at the dock in time for the six o'clock boat?'

'If we step on it we can. Come on Wend,' says Millie, grabbing her daughter's hand and leading her off at a fast jog.

'I'll see you there,' I say, as I turn and walk back along the beach towards town.

A toddler runs in front of me, trips over a bit of driftwood and cries out. I help him up, look round for a parent and see a large man looking over at us and getting up. The little lad runs off towards him and the man gives me a wave and lies down again. The boy plonks himself on the man's stomach and grins at me as I walk on. There aren't that many people on the beach and I'm feeling so hot and tired I'd give anything to have a swim in the sea and stretch out on the sand. As I walk off the beach onto the road, the shapely figure of Celeste appears before me.

'Hey, you're here already. Did you find your friends?'

'Yes I did.'

'You said her name was Millie Drake?'

'That's right.'

'Only, I was just in Bill's Bar. There were couple of English guys drinking in there and I heard one of them asking the barman if he knew her.'

My heart sinks as she says this. 'What were they like?'

'One of them was about fifty, big, bald, and kinda nasty looking, in a linen suit. The other one was younger, short hair, jeans.'

'Thanks. I need to get going.'

'Will I see you later?'

'I hope so.'

Celeste goes onto the beach and I'm about to follow Millie and Wendy up the hill and try to find them, when I remember that I'll need my passport if we're going to make the boat and I'm nothing against Jack Drake without my gun, so I need to get back to the house. I walk fast towards town and remember seeing Bill's Bar on the front when I got off the boat. It's on the corner of the lane that leads up to the house. There may be another way up there, without going past the bar but the lanes are a maze and I don't have time to find it. I put my sunglasses on, pull my hat down, approach the corner where the bar is and lurk in a nearby doorway. There are a few people at tables outside but Jack Drake isn't among them. I go closer to where I can see inside but he's not there either. There's no sign of him on the front, so I climb the hill.

I get into the house and hear Donald punching at his

typewriter. I change into a skirt and silk jacket, put on a belt and slide the Smith & Wesson into the back of the waistband with the blade alongside it. I put the rest of my stuff in the holdall, sling it over my shoulder, put on my hat and glasses and Donald is still tapping away when I go out of the door and down the stone steps.

I turn into the lane, a man steps in front of me and throws a fast punch at my jaw. I hit the cobbles and go out.

• • •

I'm on fire. There's a searing pain in my head. I open my eyes to blackness, try to move but I'm blocked on every side. I lift my head and it hits a solid surface. I'm in a box. I can feel my gun and blade are gone. I strain against the top and the sides with every last bit of strength but nothing moves. I make myself still, count to ten, try again and nothing moves. I go quiet and listen. No sound. I feel the sides of the box. Wood. I'm in a coffin. Calm down. It's just wood. I feel some holes at one end, try to twist and see them but can't. Air, at least. I won't suffocate. Rest, there's nothing you can do. Try rocking side to side. Nothing. Try banging on the wood. Can't. No room. Go passive. Wait. If they wanted you dead you would be. They'll get you out. Unless they want a slow death. Don't think that. Go passive. Wait... Voices. Footsteps... Hammer. Chisel. Top coming off... Air... Faces...

'Here it is.'

'The fucking slag in all her glory.'

'You never said it was crumpet.'

'Shit sandwich more like.'

'Look at them fucking pins!'

'All right, just get it out and bring it inside.'

'Yes, guv'nor.'

Jack Drake walks away and the other man stands above me with one foot either side of the box, I go passive and keep my eyes shut as he reaches for my wrists and pulls me up. When he puts one arm under my waist, gets me in a hug and lifts, I bring my knee up sharp between his legs. He screams and hits the deck, still holding me. I'm struggling to get on top of him and get my hands on his neck when Jack Drake runs in and pulls me off him.

'You stupid fucking wanker. Can't even bring a fucking tart to heel!' says Drake with his hands round my throat.

'I thought she was out.'

'This is Harry Walker's girl, you stupid fucking cunt.'

The other man gets up holding his balls and I see that he's big.

'Grab her arms, Webb.'

Once I'm held, Drake releases my neck, takes out a gun and puts the barrel to my temple.

'Now tie 'em.'

Webb takes a length of cord off his belt and binds my wrists together in front of me. Drake moves behind, puts the barrel against the back of my neck and I feel his breath on my ear.

'I think it's time to see the ladies,' he says, pushing me towards the door of the barn.

The night is black but there are lights in the farmhouse across the yard. Webb goes ahead, opens a door and Drake shoves me into a kitchen.

Millie and Wendy are sat on the floor, tied and gagged.

'Lock my girl in the back,' snaps Drake. 'And be careful with her!'

Webb picks Wendy up, takes her to another room and comes back.

'Get the curtain off.'

Webb unties Millie's blindfold and Drake takes me by the scruff of the neck and stands me in front of his wife. As he puts the gun to my head, I feel him trembling with rage.

'Have a good look, girl. Here it is, in all its glory. The slag who thought it could get one over. Eh? And now you're going to see what happens to a bit of mouldy skirt who takes a liberty with me. Me! Who grafted his fucking arse off so you could live the life and who you shat on like a piece of fucking dirt, soon as I went inside and took off with some fucking toerag not worth a wipe off my arse and when I go to put you right, this fucking slag pulls her bit of pantomime and sends you packing to the seaside and stealing my little girl, and my brave boy has to step up and do the right thing. You was bang fucking out of order and you fucking know it!'

'Jack, please…'

'Shut your filthy mouth before I put a boot in it! This is where you shut up and learn some fucking respect if you want to see tomorrow morning!'

Millie lowers her head. Jack lets go of my neck and stands back.

'Right. Let's have a bit of fun before we make a mess of this bird. Strip the fucking clothes off the whore and give us a bit of cabaret while she's still worth running up the pole. I've been away too long looking at a bunch of iron hoofs knobbing it in the showers. It's time to catch a good show.'

I back against the wall while Drake waves Webb towards me with the gun. He takes out a knife, cuts my hands free, rips my blouse and bra off, then my skirt and pants. His hands are all over me and he's pushing me down onto the stone.

'Get the old chap out then,' says Drake, moving for a better angle.

Webb's on top of me now, one arm across my chest and trying to get his cock out with the other hand. I look at the gun and go passive, as if I know I've got to submit. I can feel him hard against me. He takes his arm off me, leans on one elbow and tries to get himself inside me. I grab his ears, pull him over so he's between me and the gun and jam my finger in his eye. He screams, rolls off me and lies on his back with his cock deflating rapidly. Drake bellows with laughter and as he staggers round the room guffawing, I understand why he got committed to Broadmoor Hospital for the Criminally Insane.

'You fucking pussy!' he shouts, letting his gun hand drop to his side.

I jump up off the floor, hit Drake with a flying tackle and he crashes into the wall. As he slides down, I go for the gun but Webb's up and pulling me off him and I'm ducking punches, then Drake's up and he gets me in a head lock, shoves me in the corner and holds me there. Webb picks up the gun and gives it to Drake. He lets go of me, stands tall, pulls back the hammer and aims at my head.

'You're too fucking handy to live.'

As his finger tightens on the trigger, there's a noise outside. The door bursts open, a tall figure appears, darts at Drake like a cat, wraps an arm round his head, snaps it back and slices a blade across his throat. He spins round, fires a drop kick at Webb's face and when he hits the deck he lands with both knees on his stomach and stabs him in the heart. I'm still reeling from the speed of what I've just seen when the man steps forward and offers me his hand. I look into his face but he's a stranger to me. He helps me up. I look over his shoulder and my sister Georgie is standing in the doorway, with moonlight behind her.

27

Georgie comes in, steps over Drake's body and stands next to the tall young man.

'This is James.'

I try to focus on the person who's just saved my life.

'I've told you about him,' says Georgie, stepping forward and helping me into what's left of my blouse and skirt.

'Yes… you have,' I say, when my head stops spinning enough for me to speak. 'Hello James.'

'How do you do,' says James, shifting from one leg to the other, as we shake hands.

'Thank you for…'

'Oh, that's quite all right.'

'James is in the SAS,' says Georgie, putting her arm through his.

'Ah.'

'Oh, I'm only a reservist actually, although we get a proper training.'

'Clearly.'

As James chuckles modestly, I look past him and see Millie, bound and gagged on the floor, still with her head down. 'What are we thinking? Come on,' I say, rushing to her side.

James pulls the knife out of Webb's chest, wipes it on

his shirt and cuts the cords binding Millie's wrists and ankles, while I take her gag off.

'Get Wendy!' she says.

'Not yet.' I say.

'Get her!'

'You want her to see that?' I say, pointing at Drake's body.

'Is he dead?'

'Yes.'

'Thank fuck. Get him out of here.'

'Of course.'

I'm about to take his feet when James kneels down, puts one arm under his knees, the other below the middle of his back and picks him up. Georgie opens the door and James carries Drake outside, comes back moments later and removes Webb.

'Compost heap for now, I think,' he says, when he returns.

I go in the direction Webb went with Wendy and beckon James to follow me. I open the first door off the hallway and find her trussed up on a bed. We set her free, help her into the kitchen and she falls weeping into her mother's arms.

'Oh, my poor darling,' says Millie, holding her tight and guiding her to a chair. James puts another one next to it and mother and daughter cling to each other and rock gently back and forth, as Wendy's sobs gradually subside.

'There there, my darling, it's all right now… everything's all right now.'

Wendy opens her eyes and looks at the blood on the floor. 'Where's Dad?'

'He's gone. He'll leave us alone now,' says Millie.

'Who are these?' asks Wendy, after taking a moment to focus on the three of us.

'Our friends. You saw Rina on the beach, earlier.'

'Oh, yeah.'

'This is my sister Georgie and her boyfriend James,' I say.

'Are we going on the boat still?' asks Wendy.

'Not tonight,' says Millie.

'If Dad's gone, we can stay here, can't we?'

'I'm not sure, we'll have to have a think about that.'

Wendy looks at the blood, then at the knife James is still holding.

'I could hear all the noise.'

She looks into her mother's eyes. 'He's dead, isn't he?'

Millie holds her look for a moment, then she nods her head, puts her arms firmly around her daughter and holds her close, as the tears come.

I nod to James and Georgie and they follow me outside.

'They need some time,' says Georgie when we're in the yard, beneath a full moon in a crystal clear sky.

'We should do something with those two,' says James, looking across to where Webb and Drake lie on a heap of dirty straw. I'm relieved to see my holdall lying in a corner of the yard.

'Bury them?' I suggest, as I go and retrieve it.

'It's pretty isolated here, we could burn them, if we can find petrol. It'd be quicker.'

'No cars on the island, so there probably isn't any.'

'I'll see what I can find in that barn.'

When he goes inside it, I turn to Georgie, 'I owe him my life.'

'He's a good man.'

'How on earth did you know I was here?'

'Lizzie.'

'What?'

'I went to the flat to pick up some clothes for the trip and she told me you'd just left for Hydra. I thought it was strange that you hadn't mentioned it when we talked about me going away with James and I guessed there was something going on. When I pressed her, she gave me the whole story.'

'I see.'

'When I told James and gave him the background about why Drake was after you, he really wanted to come.'

'Just as well.'

'I met Jack Drake once with Bert Davis. I remember him because he put his hand up my leg and Bert shouted at him to knock it off and took me home and bought me an ice cream.'

'He got his payback then.'

'He did. As soon as we got off the boat and walked along the front I recognised him in a bar with the other bloke. We followed them up the hill, watched them grab you and take you to the farmhouse on the back of a donkey.'

'On a donkey?'

'Yes. They took you to the barn and then went into the house. I wanted to go and get you out then but James said it wasn't safe and made me wait. Then they got you from the barn and took you into the house and we could hear Drake shouting and laughing. James crept to the wall and opened up a crack in the wood with his knife, so he could see what was going on, then he shouldered the door and crashed in.'

'He was amazing.'

'He's very strong.'

'And a lovely boyfriend.'

She smiles and I open my holdall, take out a pair of flares, a T-shirt with a peace sign on it and some sandals. I put on the flares and I'm pulling the T-shirt over my head when James comes out of the barn carrying two spades.

'We're in for a bit of hard labour, I'm afraid.'

'What about inside the barn?' I ask.

'Good idea.'

'Is there another spade?' asks Georgie.

'Afraid not.'

'Why don't you go and see how Millie and Wendy are doing?'

'OK.'

As Georgie goes to the farmhouse, James and I enter the barn. The soil is loose on the floor and we agree on a grave in the corner, near the box I was kept in. I start digging while James gets the bodies. When he dumps Drake near me, I see that he's shat himself.

James picks up the other spade and starts shifting earth like he's out to win the Olympics. I'm glad to be digging myself. I always find exercise is the best thing after I've been knocked about and before long we've made a hole that's more than deep enough for both men. We kick them in, fill it up and drag some old boxes and crates over, to hide the disturbed soil.

In the kitchen, Millie's made a pot of tea, put the table back where it should be and she's sitting with Georgie and Wendy, who is looking a lot stronger.

'Tea? Or there's some wine?' says Millie.

'Tea's great, thanks,' I reply.

'Me too,' says James, setting chairs at the table for us.

As we relax and sip our tea, I become aware of Millie looking at me. There's so much that could be said about Ronnie offing Joe and getting away with it and where that leaves him with Millie and Wendy. As if she's reading my mind, she nods towards the hall door, 'Can I have a word, Rina?'

'Sure,' I say, following her out of the kitchen and into the room Wendy was in. Millie sits on the bed.

'I can never repay you for what you've done for us.'

'You don't have to.'

'I wish I could but I can't.'

'Please don't worry about it.'

'I want to tell you what I've decided.'

'Go on.'

'Because of Ronnie and what he did to Joe, I can't risk him finding us. It might be safe but I can't take the chance, in case he's going the way his dad did.'

'I think you're right.'

'I'm taking Wendy to Australia.'

'Good.'

'You mustn't tell anyone.'

'Of course not.'

'I've got enough left from the money you gave me to get us there. We'll go overland so we can get round the visa thing easier.'

'Good decision.'

'Change our names and start afresh.'

'Yes.'

She stands, puts her arms out to me, we hold each other and I can feel her trembling. She pulls back, wipes her eyes and looks into mine. 'Think of us sometimes, won't you?'

'You know I will.'

She stands up, takes some deep breaths, opens the door

and we go back into the kitchen. Something tells me that it's time to leave.

'Who fancies a midnight dip?' I say.

'Oooh, yes!' says Georgie.

'Excellent idea,' says James.

They say goodbye and as they go out of the door, I turn back to Millie and Wendy,

'I don't suppose…'

'No thanks,' says Wendy.

Millie comes to the door and kisses me. 'Take care.'

'You too.'

We pick up our bags and walk down the winding lane to the beach. James and Georgie throw their clothes off, put on their swimming things, race each other to the sea and dive into the waves. James ploughs off at a fast crawl that looks like it'll take him to Africa. When Georgie chases after him and shouts, he turns round, picks her up, throws her in the air and catches her, then they both disappear beneath the waves before coming up for air and pelting each other. I change into my swimsuit, walk to the water's edge and make a more leisurely entrance. The moon is dropping towards the horizon and I swim out towards it, turn on my back and gaze at the infinite number of stars above me. I glide through the warm silky water, looking at The Plough and The Bear, wishing I could float up among them and wondering if all the talk that's going on about sending men to the moon will mean they'll really be able do it and if we'll all be flying into space before long and up among the stars.

After I've drifted about some more, done a few strokes and breathed the balmy sea air, James and Georgie swim past me and get out of the water. I follow them to where our clothes are.

'That was so good,' says Georgie, lying down on her towel.

'You can't beat the Med,' says James, settling beside her.

I look at the two of them stretched out on the sand, all lithe and handsome and I'm so glad to see my little sister with a good man in her life after all the sadness and trouble she's seen, that made her pull back from the world and hide behind her books and her schoolwork, and the way all the effort she's made has paid off for her and taken her to Cambridge and a life among people who use their brains instead of their fists. When I see they're both asleep, I lower my aching body onto the warm sand.

• • •

Someone takes my hand. I open my eyes and Georgie's looking down at me.

'You OK?'

'Mmm…' I say, turning onto my side. 'A bit hot.'

'You're burning.'

I look at my shoulder and arm and see that she's right. The sun has risen and started to slow roast me.

'You were talking in your sleep.'

'What was I saying?'

'Something about a goat, I think.'

'I met one on the boat over.'

'Nice?'

'Delightful.'

James sits up and puts on his shirt. 'I think breakfast, don't you?'

'Mmm,' says Georgie, pecking him on the cheek. 'Sister?'

'Great idea.'

'I could eat a goat.'

'Easy,' I say, getting up and putting on my T-shirt and flares.

'To town!' says James, jumping up and leading the way along the beach, which is beginning to welcome some swimmers and loungers as the sun climbs in the sky.

We get to a café on the port and sit at a table in the shade. As we're finishing breakfast and ordering more coffee, I see Celeste and Donald approaching along the front. I return Celeste's wave and they come to the table.

'Hey. You look like you've been on the beach,' she says.

'It was so good. Swimming and sleep,' I reply.

'Nothing better,' says Donald, sitting down.

'Are these the friends you were looking for?' asks Celeste.

'No, actually, this is my sister, Georgie, and this is James.'

'Oh, wow. Good to meet you both,' says Celeste, shaking hands.

'Welcome to Hydra,' says Donald.

'Oh my goodness,' says James, taking his hand, 'You're Donald Lewin.'

'Guilty.'

'I love your work.'

'Oh… well, that's…'

'He's obsessed with your poems,' says Georgie.

'So moving, poignant. The irony…'

'He thinks you're better than Walt Whitman,' says Georgie.

'At last!' says Celeste, laughing and nudging the smiling Donald.

'Is it true you have a record coming out?' asks James.

'Oh, just some songs, you know?'

'I'm sure he'll play some of them for you if you want,' says Celeste.

'That would be wonderful.'

Donald stands up, 'I ought to get back now but if you maybe want to come by the house later?'

'We'd love to,' says Georgie.

'Cool. See you then.'

As Donald walks up the hill, the waitress arrives and Celeste orders coffee. When she's gone, James lets out a long breath. 'That was amazing.'

'He's going to be so chuffed,' says Georgie, pointing at her boyfriend.

'So's Don but he'll do his best not to show it,' says Celeste.

'Are you sure it's OK for us to come…?' asks James.

'Absolutely. He loves performing his stuff. You might even get a few pages of my novel.'

'I'd like that,' says Georgie.

'Just kidding.'

'No, really…'

I hear a blast from a ship's horn and look round. The ferry is approaching the quay and as I look at the bow dipping and rising, I suddenly miss Lizzie and now the job's done, I know I want to be at home.

'Do you two think you might stay for a while?' I ask.

'I'd certainly like to,' says James.

'Wild horses wouldn't drag him away now and I'm in no rush to get back.'

'In that case, I think I might just hop on that ferry.'

'OK,' says Georgie.

I give my sister a hug, 'Have a great time and I'll see you at home.'

I say goodbye to Celeste, give her my number and tell her to get in touch if she's ever in London. I turn to James and when I look into those dark eyes I want to thank him again for saving my life and taking care of my sister, but Celeste is there. I grasp his hand and hold it for a moment, while we share a smile and say goodbye.

Georgie picks up my bag and walks with me towards the

boat. When we get to the quayside they're still unloading some crates from the stern so we linger by the rail.

'James is so nice,' I say.

'Yeah, he's great.'

'When you told me about him on the phone, I assumed he was a student.'

'He was. That's how we met. He got a first in Classics last year, then he took the SAS Reserve test. After that he went off to Catterick and did his training.'

'Does he want to join up full time?'

'I don't think so.'

'Are you glad about that?'

She looks across to where he's sitting and then smiles.

'I think I am.'

The last of the crates arrives on the quay and there's a blast from the hooter.

I give Georgie another hug, 'Thanks for looking out for me.'

'You've done it for me for long enough.'

'I always tried to shield you from the nasty stuff.'

'I know.'

'Didn't work, did it?'

'Not always.'

'I'm sorry.'

'You did what you could.'

'I suppose.'

'You've been great.'

'Thanks,' I say, wiping away a tear.

'And I'm fine.'

'Yes… you are.'

We hold each other one last time and I go down the gangplank.

28

The plane lands at Heathrow soon after six o'clock. I breeze through customs, pick up a cab outside the terminal and head home. While I was in the air, I read an article in the *Daily Telegraph* reflecting on the arrest of Mrs Dorothy Pargeter-Smythe for espionage and the continuing scandal of the legacy of Burgess and Maclean with the addition of a woman to the roster of Cambridge spies who have betrayed our great country. I reckon Mayfield's story must have broken in one of the tabloids yesterday.

By eight I'm climbing the stairs and letting myself into the flat. I unpack my bag and take a long shower. I dry off, pour myself a large drink and put on The Yardbirds 'Having a Rave Up' and I'm listening to Eric Clapton and Jeff Beck on the same album, while I look through the wardrobe and decide that I must get down the King's Road and do some serious shopping. I pick out a black sleeveless wrap dress by Guy Laroche, seamed stockings and my Delman heels. When I've done the make-up and hair, I'm just about to leave for the club and surprise Lizzie when it occurs to me that I might as well give George the news about Jack Drake before I go. It should be a phone call but George won't allow anything to be said over the wire, so I'll have to drive round there. I go into the hall, dial his number and Bert answers.

'I'm just off the plane.'

'You coming round?'

'Give me ten minutes.'

'OK.'

I walk along Randolph Crescent and try to spot the car, then I remember I left it in Sutherland Avenue the other night because I couldn't find anywhere else to park. I walk round past the drinkers sitting outside the Warrington and get a whistle and some lip from a team of builders who should have gone home hours ago. I get into the Mini and enjoy giving it some welly down Sutherland, across Harrow Road, then I pull it round the corner into George's street.

Bert lets me into the house and I go along the hall into the empty lounge and wait. Bert comes in, closes the door and picks up a bottle of scotch off the dresser.

'Want one?'

'Don't mind if I do.'

As he pours a glass and hands it to me, George comes in from the back, breathing heavily. He's in the vest and shorts he wears to lift his weights. He wipes his forehead with a towel and chucks it on the sideboard.

'Good news?'

'He's gone.'

'Any aggro?'

'Not much. He had a face called Webb with him.'

'He's one of them who got him out. Done?'

'Yeah.'

'Nice job.'

'Ta.'

'What about Millie and the girl?'

'They're fine. Taking it on their toes.'

'Do you know where?'

'I didn't ask.'

'Fair enough.'

Bert pours George a drink, hands it to him and tops mine up.

George sits in his usual armchair, takes a pull on his whisky and looks at me. He's about to say something and I'm pretty sure of what's coming.

'You know about Ronnie?'

'They dropped the charge.'

'And he's out. Which gives you and me a problem.'

'I'm not doing it.'

'Oh yes, you fucking are.'

'He's a kid.'

'A kid who's out to do you if you don't get to him first!'

'He got lucky once, I doubt if he'll try it again.'

'What are you, fucking mad? He's building his form, getting his reputation, he's tried to off you once, of course he'll go again.'

'And you done his old man since then,' says Bert.

'He doesn't need to know that.'

'Now you listen to me girl!' says George, sitting forward in his chair with that steely look he gets. 'This whole fucking mess is down to you taking an almighty fucking liberty and not doing that fucking builder when you were told.'

He moves further forward, his eyes drill into me and his voice softens. 'I went easy on you for that because you're who you are and you've done a lot of good work for me but I'm telling you now, if you don't take care of this kid fucking sharpish, I'll come down on you like a ton of fucking shit and you'll wish you were never born. Now get the fuck out of here and don't come back till it's done.'

He sits back in the chair, drains his glass and closes his eyes. After a moment, Bert moves to the door and opens it. I walk along the corridor and out of the front door. Bert joins me on the pavement.

'He's not fucking about.'

'I know.'

George is right. Ronnie will kill me the first chance he gets. Much as I hate the idea of doing someone that young, I know I've got no choice. It's him or me.

'I need a clip for a Beretta 950.'

'Handy little tool. Point 25 ACP ain't it?'

'I don't know.'

'I can check at the yard.'

'Can you come now?'

'Sure.'

I drive us round to Westbourne Park Road and stop outside the coal yard opposite the Royal Oak. Bert gets out and goes through to his lock-up at the back of the yard, stopping to have a word with the bloke on the gate. I look across at a West Indian dealer outside the El Rio café, a gambling joint where Christine Keeler and Profumo used to go. He gets a lump of hash out of his pocket, cuts off a slice and sells it to a couple of white kids who move off sharpish. Bert gets into the car.

'You're in luck,' he says, handing me a clip. 'There's eight in there and I've got another one, if you want it.'

'May as well.'

He takes one out of his pocket and gives it to me. With the eight in the gun and two clips, I've got twenty-four rounds.

'What do I owe you?'

'Have it on the house.'

'That's kind.'

'I know how you feel about this one.'

'Thanks, Bert.'

'If you need any help, give us a shout.'

'I will. Are you going back to George's?'

'I think I'll have one in there first,' he says, nodding towards the Royal Oak.

'Take care, Reen.'

I give him a peck on the cheek and watch him cross the road and go into the pub, then I turn the car round and drive back to Randolph Crescent. I go up to the flat, get the Beretta from under the floorboard, check the magazine, put on a leather belt, slide the gun in behind it and put on my black Yves Saint Laurent jacket to hide the bulge. The belt rather spoils the line of the dress but it can't

be helped. I slip a blade into my suspenders and I'm ready
to go.

The club's humming when I get there. The tables are
mostly occupied and they're three deep along the bar. The
band are playing 'In the Heat of the Night', Tim's doing
his best Ray Charles impression and the dance floor's full
of clingy couples. I see Kelly coming out of the dressing
room and I ask how Mary is. She tells me she's doing fine
in the kitchen and still living at her flat in Meard Street. I
make my way through the tables to the back, open the door
to the office and Lizzie's at the desk, writing.

'Darling girl!' she says, getting up and hugging me
tight. We kiss and sink onto the sofa.

'Tell me all.'

'It's done.'

'Thank God.'

'But it wasn't down to me.'

'How come?'

'You know you told Georgie and James where I was?'

'I've been so worried that I did the wrong thing.'

'You didn't.'

'It just slipped out when they said they were going to
the continent, then I realised how dangerous it could be
for them if they found you.'

'It's just as well they did.'

'What happened?'

'Pour me a drink and I'll tell you.'

We sit down with glasses and I give Lizzie the full story.

When I get to James's forced entry and what followed, she's on the edge of her seat.

'I guessed he could take care of himself, but I never knew he'd be that good.'

'I've never seen anyone so fast.'

'And that's coming from you.'

I laugh and refill our glasses.

'I really wasn't sure if I should tell her where you were but I knew you were in danger and I couldn't bear the idea of you being on your own against that monster.'

'He had a bloke called Webb with him too.'

'Oh, he's a right git. He was in here the other night, shooting his mouth off about getting Drake out of the Moor. Tried to start a ruck but the boys got him out before he could do any damage.'

'He won't be starting anything now.'

'I'm so glad it worked out and you're home safe.'

'I wouldn't be if you hadn't sent Georgie and James.'

'Where are they by the way?'

'They're staying on Hydra for a bit. James's favourite poet is there and he's dead excited about it and it's a beautiful island for a holiday.'

We sit close and enjoy the warmth of each other for a while and I'm wishing the moment would last forever when a young bloke with dark hair in a mod suit walks past the one-way glass panel and I think of Ronnie Drake. He could well be dealing in a club nearby right now and I need to work out what I'm going to do about him before he's on me and has me in the river, like before. Lizzie senses I'm worried and when she asks me if something's wrong, I tell her the score.

'It never ends for you, does it?' she says, when I've finished.

'It's all because I broke the code.'

'You did a good thing.'

'And caused a load of aggravation.'

'Millie and Wendy are free and a vicious fucking mental case is in the ground.'

'And now I've got to kill his son.'

'If he's going to grow up anything like his dad…'

There's a knock on the door. Lizzie opens it and Jeremy is standing there with a bottle of champagne in his hand.

'Good evening to you both,' he says, giving a slight bow. 'Rina, how good to see you. They told me at the bar that you were here.'

'Hello, Jeremy.'

'I wondered if I might have a word with you, alone?'

'Anything you want to say, you can say in front of Lizzie.'

'Very well.'

'Come in and sit down, Jeremy,' says Lizzie, putting a chair in front of the desk for him and sitting behind it.

'Champagne?'

'Not right now.'

He offers me the bottle and I shake my head.

'I believe I'm in a position to give you some good news.'

'Don't hold back,' I say.

'But first I want to thank you for disentangling me from the web of deceit, spun by my wife, putting the revolting bitch where she belongs and giving me my freedom.'

'She's a piece of work all right.'

'I had no idea quite how devastatingly ghastly she was until she had me arrested. Her father's no better. Absolute horrors, the pair of them.'

'So what's the good news?' I ask.

'Ah. Yes,' he says, taking a cigarette out of a silver case and lighting it. 'I imagine you might be contemplating reducing the life span of a certain Ronald Drake.'

'Maybe.'

'Well you needn't bother.'

'Why?'

'He's just been arrested and is currently on remand at Bow Street Police Station.'

'What?'

'A large quantity of heroin, a pound and a half, to be exact, in half ounce bags, was found in the boot of his car earlier today along with six hundred pounds in cash. He is being charged with drug dealing and I have arranged for a witness to testify that Drake supplied him with heroin on two occasions.'

'Fuck.'

'I knew you'd be pleased.'

'Is the witness solid?'

'As a rock.'

'Why have you done it?'

'I think you're both aware of my father-in-law Sir David's appetite for smooth-skinned young men?'

We both nod.

'Drake, in addition to selling drugs, although not on the scale he's been caught with, has entered the business of introducing young men...'

'Running rent boys,' says Lizzie.

'Exactly, and in Sir David's case, demanding payment to remain discreet about the transaction. As you know, we had occasion to deal with a similar situation recently but I felt that Sir David's body count might be running a little high if we applied the same remedy in this instance and so incarceration became the favoured option. I'm told that he is likely receive a sentence of approximately twelve years.'

Relief is running through me as I hear this but I know there's a sting coming. He'll want payback, like he has before, but this time he's not going to get it. I whip the Beretta out of my belt, shove him up against the wall, put my forearm across his throat, press the gun against his cheek and pull back the hammer.

'You'd better get the fuck away from me now before I put a bullet in your brain.'

'What the..?'

'If I see you again, I will kill you. Do you understand?'

'I...'

'And if you come at me with that nonce at Kesgrove,

like your fucking bitch wife did, I shall kill him first and then you. Slowly.'

'Right.'

'Now fuck off.'

'Yes.'

I keep the gun on him while I open the door. He scurries out, pushes through the crowd and almost runs up the stairs.

I close the door and put the gun away.

'Blimey,' says Lizzie, refilling our glasses.

'Sorry,' I say, sitting on the sofa.

'No, it's good. I can't stand him and with any luck we won't get his seedy old father-in-law coming in any more either.'

'Right.'

'What's the nonce at Kesgrove bit?'

'You remember he made me do Weston, the one who was blackmailing that father-in-law?'

'Yeah.'

'There was another scum at the kid the night I did it and Dorothy said he could identify me. I doubt it would stick, without Weston's body, but it would mean getting my collar felt.'

'Where's his body?'

'In the crusher.'

'And Ronnie's inside.'

'Open that champagne!'

29

Three weeks later we're queuing up to see Grim Reaper at the Flamingo. Georgie and James have just got back from Hydra, looking tanned and fit and full of tales of Donald and Celeste, who they stayed with after I left. James certainly got his wish to hear Donald reciting his poems and singing his songs, apparently the problem was getting him to stop. There's only so much mournful longing you can take, it seems, and even James had had enough by the time Donald's girlfriend Julianne arrived from Norway and distracted him. Georgie said Celeste was lovely and her novel is wonderful, about a young Japanese girl at the end of World War II, whose family are all killed at Hiroshima and her struggle to survive after she stows away on a boat to America. Georgie's got a copy of the manuscript and she's going to show it to someone she knows, who works for a publisher in Cambridge. They spent a lot of time walking in the hills and lazing on the beach and I'm so glad they had a good time after such a tough start.

We get into the club and get a good position near the stage. A German band called 'The Scorpions' are supporting and they kick off with a fast, heavy rock number which has the crowd jumping right away, then they slow it down with a ballad that gets a few dancing and when Georgie and James start holding each other and swaying a little, me and Lizzie give it a bit too. The band are good movers and when they up the tempo again, the guitar players start whirling around and chopping the air while the singer stands tall in the front. They power on through a good varied set and finish up with a fast number that has the singer screeching a long high note at the end in sync with the guitars and they finish off with a drum roll and a final chord that has me stuffing my fingers in my ears and longing for Perry Como.

I'm on my way to the bar to get drinks in the interval when I run into Clarke, the engineer from Chappell Studios, who copied the tapes for me. He tells me he's heard the Grim Reaper album and reckons it's going to be big. It's due for release in a month and the band are in London doing a few warm up gigs before going on a world tour to promote it. He knows the plugger who's handling it and the airplay is going to be massive. I ask if Bobby Grant is doing all this and he tells me he's been dumped. I ask how come but he doesn't want to tell me. After I've worked on him a bit he swears me to secrecy and tells me that Grant came a cropper when the Mafia got interested in the band. Instead of doing a deal with them, like everyone does, he told them to fuck off so they smashed his legs, put him in a wheelchair, gave the boys a sweetener and took over the band. I ask where Bobby is now and he says he's stayed in the States.

I can't believe this is happening. First Jeremy fits up Ronnie Drake so he's going away for a twelve, instead of coming after me, then those nice Italian gents in New York put Bobby Grant out of the game, who also had it in for me. For the first time in a long while I reckon I can walk down the street without looking over my shoulder. I feel like kissing Clarke all over but I buy him a vodka and tonic instead.

A blistering guitar riff announces the arrival of Grim Reaper so I forget the rest of the drinks and elbow my way back through the crowd. I join the team and watch Caesar, all in black, standing dead still in a spotlight centre stage, playing the fastest guitar I've ever seen. The band are behind him, in the dark, giving him a raw, driving backing that he's threading a brilliant solo around. He builds to a screaming climax, stops dead and steps back while the drummer counts in on his sticks. Lights go up, the band crash in with stomping chords and Denny the singer bounds on, grabs the mic and shouts his heart out about a dark creepy spirit that's got inside his girl and won't let go. I manage to give Lizzie the news about Bobby Grant and she squeals with delight, grabs me and gives me a stonking kiss which makes James look twice, although I'm sure Georgie has told him the score. When Caesar steps forward for a solo, Denny does his leaps and jumps in front of the drum kit like he did at Woburn, but everyone's looking at Caesar.

The crowd are packed so tight towards the front that dancing's out and we can only move along with everyone else as the band get heavier and louder through the set.

Denny's voice gets rougher and the songs get darker and more devilish and while they're great at what they do, it's not really my kind of stuff and I'm happy to leave it to the bikers. When they finish off with a real pile driver I'm quite relieved and I think the others are too. We've booked a table at Rules and Georgie and James decide they'll go straight there and wait for us, while Lizzie and I try and get a quick word with Caesar.

There's a couple of men on the pass door to behind the stage but Lizzie knows them, of course, and they let us through. The roadies are humping gear along the corridor and setting up for the all-nighter. I ask one of them who's on and it's Atomic Rooster and Brian Auger so they're in for a good night. We get to the dressing room just as the door opens and Denny comes out smoking a fat spliff. I can see Caesar standing inside drinking from a bottle of red pop and I give him a wave and he comes into the corridor.

'You get better and better!' I say.

'Oh, no really, it is the band who…'

'Stop being so modest. You are fucking amazing,' says Lizzie.

'Well, thank you.'

'How was the recording in New York?' she asks.

'It was good.'

'Did you get any aggravation from that Tony?'

'Only a bit to begin. Then new managers and no more troubles.'

'We heard what happened to Bobby.'

'Yes,' he says, allowing himself a slight smile.

'Did you get your Mexican debt sorted?' I ask.

'All is good. New managers took care.'

'They gave you enough to pay it?'

'No... They took care.'

We're left to imagine how the US Mafia took care of a Mexican drug dealer.

'We have party at hotel. You want to come?' asks Caesar.

'We'd love to but we're meeting my sister. Thanks for a great gig.'

'Always thanks to you two for giving me to play in your club.'

'Great to see you doing so well,' I say.

We both give him a hug and make our way round a big Leslie speaker that's blocking the passage. We walk back through the club which is filling up with the all night crowd and I can see a few mod-suited lads are standing round the walls, selling pills.

We walk down Wardour Street, up Shaftesbury Avenue, through Covent Garden and along Maiden Lane to Rules. The receptionist checks the name, indicates our table and I take a moment to enjoy the sight of my sophisticated sister sitting with her boyfriend at a corner table. One thing I always tried to do for Georgie was to make sure she always had nice clothes and she's certainly looking good tonight in her Cardin tunic dress. James stands as we approach and pulls out chairs for us.

'We thought a little Montrachet Grand Cru,' he says, offering the bottle.

'Good choice,' says Lizzie as we hold up our glasses.

James pours the wine and we savour its warm round taste.

'I can't say that's quite my kind of music, although I did enjoy it and I thought that young guitarist was simply stunning.'

'He was,' says Georgie.

'Incredibly fast.'

We all nod in agreement as the waitress arrives and gives us menus. We study them in silence and when she returns to take our order it seems like Grim Reaper have given us a desire for red meat. James and I are going for fillet steak, Lizzie's having a porterhouse and Georgie's chosen entrecôte.

'Wasn't he at the club for a while?' asks Georgie.

'Yes, he was,' I reply.

'Club?' says James.

'Lizzie and Rina have a club.'

'Oh. Ladies… Or?'

'Mixed,' says Georgie, stifling a giggle with her napkin.

'I suppose that's more and more the way of it now, isn't it?'

'We try to move with the times,' says Lizzie.

James circulates the bottle again.

'Has your sister told you that she's begun writing a novel?'

'I told you it's a secret, you rotter,' says Georgie.

'Oops, sorry.'

'That's wonderful,' I say.

'We'll see.'

'What's it about?'

'I don't really know yet.'

'She was inspired by all those scribblers on Hydra.'

The waitress arrives with our steaks, we order another bottle of wine and eat in silence for a bit. After a while Lizzie looks up from her plate.

'Where are you from James?'

'Er, Bedfordshire.'

'Oh. Whereabouts?'

'Near Shuttleworth.'

That name rings a faint bell with me.

'Do you have family in the services?'

'Well, er, I did but... My father was with Military Intelligence but he was recently discharged. You might have seen it in the papers, actually... he was up on spying charges, then they were withdrawn.

'So he was cleared?'

'Not fully. It was all a stupid mess.'

Georgie moves closer to him and puts her hand on his.

'Now my mother seems to be caught up in the same ghastly business.'

'Is she with the Intelligence Services too?' asks Lizzie.

'She was at GCHQ. She's now in prison.'

'Poor woman. Will you be able to visit her?'

'I hope so. It happened just as we were about to go on holiday. As soon as it hit the papers I had the press after me like bloodhounds and the family lawyer advised me to get out of the country until we got a trial date, so a Greek island seemed like a very good idea.'

'The press can be a pain,' says Lizzie.

'There was one fat, baldy little creature I would happily have taken out.'

'Is your lawyer hopeful?'

'Oh, I think so. I expect it's the same sort of mix up that my father was caught up in. The whole world of spies is incredibly convoluted and complicated. I'm sure it's all been a big mistake and she'll be exonerated.'

'I do hope so,' says Lizzie.

I look round for the waitress and signal for the bill.

• • •

We get a cab back to Randolph Crescent and say goodbye to Georgie and James. They have to get back to Cambridge tonight because Georgie's got a seminar in the morning. We see them off in their Austin Seven and go up to Lizzie's flat. She pours us a nightcap and we settle on the sofa.

'What a turn up, eh?'

'I couldn't believe it.'

'No wonder you didn't speak.'

'I was so shocked.'

'He's such a lovely boy.'

'And they seem so happy together. I feel terrible.'

'Well, you mustn't.'

'I got her done.'

'She got herself done.'

'But if I hadn't told Mayfield…'

'She was a spy. They get caught. Anyway, she was fitting up James's dad, which would have been worse for him.'

'I suppose.'

'He's a strong boy, in all ways. He'll get over it and live his life, with Georgie, if it's meant to be.'

'Let's hope.'

'They make a lovely couple.'

I sit back, sip my drink and start to relax. I know Lizzie's right. Dorothy was always living on the edge and it's not my fault she fell off. James has a good heart and he's showing every sign of being able to handle it. Now that everything's calmed down, I'm hoping we can get away somewhere quiet for a while.

As we're moving towards the bedroom, the phone rings. Lizzie picks it up and listens.

'On my way,' she says, putting the receiver down and reaching for her car keys.

'There's been a tear-up at the club.'

'Oh no.'

'Blood on the dance floor.'

'Hang on, while I get a tool.'

The End

Hugh Fraser is best known for playing Captain Hastings in Agatha Christie's '*Poirot*' and the Duke of Wellington in '*Sharpe*'. His films include *Patriot Games*, *101 Dalmatians*, *The Draughtsman's Contract* and Clint Eastwood's *Firefox*. In the theatre he has appeared in *Teeth'n'Smiles* at the Royal Court and Wyndhams and in several roles with the Royal Shakespeare Company.

He has also narrated many of Agatha Christie's novels as audio books.

You can follow Hugh on Twitter @realhughfraser

DON'T FORGET TO ENJOY RINA WALKER'S OTHER GRIPPING THRILLERS!

HARM

ISBN: 978-1-910692-73-8 • £8.99

Acapulco 1974: Rina Walker is on assignment. Just another quick, clean kill. She wakes to discover her employer's severed head on her bedside table, and a man with an AK-47 coming through the door of her hotel room. She needs all her skills to neutralise her attacker and escape. After a car chase, she is captured by a Mexican drug boss who exploits her radiant beauty and ruthless expertise to eliminate an inconvenient member of the government. Notting Hill 1956: Fifteen-year-old Rina is scavenging and stealing to support her siblings and her alcoholic mother. When a local gangster attacks her younger sister, Rina wreaks violent revenge and murders him. Innocence betrayed, Rina faces the brutality of the post-war London underworld – a world that teaches her the skills she needs to kill...

THREAT

ISBN: 978-1-911129-75-2 • £8.99

London 1961: In the dying days of the Macmillan government, George Preston is in control of crime in West London and Rina Walker is his favoured contract killer. When Rina is hired by Soho vice king Tony Farina to investigate the disappearance of girls from his clubs she discovers that they are being supplied to a member of the English aristocracy for the gratification of his macabre sexual tastes. Rina's pursuit of the missing girls and her efforts to save the innocent from slaughter become increasingly perilous as she grapples with interwoven layers of corruption and betrayal and makes her way, via the louche nightclubs of Berlin, towards a final confrontation with depravity.

MALICE

ISBN: 978-1-911583-06-6 • £8.99

Malice is book 3 in the bestselling Rina Walker series,
following *Harm* and *Threat*. London 1964. Gang warfare is
breaking out and Rina Walker's struggle to survive amid
the battles and betrayals of a gruesome cast of racketeers
and gangsters requires all her considerable skills as an
assassin. Playing one side off against the other to protect
those she loves, Rina is caught in a deadly game of cat and
mouse where her life is just one of many at stake...